D0397419

DISCARDED FROM
GARFIELD COUNTY PUBLIC
LIBRARY SYSTEM

Garfield County Libraries
Glenwood Springs Branch
815 Cooper Avenue
Glenwood Springs, CO 81601
(970) 945-5958 • Fax (970) 945-7723
www.GCPLD.org

just
kiss me

Center Point
Large Print

Also by Rachel Gibson and available from Center Point Large Print:

Run to You
What I Love About You

This Large Print Book carries the Seal of Approval of N.A.V.H.

just kiss me

RACHEL GIBSON

CENTER POINT LARGE PRINT
THORNDIKE, MAINE

This Center Point Large Print edition is published
in the year 2016 by arrangement with Avon Books,
an imprint of HarperCollins Publishers.

Copyright © 2016 by Rachel Gibson.

All rights reserved.

This is a work of fiction. Names, characters, places, and
incidents are products of the author's imagination or are
used fictitiously and are not to be construed as real. Any
resemblance to actual events, locales, organizations,
or persons, living or dead, is entirely coincidental.

The text of this Large Print edition is unabridged.
In other aspects, this book may vary
from the original edition.
Printed in the United States of America
on permanent paper.
Set in 16-point Times New Roman type.

ISBN: 978-1-68324-124-9

Library of Congress Cataloging-in-Publication Data

Names: Gibson, Rachel, author.
Title: Just kiss me / Rachel Gibson.
Description: Center Point Large Print edition. | Thorndike, Maine :
Center Point Large Print, 2016.
Identifiers: LCCN 2016030052 | ISBN 9781683241249
    (hardcover : alk. paper)
Subjects: LCSH: Large type books. | GSAFD: Love stories.
Classification: LCC PS3557.I2216 J87 2016 | DDC 813/.6—dc23
LC record available at https://lccn.loc.gov/2016030052

A huge thanks to the readers who've supported me for the past eighteen years. I can't answer every e-mail, but just know that I appreciate the time you take to write me. You all are awesome.

A special thanks to Lucia Macro and Claudia Cross for flying across the country to come to my aid. Your help and guidance is truly immeasurable.

And to HHH—you know why.

— Chapter 1 —

The Diary of Vivien Leigh Rochet
Keep out! Do NOT read under Penalty of Death!!

Dear Diary,
  It's official!!!! I <u>hate</u> Ms. Eleanor Whitley-Shuler. Everyone calls her Nonnie. Not me. I call her the Mantis because she is long and skinny and has bug eyes. Mr. Shuler died the year after Momma and I moved into the carriage house. His name was Fredrickk, but I don't remember him or how he died. I was just a baby, but I bet the Mantis bit off his head. I know she wants to bit off mine. Momma says the Whitley-Shulers are our friends, but I said they aren't. We work for them and live in their carriage house. Momma says I need to be sweet, but I don't want to be sweet. Momma says I can't hate anyone, but the Mantis told Momma I'm as plump as a drop dumpling, and I shouldn't eat so much ice cream. When she wasn't

looking, I knocked over a stupid dog figurine. ON PURPOSE!!

Dear Diary,

I hate school!!! Every year my teachers say my last name wrong. They say, Vivien Ro-_chet_. I have to tell them it's pronounced Ro-_shay_. I've been going to Charleston Day School since kindergarten. For _eight_ years, the teachers get my name wrong on the first day every year. (Okay, so maybe I don't remember the first day of kindergarten.) The kids at school laugh and call me roach-ette. I hate them and they'll all be sorry someday when I'm a famous movie star. They'll all want to be my friend, but I won't let them. I won't let them see my movies or come to the big house I'm going to buy my momma someday. Except Lottie and Glory. They can come. They're my friends and we eat lunch together. Glory gets to wear a bra this year. Momma says I don't need a bra. NO FAIR!!!

Dear Diary,

Death to the Mantis!!! When me and Momma were cleaning the big house today, the Mantis said I have to

8

vacuum because she doesn't trust me to dust. She says I have too many accidents. She says I'm clumsy and she's afraid I'll knock over pictures of her super stupid sons, Henry and Spence, again. I'm twelve—almost thirteen. I'm not clumsy and I don't have accidents. I have on purpose, and who cares about Henry and Spence? They go away to school and only come home for holidays. They're buttheads. Especially Henry. He doesn't laugh or smile or anything. I call him Scary Henry or Butthead Henry. ☺ He's five years older than me but acts a lot older. His black eyeballs glare into mine like he can read my brain. He looks at me as if he knows I knock things over on purpose and lie about it. But he never says anything. Like last summer when someone knocked over the stupid lawn jockey and broke off its stupid arm. The Mantis said it was really old and had been in their family since before the war. She said it was probably my fault. She said I must have messed with it and knocked it over, but I said I didn't. Henry stared at me with his black eyes like I'm a liar and Spence laughed because . . . Spence is crazy and laughs

9

at everything. I cried really loud and ran inside the carriage house before the Mantis could bite off my head. Who cares about a stupid lawn jockey? It's so heavy it could kill a kid. It's not a kid's fault that it can fall over if you stand on its shoulders to see a bird's nest in the tree. In case anyone finds this and reads it, I'm innocent!!!

Dear Diary,

I ran all the way home from school because Momma said she was taking me to see the sand castles on Folly Beach. When I walked in the door, I knew we wouldn't go. Momma was on the couch with the patchwork blanket that Mamaw made her. She was rubbing it with her fingers and staring at the ceiling like she does when she has a sad spell. I'm not calling Mamaw Roz to come and get me this time. I'm almost thirteen (in seven months) and can take care of myself. I can take care of Momma now, too. I hate her sad spells. I hope this one doesn't last really long. ☹!!!

Dear Diary,

Today me and Momma walked to the store for strawberry Moon Pies and

Coca-Cola. Momma was in one of her happy moods today and we walked to Waterfront Park, too. We got our feet wet in the Pineapple Fountain then looked at boats in the harbor. Momma says we're going to sail away someday. She pointed at a big yacht and named all the places we were going to go. Aruba, Monaco, Zanzibar, she said it was going to happen, but I know it won't. On the way home, Momma said she was going to buy a house on Rainbow Row someday because they look yummy. Like a row of pastel Candy Buttons they sell at Kroger. She said she could be happy forever in a yummy house. When I'm a rich movie star, I'll buy her the pink one so she can be happy forever. ☺!!

Things To Buy
When I'm Rich List

1. Pink candy house
2. My own ice cream store
3. Beeper—Momma says only drug dealers have beepers—as if!
4. A pool
5. A rabid monkey to bite Henry

— Chapter 2 —

Beneath the wide brim of a black straw hat, Vivien Leigh Rochet put a hand to her forehead and let out a slight moan.

"A few too many appletinis last night?"

"A few." Vivien reached for a bottle of water in the console separating her from her assistant of five months, Sarah. The two sat in the back of a black Cadillac Escalade speeding down Interstate 26 toward Charleston and the thunderclouds gathering above the historic city. "Christian told me they matched my eyes." Christian Forsyth—real name, Don Smith—was Vivien's latest leading man and, according to the tabloids, her newest Hollywood lover.

"Today your face is a nice shade of appletini."

Vivien took a long drink and hit the button in the armrest. "Don't say *appletini*." The window slid down and she tilted her face toward the wind spilling over the top of the glass. The heavy air fluttered the brim of her hat and smelled like the tall pine and scrub growing along the interstate. It smelled like magnolia and sunshine. Like rain and sea breezes. Like chaos and comfort. Like home.

Next to her, Sarah's fingers tapped the screen of

her notebook, and in the front, the driver spoke into his cell phone as he changed lanes. If he didn't stop jerking the wheel like that, Vivien was going to puke all over the black leather seats. The humid air slipped across the sharp edge of Vivien's bare shoulder and collarbone to play with the ends of the loose ponytail resting against the chiffon top of her Zac Posen bandeau dress. The breeze ruffled the rolled hem of the floral skirt and brushed her thighs.

It had been three years since she'd been home, working in a quick visit on her way to the New York City premier of *End Game*, her third and final film in the Raffle trilogy. The wildly popular dystopia films, based on the equally popular books, had launched Vivien Rochet from minor-role obscurity to major stardom. At the age of twenty-two, she'd been picked from thousands of hopeful actresses to play Dr. Zahara West, archeologist, assassin, and revolutionary leader in the blockbuster series. By the time that third and final film had come out three years ago Vivien had a resume filled with six major movie roles and multiple television appearances. Her star on the Hollywood Walk of Fame was just down from Charlie Sheen. Fitting she supposed since she lived down the street from him in real life.

Three years ago, when she'd rolled into town, she'd been a little cocky, riding a wave of success and money. She'd just been nominated for a

People's Choice award, and learned that her seven-inch Zahara action figure—metal bikini edition—had sold more than all the other Raffle figures combined. Back then, she'd returned to Charleston to help her momma host a house-warming party, and she'd felt like she was hot shit. This time, she just felt like shit. This time she was home to plan her momma's funeral.

"You're on the cover of the *Enquirer* again. Apparently you were caught in a sex romp."

Who cares? Vivien's perfect brows scrunched together and reminded her of her headache. Sarah was just doing her job. Or perhaps her assistant was trying to take Vivien's mind off the awful details of the past twelve hours when her life had been sliced to pieces like celluloid on the cutting-room floor.

Twelve hours ago, she'd been drinking apple-tinis at a lavish party on Mulholland Drive and pretending interest in the latest Hollywood news and gossip. Scoring an invitation and getting seen at parties of the rich and swanky was part of the business. Flashing a smile for photographers and having her picture taken on the arm of men like Christian Forsyth was good for Vivien's career, no matter that he was the most boring man to walk upright and she had no romantic interest in him at all.

Twelve hours ago, her life had been about the right film roles and spending time with the right people. Twelve hours ago, she'd been playing the part of glamorous Vivien Leigh Rochet. Actress. Movie star. Hot shit.

Roll camera. Sarah's sudden appearance at the party should have tipped Vivien off that something was wrong, but she'd had a few too many cocktails on an empty stomach to give it a thought. If she hadn't been intoxicated, she might have noticed the worry in her assistant's blue eyes. She might have had a little forewarning before Sarah stepped close and whispered the impossible in her ear.

Her momma was dead. Twelve hours later, Vivien didn't know any real details. She'd been told that paramedics had tried to revive her at home but that she'd died on her way to the emergency room. Her death appeared to be natural. Natural? Nothing that had happened in the past twelve hours felt natural, and Vivien could hardly breathe past the pain and guilt slashing her heart.

"I guess it sells more than the usual anorexic stories," said Vivien.

Macy Jane Rochet was dead and fake stories in gossip papers seemed so trivial. So stupid. There had been a time when no one had cared enough about Vivien Rochet to print her name, let alone make up entire stories about her. A time when she would have killed to get a mention in the tabloids and to see photos of herself splattered across magazine covers. Her mother was dead and Vivien's life suddenly seemed stupid and trivial.

And completely empty now.

Before Sarah's sudden appearance last night, everything in Vivien's life had been so clear. So charted. She was a bright star blazing a trail toward mega stardom. Now it was blurred and her head was congested with pain and caffeine and booze. She could hardly think past her raw emotions, and so much had happened in the past twelve hours, she wasn't even sure if it was Sunday or Monday.

It had to be Sunday. Maybe. "What day is it?"

Without looking up, Sarah answered, "June sixth."

Vivien reached into her red Kelly bag and pulled out a pair of sunglasses. She slid the black frames on her face and leaned her head back. That didn't really answer her question, but it had to be Sunday. She'd been at the party on Saturday night. Had that been just last night? It seemed like more time had passed since when she'd learned about her momma.

Her mother had been kind and loving, delicate and beautiful. She'd also been difficult and exhausting, and if truth be told, sometimes crazy as a bessie bug. She'd certainly embarrassed Vivien more times than she could count. With her erratic highs and lows. Her overblown elation one day and her utter despair the next. Her huge dreams of a happily ever after and difficulty with men. The earth beneath her feet ebbed like the tides, changeable, predictable, and leaving those around her restless and worn out at the same time. But even when she'd been at her most difficult, she hadn't been difficult to love. Not for Vivien, because no matter the highs and lows and instability, she'd always known that her mother loved her as no one else on the planet loved her. No judgments. No expectations. Just warm and generous love from her wide-open heart.

Macy Jane hadn't been perfect, but she'd done her best to take care of Vivien. When she'd fallen short, Vivien's Mamaw Roz stepped in. After Mamaw Roz died, Vivien took care of herself. She took care of her momma, too. It had been the two of them against the world. Together.

Always.

The Escalade took one of the last exits and headed into the heart of the Holy City, church spires and steeples pointed toward heaven, heavy with thunderclouds typical of July. The SUV continued down Meeting Street and moved toward the harbor, toward cobblestone streets lined with palmetto and plumeria. Toward the genteel opulence and polished grandeur south of Broad Street. Vivien had grown up in the middle of the elite class. Smack-dab in the middle of old families with old family names. Names that could be traced back to the founding of the St. Cecilia Society and beyond to the original thirteen colonies. She'd grown up surrounded by "good families," but she'd never belonged. Her "people" didn't have towns or bridges or golf courses named after them. Her "people" worked hard to scrape by and her family tree looked more likea spindly shrub than a stately live oak.

"Take a left on Tradd," she told the driver. "Then another left on East Bay." Instead of returning to the only home she'd known for the first eighteen years of her life, the SUV headed for a set of row houses, each painted in a different bright color. Her mother had once said the row resembled a strip of Candy Buttons and that she could be happy in a yummy house. Three years ago, Vivien bought her momma the pink button so she could be happy and so she never had to live in anyone's backyard again.

"In the front is fine," she said and the Cadillac pulled to a stop next to the curb. She put her bottled water into her purse, and waited for the driver to open the back door before she slid from the vehicle. From beneath the brim of her wide hat, she looked up at the pink stucco, and the three stories of white window frames and gray shutters. A drop of rain hit her bare shoulder and dotted the stones around her black, four-inch heels. The one and only time she'd been at the row house, her mother had been excited and animated, directing florists and caterers all at the same time. Her mother had indeed seemed happy, and Macy Jane in a happy mood was always infectious—if you didn't let yourself worry about the subsequent sadness.

Several pieces of furniture had been delivered the day before, and Vivien and her mother had run around, pulling plastic off of the sofa and chairs in the grand drawing room and a small dining set in the kitchen. Movers unloaded an Elizabethan four-poster bed and an antique Aubusson rug that Macy Jane had discovered at an estate sale. Vivien wasn't shocked that her mother had done very little to furnish the 4,200-square-foot townhouse before the housewarming party. She was a bit annoyed, but not in the least surprised by Macy Jane's indecision.

"I don't need to have every room furnished with stuff to host my party." Macy Jane had defended her laissez-faire approach to home ownership and to life in general.

Which Vivien supposed was true and hadn't bothered to argue that the point of having the party was to show off to her friends and impress them with her home and "stuff." It wasn't to show off an empty house.

Not that it had mattered. The party had taken place in the private courtyard and caterers had provided everything from tables and chairs to the fine pink linens.

"Is it always this muggy?" Sarah asked as she and the driver unloaded their bags.

"Yes ma'am," the driver answered, appearing not in the least bothered in his black suit and tie. "After it rains, it won't be so bad."

Vivien pulled a house key from her purse and stepped inside the small alcove. Her hand trembled as she unlocked the door and pushed it open, half expecting to see her mother, arms open wide. "Let me hug my sweet girl's neck," she would always say in her smooth drawl. Instead the foyer was dark and empty. Her mother had died here. Somewhere.

A tear slipped down her cheek and she pulled off her glasses and hat. The coroner hadn't determined the cause of her mother's death yet. Only that it appeared to be natural. She moved into the drawing room, and her feet came to an abrupt halt as she took in the room within her watery gaze. White sheets covered the furniture and a thick layer of dust covered everything else. The Aubusson rug was rolled up in front of the fireplace and someone had pulled down the mahogany mantel. Vivien blinked as if she didn't trust her eyes. When she'd spoken to her mother just last week, she hadn't mentioned that the floors were being sanded and the mantel was torn out. She hadn't mentioned any sort of renovations at all. Then again, she hadn't mentioned feeling the slightest bit ill, either. She hadn't mentioned much of anything beyond signing up for the seniors' Zumba class in hopes that they didn't "work up a glow." Which Vivien had argued was the whole point of Zumba.

Vivien wiped her cheeks and set her purse on the covered couch. She had so many questions, and the more she looked around, the more came to mind. She walked past the winding staircase and through the light pouring in from the cupola above. The dining room and library were as empty as the last time she'd been in the townhouse. No towels hung in the bathroom, and the small table and four chairs sat exactly where they'd been placed several years ago in the brick kitchen.

A baggie of apples sat on the granite counter and a thermos and a drinking glass had been placed on a towel, upside down as if they'd been recently washed and left there to dry.

"It looks like your mother was remodeling," Sarah said as she walked into the kitchen.

"This is so strange." Vivien opened the refrigerator. Empty but for one can of Coca-Cola and a bag of carrots. Old shriveled carrots.

"Yuck. Do you want something to eat?" Sarah asked as she opened and closed cabinets and drawers. "I'm starving to death."

The thought of food made Vivien's stomach roll, either from grief or hangover, she wasn't certain which. Maybe both. "Find anything in there?"

Sarah shook her head and moved through the open pantry door. "Just a box of teas and some cups in here." She returned and pulled out her phone. "I can call around and have something delivered. After that, I need a bath and a nap."

At the moment, Sarah's stomach and bath and nap seemed too much for Vivien to take on. The responsibility too daunting. She had so much to do and think about. She wanted to scream and hit something. She wanted to curl up on her momma's bed and catch the smell of her momma's hair on a pillowcase. She wanted to cry big sloppy tears until her mind was as empty as her soul.

"I have a better idea. Pick a hotel somewhere nearby and stay in it." She wanted to cry until she succumbed to exhaustion. She wanted to be alone, and she wasn't a bit surprised when her assistant didn't bother to even put up a token resistance. Sarah loved nothing as much as room service and a pool bar. She handed Sarah an American Express, and twenty minutes later, waved good-bye as her assistant wheeled her suitcase to a waiting cab.

Once alone in her mother's Candy-Button house, Vivien moved to the French doors and looked out onto the stone courtyard spotted with splashes of rain. The last time she'd stood beneath the shade of flowering maple, breathing in the sweet scent of camellias, her mother had been alive with the kind of energy that lit up her eyes and made her buzz around like a hummingbird.

"Momma, you're going to wear yourself out before anyone arrives," Vivien had warned as she'd stepped into the courtyard after she'd showered and changed into the appropriate floral dress, yellow heels, and yellow hat.

Her mother looked up from a bottle of Moet and Chandon champagne, rose of course. "If everyone who RSVP'd makes it today, we'll be quite the fancy group." Macy Jane wore pink from hat to heels to match her house.

"Why wouldn't everyone make it?"

"It's hot as hades. Some of the ladies might just want to stay cool with their bought air." The cork popped and flew across the bricks to land in a bed of red impatiens. "Did you see that? Your mamaw always said popping corks brought luck. The bigger the pop, the bigger the luck."

To Vivien, the bigger the pop, the more likely it was you got hit in the head with a flying cork. "How many people did you invite?"

"Twenty, including Nonnie and her boys."

Vivien reached for a crab puff from a three-tier serving stand. "Why would you invite the Whitley-Shulers?" She carefully bit into the little hors d'oeuvre.

Macy Jane looked up from two champagne glasses. "They're some of our oldest friends." She set the bottle next to a silver urn filled with a gorgeous mix of lilies and hydrangea and roses.

"They were never our friends, Momma."

"Of course they are, sugar." She shook her head as she poured. "Don't be silly."

Sometimes Macy Jane stretched the truth until it fit her reality, but she never told a flat-out lie. Lies made baby Jesus cry, and her momma had always been very concerned about landing in a fiery hell for upsetting baby Jesus. Vivien took the flute her mother offered. The smooth crystal cooled her palm. "We worked for them."

"Oh that." Macy Jane waved away that tiresome bit of truth with her hand. "We just did a little light house cleaning for pin money. You practically grew up with Henry and Spence."

Now that was certainly stretching the truth to its snapping point. She'd grown up across the formal lawn of the Shuler mansion. She'd grown up in the converted carriage house, but more than sculpted hedges, fountains, and rose arbors separated the two families. More than money or manners, her last name alone separated her from Henry and Spence. The brick courtyard between them might as well have been an insurmountable brick wall. The boys attended an exclusive boarding school in Georgia. Vivien walked to school fifteen minutes from her front door. Henry and Spence passed the lazy days of summer in the big house in Charleston, or at their granddaddy's beach home in Hilton Head. They vacationed in Paris, France. Vivien spent her summers at public beaches and vacationed at Uncle Richie's split-level in Paris, Texas.

Vivien raised the glass and took a sip. They weren't friends, yet they weren't just neighbors, either. They all resided in a weird space that was neither. She'd spoken to the Whitley-Shuler boys a few dozen times. She'd played basketball with Spence once while Henry walked around like he had a stick up his ass.

The bubbly champagne tickled her throat and she lowered her glass. For people who had lived in such close proximity, she couldn't say they knew each other. Although, she certainly knew a lot more about the Whitley-Shuler boys than they did her. She had the kind of knowledge that had come from years of dusting their bedrooms and snooping through their lives. Playing with Henry's switchblade comb and Spence's fake barf. She'd touched their pocketknives, read their private letters, and looked at their appalling porn.

"This is good." Vivien touched the rim of her glass to her mother's.

"Cheers!"

"Here's to your Candy-Button house, Momma."

"I still can't believe we're here." Macy Jane raised the glass to her smiling lips. At fifty, strands of silver streaked the glossy curls of her brunette hair. Today her green eyes were bright

25

and alive, reflecting happiness in her beautiful face. Vivien hoped like hell everyone who'd RSVP'd showed up today so her mother didn't tailspin. "Remember all the times we dreamed about moving to Rainbow Row, Vivie?"

That dream had been more Macy Jane's than hers. "I remember." Her dreams of moving had usually started with buying the Whitley-Shuler house and had ended with her tossing Nonnie out on her skinny ass—Tom-and-Jerry style.

"Is Ms. Whitley-Shuler coming for sure?"

"She said she had a Preservation Society meeting, but she'll try her best to make it."

"Hmm." Vivien took another sip from her fluted glass. That meant Nonnie wasn't planning to step foot in the row house.

"Mind your manners, Vivien Leigh."

She lowered her champagne. "I didn't say anything."

"Not yet, but I know that look. You're fixin' to make an ugly comment about Nonnie." Macy Jane shook her head. "Jesus doesn't like ugly."

There were a lot of things in Macy Jane's world that Jesus didn't like. However, Vivien had a suspicion that Jesus liked nasty bitches even less than he liked ugly comments. She reached for a little weeny on a toothpick and said, before she popped it into her mouth, "I sure can't wait to see our good friends again." She smiled as she chewed.

If Macy Jane noticed the sarcasm in Vivien's tone, she chose to ignore it. "Of course the boys can't make it. Spence is in Italy with his new wife. He married one of Senator Coleman's girls, you know, and Henry works in some fancy office in New York. He's a real big shot but took the time to send his regrets. Henry always did have beautiful manners."

Vivien had been vaguely aware of Spence's recent wedding, and she wasn't a bit surprised he'd bagged a Coleman. It would have been more shocking if he hadn't married into a family with an old name and political ties. She didn't recall Henry having beautiful manners at all. In fact, she was fairly certain she recalled his appalling manners and she really didn't care if she everlaid eyes on him again. Not after the horrible condom incident, when she thought Henry might choke her to death.

The horrible incident had taken place when she'd been thirteen, but she still recalled the fire in his black eyes as if it had happened yesterday.

That summer, Henry had just graduated from his fancy prep school, and he and Spence had spent the summer like always, lazing the days away at Hilton Head. As usual, Vivien spent her summer in Charleston, working in the big house, dusting tables and shelves and massive bedroom furniture.

And, of course, snooping.

The day of the condom incident, she'd popped her latest *NSYNC CD into her Discman, stuffed in her earbuds, and rocked out as she cleaned. She sang along to "Tearin' Up My Heart," practiced her dance moves, and brushed the top of Henry's empire dresser with her feather duster. She'd glanced behind her for good measure, then she slid open the first drawer. Behind a row of socks, she just happened to discover a box of Trojans. The words of her favorite song died on her lips as she took a closer look and read, "Extended pleasure, climax control lubricant." Whatever that meant, she hadn't a clue. Vivien had pathetically little experience with boys. At least she thought it was pathetic. While *NSYNC sang about the pain tearing up their hearts and souls, Vivien counted six condoms in the box that originally had held a dozen.

Gross.

"What the hell are you doing?" she heard above her music.

A squeaky scream escaped her lips as she spun around. The box of Trojans fell from her hand and her heart pounded *boom-boom-boom* in her chest. Butt Head Henry stood several feet away, his dark brows lowered over his scary, dark eyes.

She pulled out the earbuds with her free hand and turned off her Discman. "What are you doing home?" He was supposed to be in Hilton Head.

"I live here." He looked bigger than usual. Taller. His shoulders wider, and he was better-looking than before too. Like her Mamaw Roz always said, "He's as handsome as wet paint." Vivien didn't know what that meant, but if she liked him at all, even a little, she might think of changing his name from Butt Head to Handsome Henry. Only she didn't like him and he was mad. Real mad. So mad he looked scary. So scary his squinty eyes shined like wet onyx. His cheeks turned a deep red with it, but no matter his anger, Henry was a Southern boy. He'd been raised with manners and morals that would never allow him to hit a girl. Just because he wouldn't hit her, didn't mean he wasn't scary as all get-out.

"What are you doing in my room, Vivien?"

She held up the feather duster. "Cleaning."

"My underwear?" He developed a worrying little tic at one corner of his mouth.

No, she didn't fear him physically, but that didn't mean she wasn't in trouble. If he ratted her out, she was in deep, deep do-do with her momma. "Your sock drawer, actually," she corrected him.

He pointed to the box at her feet. "Those were in the back of my sock drawer."

In the middle, but she thought it best not to quibble. Instead, she looked behind his back to the empty doorway and wondered if she could get around him and make a run for it.

"Does your momma know you snoop?"

The best defense was always a good offence. "Does your momma know you have condoms in your sock drawer?" She slid a bit to her right and figured her best hope for an exit was to distract him until she could get between him and the door. "What does climax control mean?"

The little tic got a little scarier. "Ask Macy Jane when you tell her what you do up here when no one is watching you."

"I'm not going to tell my momma."

"Oh, I think you are." He took a step forward and towered over Vivien.

She shook her head, more scared than she thought possible or wanted to let him know. No way could she tell her momma. She'd get mad then sad and might stay in bed for a week. She might even "take a switch" to Vivien like she always threatened. This time she might actually get around to it. "If you don't tell on me, I won't tell on you."

"No one cares about condoms at my age." As if to prove he was eighteen, he lifted a hand to scratch the dark stubble on his jaw.

That was probably true. Vivien crossed her arms over her chest and brought out the big guns. "Your momma will care when I tell her about Tracy Lynn Fortner."

His hand fell to his side and his voice got real low. "What did you say?"

"You heard me."

He stared at her without blinking. "How do you know about that?"

Years of snooping, of course.

"No one knows about that."

"Not yet."

He took a step closer and grabbed her shoulders in his big hands. "You whisper a word about that," he said through clinched teeth, "and I'll choke you to death."

She believed him. His black eyeballs bored holes in her and she tried to swallow past the sudden lump in her throat. She guessed she'd been wrong about him and his manners and could practically feel his hands on her throat.

, He shook her. "Do you hear me?"

Her head snapped back.

"If I hear one word about that, I'll know it came from your mouth." He shook her one last time and dropped his hands. "I'll hunt you down like Ole Yeller. Got it?"

"Yes." The second his grip had eased, she'd run like hell and hadn't stopped until she was in the carriage house, locked inside her bedroom.

Fifteen years had passed since the horrible condom incident and Vivien saw little of Henry after that day. She'd steered real clear of him. Not that it had been necessary. Once Henry went off to college, he hadn't returned very often to Charleston.

Vivien pushed open the French doors to the courtyard and kicked off her shoes. Strong winds blew the tops of the trees and scattered leaves about the old brick. She hadn't ever breathed a word about Tracy Lynn Fortner. Not because she feared Henry's wrath, but even at thirteen, she knew that Tracy Lynn would suffer much more than Henry. Vivien might have been a little bratty, and a lot nosey, but she'd never been intentionally mean and hurtful.

Barefoot, she stepped outside and into the courtyard. Patches of sand and dead azaleas covered the brick, and she walked past a concrete angel partially covered in ivy. She moved to the bed of impatiens and knelt down beside the brick border. Her mother had loved impatiens, and Vivien picked one of the little red flowers.

The clouds above her head boomed and she felt the vibration in the air and beneath her knees. She brought the little flower to her nose as the skies opened and showered her with big fat drops.

Tears filled her eyes as she picked flowers and made a delicate posy like her momma had taught her. She set it by her knee then bent forward and parted plants. She searched the ground beneath the thick leaves. With each drop of rain, each tear that rolled down her cheek, her search got more frantic. The champagne cork from her mother's party had been so insignificant. She'd ignored it at the time and forgotten it until now. Now it took on an importance beyond a mere stopper. It was a tangible trace, a link to that special day filled with pink champagne and her mother's bubbly laughter. The rain soaked her hair and dress. Her hands got muddy and sand dug into her knees. She didn't care. She leaned farther into the bed of wet flowers, her deep sobs rushing from her lips and pulling at her chest. As if she was just inches away from discovering a lost horde of gold, her search got more frantic.

"What are you doing out here?" a man's voice boomed over the thunder.

A startled gasp escaped her dry mouth and her heart stopped.

"Besides digging in the mud."

She looked over her shoulder, and through the rain and tears blurring her vision, she stared at a pair of dark jeans and work boots. A single raindrop fell from her lashes as her gaze moved up his long legs, over the bulge of his button fly to the gray Henley splattered with rain. She looked up past his tan jaw and lips and into his dark eyes. Dark eyes that had once threatened to hunt her down like a coonhound and choke her to death.

"Hello, Ms. Vivien," Henry Whitley-Shuler drawled, pulling the vowels like warm taffy. "It's been a long time."

— Chapter 3 —

The whistle of a chicken-shaped kettle pierced the musty air and drowned out the sound of raindrops splattering old glass windows and the ornate cupola. Inside the historic row house on East Bay Street, Henry Whitley-Shuler removed the kettle from a back burner on the gas stove. Clouds of steam rose from a chipped celadon pot as he poured scalding water over the stainless strainer he'd packed with loose tea. The irony of pouring tea for the girl who'd snooped in his drawers while pretending to clean was not lost on him.

He'd been just five years old when Macy Jane and Vivien had moved into the carriage house. His memory of that day was like an old jigsaw puzzle in the bottom of an equally old trunk. The picture was faded and half the pieces were missing, but he did remember standing beside his mother on the back porch shaded by the old magnolia tree, and the scent of sweet lemon heavy in the air. He remembered looking up at his mother's blank face and at Spence balanced on her hip. The recollection of a dark-haired woman had faded to a gossamer outline in his memory, but he knew the woman was Macy Jane.

His memory of Vivien in subsequent years was much clearer. He remembered her and her mother dusting furniture and mopping floors. He could recall a Christmas or two when he'd walked into the kitchen and seen her standing on a stool next to her mother, polishing *his* mother's silver. God knew his mother had a lot of silver, and he could clearly recall the flash of temper in her green eyes and the rebellion pursing her lips whenever his mother had corrected her grammar or suggested that she not eat an entire bag of Oreos.

He might have felt bad for Vivien's situation in life if she hadn't been so damn annoying. He might have cut her a break if she hadn't broken into his personal belongings while she ransacked every room in the house. Growing up, he'd seen little of the girl with the big green eyes and pale white skin. He and Spence had come home to Charleston on school breaks but spent most of their summer months at the beach house with their grandfather Shuler. He hadn't had to see Vivien on a daily basis to know she had sticky fingers. He hadn't had to see her in action to know that she'd pawed through his and Spence's bedrooms. He and his brother used to set books and knifes at specific angles and put thread on the handles of their closets. Every time they returned, the thread was gone and the books were at slightly different positions. One time, Spencer put a mousetrap inside his sneakers, and when they'd returned home, the trap was stuffed in his dress shoes. Another time, he'd put sticks of hot pepper gum in a pack of Wrigley's Doublemint. They'd come to Charleston for spring break and had found one piece missing. One piece. They'd laughed about that for the entire week.

Henry set the kettle back on the stove and he combed his damp hair from his forehead. Rainwater soaked the shoulders of his shirt and he lowered his hand to flick a glob of mud from his chest. Mud smeared his forearms and he had a muddy handprint on his shoulder. He probably had mud on other places he couldn't see. There had been a time in his life when he would have suspected that Vivien got him muddy on purpose. A time when her lips would have said "sorry" but her eyes would have spoken of unapologetic glee.

He fit the little lid on the pot and moved to the pantry. What he recalled most about Vivien was that she'd always been a little actress. He'd never met anyone in his life, and he'd known some shady characters, who'd managed to look so damn innocent while lying her ass off. She could get caught with chocolate on her face and her hand still in the cookie jar and convince everyone that she'd been set up, wronged, and wasn't the least bit guilty.

A set of pink cups and saucers sat on a shelf next to empty canisters in the bare pantry. Henry was a coffee man himself, but he'd have to move north in shame if he didn't know how to make hot tea. Which was a good thing, because Ms. Macy Jane hadn't filled any of her cupboards with much at all. A few dishes and loose tea were about it, but then Macy Jane hadn't lived in this house.

He carried a cup and saucer across the eat-in kitchen to a small table beneath a window that looked out into the garden. Vivien had a lot of fans here in Charleston. The hometown girl turned big Hollywood movie star. Macy Jane had been her biggest fan and had never even tried to contain her pride. Not that she'd ever tried to contain any emotion. She'd been so proud of her only child. She had Vivien's pictures everywhere and starlight seemed to beam around her whenever she talked about her "sweet girl." Yet Vivien had rarely come to see her momma.

If the town knew Vivien Rochet was in Charleston, the mayor would likely throw a parade and her fans would dress up in various *Raffle* costumes. They'd squeeze themselves into neon pleather and stiletto boots, black togas and metal bikinis. They'd line up to pay homage to Zahara West, but Henry wouldn't be among them. First, he didn't dress up in any sort of costume for anyone, and two, he was not a fan of Vivien Rochet.

There had been a time in his life when he'd dated models and heiresses and debutants. When he'd lived at breakneck speed and had gone through his share of beautiful and smart women. Hell, he'd even dated an actress or two. Vivien's fame and beautiful face did not impress him. He didn't care if she appeared on coffee mugs and movie posters; he just wasn't impressed by a woman who seemingly cared so little about anyone but herself.

The heels of his work boots stirred up some dust as he returned to the stove. One of the last times he'd laid eyes on Vivien in person, she'd been snooping through his chest of drawers. He couldn't remember her age, but it was the summer before he'd entered Princeton. At the time, she'd still been a chunky kid with a smart mouth and sticky fingers. He shouldn't have been surprised to see her counting his condoms, but he actually *had* been surprised to catch her in the act. He'd been so pissed off, he'd tried to scare and intimidate her so that she'd think twice about entering his room ever again. She'd been anything but scared or intimidated. Her green gaze had held his and she'd had the balls to throw Tracy Lynn Fortner's name in his face. No one had even known about Tracy Lynn, but Vivien had found out. He could guess how the little snoop learned of his old girlfriend and the secret that neither of them wanted anyone to discover. Not her family and certainly not his mother. The Whitley-Shulers already had a closet stuffed with scandals and the last thing he wanted was to add one of his making. Teen Mom might be popular on MTV, but teen pregnancy wasn't done in families like the Fortners or Whitley-Shulers. While the rest ofthe world may have relaxed views on children born outside of marriage, the rules in his world had not changed. It was just as scandalous and disgraceful in his generation as it had been in his mother's. Like his mother, he and Tracy Lynn had had two choices, but unlike Nonnie, they'd made a different decision.

No one but he and Tracy Lynn knew what had happened that summer. No one but he and Tracy Lynn—and Vivien. He'd never known how much Vivien had discovered, but she'd known Tracy Lynn's name, so he'd assumed she knew everything. He'd spent the first two years at Princeton living in fear of her dropping the bomb on him. She'd obviously never told anyone, and he'd always wondered why she'd never used her knowledge against him. Shocking really, given her penchant for snooping and bad manners, and her disagreeable character in general.

He glanced up as Vivien walked into the kitchen with her dark hair messed up as if towel dried. She held a brush in one hand and her cell phone in the other. She'd changed out of her muddy dress and into a pair of jeans and a T-shirt that matched her deep green eyes.

"Are you warmed up, Ms. Vivien?"

"No. I'm freezing and wish I'd packed a sweater or a jacket." She looked a lot like her momma. A contrast of dark hair and white skin and eyes like shamrocks on the Hill of Tara. Vivien's lips were more lush than her mother's, though. Redder and fuller, like she'd been kissed all night. "I looked for a blanket, but didn't find one," she said as she walked across the kitchen toward the window overlooking the courtyard. Light from the converted chandelier slipped through the tangled length of her damp hair. The T-shirt fit loose across her small breasts, but not loose enough to hide her hard nipples raking the soft cotton. "Not even on Momma's bed."

Henry glanced at his watch and then grabbed the lid off the pot. She hadn't been kidding. She was freezing. "I have a jacket in my truck. I can run and get it for you." She didn't politely insist that he not trouble himself on her account, like any good Southern woman would do, and he was forced to run back out into the pelting rain and grab his hunting jacket from the truck box in the back of his Chevy. The ribbed cuffs were frayed and the quilted lining worn thin in places. A three-corner tear split the camo weeds on the left elbow, and there was probably a few twelve-gage loads in one of the pockets. It had definitely seen better days, but he never hunted without his lucky Carhartt. When he returned, he found Vivien sitting at the small kitchen table.

She held her face in her hands in grief, and he felt a little bad for thinking she had a disagreeable character. Maybe that had been a little harsh. "This is old but will warm you up," he said as he draped the jacket across the back of her shoulders.

"Thank you." She looked up through teary green eyes.

Now he felt more than a *little* bad. "My pleasure." Maybe she wasn't so bad. Maybe her manners had improved, too. He moved to the stove and breathed in the steam rising from the rich brown tea.

"This coat smells like swamp water."

Then again, maybe not. He glanced over his shoulder at her. "Probably. Last time I wore it, I was knee deep in the Little Pee Dee." Her nose wrinkled and he added, "You'll likely find some bird guts on it, too." He expected her to shrug herself out of the jacket he'd just run through the rain to retrieve for her, but she didn't. Her need for warmth must have been greater than her objection to his "swampy" jacket. He chuckled and turned back to the stove. "When did you get in?" He pulled the strainer from the water and placed it in the sink.

"About an hour ago."

"Did you travel by yourself?" He grabbed the teapot by the handle and carried it to the table. His lucky hunting jacket was so big on her, she looked like she'd been swallowed up in weeds. Stinky weeds, apparently.

"No. My assistant is down the street at the Harbor View."

He was surprised Vivien wasn't with her assistant, kicked back in the top-floor suite, sipping chardonnay instead of in the dusty row house. "What were you doing in the mud?"

"Looking for something important," she answered, but she didn't elaborate.

"I'm surprised to find you here." Soaking wet and digging in the dirt, drops of water falling from her lashes as she looked up at him through the rain with raw anguish in her eyes. She should have looked a mess. She was a mess. A hot mess.

"Why?" Damp strands of hair clung to the side of her neck as she dragged the brush through the back of her hair. "Why wouldn't I be here?"

Henry pulled his gaze from Vivien's smooth throat and poured tea into the pink cups. "Because the place is in the middle of a renovation."

"I can see that. Momma never mentioned a renovation." Her voice trailed off and she added as if she was talking more to herself, "I don't understand why she never said anything."

In the past year and a half, he'd gotten to know Macy Jane better than he had the entire first thirty or so years of his life, but there were a lot of things about the woman that were a mystery to him. He pushed the cup across the table, next to Vivien's brush and cell phone. "I didn't see any sugar in the pantry, and I think it goes without saying that there isn't milk in the refrigerator."

"I gave up milk and sugar in favor of Truvia."

"In these parts, that's as blasphemous as giving up religion."

She wrapped her hands around the hot cup and warmed her palms. "That, too." Her gaze swept across his face, studying him as if looking for changes since that last time they'd been in the same room.

He sat in the chair across from her and combed his hair back from his forehead. He'd changed a lot, and not just physically. "Did you choose sin over the Episcopalians?"

"I chose sleeping in on Sundays."

Choices. Vivien had been raised with a diversity of choices. The choice to sit among the Episcopalians or sleep in. She'd been given the freedom to eat ice cream until she got sick or run off to Holly-wood to become an actress. Growing up, Henry's life had been very different. He'd always known that there were limited career options open to him. Males in his position had three choices: doctor, lawyer, or banker. If one of those three choices morphed into politics, even better. He'd never questioned his options. Never contemplated a different future. He'd taken up finance and the world of finance had taken up him.

As if suddenly recalling her manners, Vivien asked, "How's your momma?"

"Mother is healthy as always."

"Glad to hear it."

Henry was fairly certain that was a lie. He looked into her gaze, and if he'd forgotten exactly why he was in Ms. Macy Jane's kitchen with Vivien, her eyes, red from crying, reminded him.

"Momma mentioned you'd moved back to Charleston. A little over two years now." He wondered what else her momma had mentioned. Had she told Vivien why he'd moved back? Had she mentioned that he'd run full tilt into the turbulence of Wall Street? That he'd been one of the youngest traders at New York Securities and by the age of thirty-three, he'd had a big desk and was on track for a corner office? No. He doubted Macy Jane knew much about that life. "Nonnie must love having you at home again."

Not really.

"I don't live with my mother." If Vivien wanted to distract herself with idle conversation, he'd oblige her. Unless she went on too long. He'd planned to just make a quick stop by the row house to make sure it was locked up. He hadn't planned tea and chitchat. He had a new life and work that needed him. Work that had nothing to do with a corner office at 200 West. Nothing to do with making millions and the traps that came with that kind of money. He'd fallen victim to his enormous ego and the allure of power and sex. Then every-thing crashed. A crash that had nothing to do with the stock market and everything to do with a heart attack at the age of thirty-three. A heart attack that had made him take a hard look at his life and at the power that was easier lost than gained. His inflated ego that had almost killed him, and for what? Money that had become as meaningless as sex?

She studied him for several more seconds before she hooked one thin finger through the cup handle. "I know why I'm at my momma's house, but the question is, why are you here, Henry?"

He'd known her his entire life, but he could not recall a time that she'd ever said his name. Just his name. Not Scary Henry or Butt Head Henry. She raised a brow and pursed her lips to blow a steady breath into the tea.

"I was just making sure the place was locked up tight." Two years ago, he'd been given two choices. Slow down or die. He might have chosen the former, but he wasn't so slow that he didn't notice red lips pressed like a kiss against pink porcelain. "I don't think I got the chance to tell you how truly sorry I am for your loss. Your momma was a nice lady."

"I can't believe she's really gone. It just doesn't seem real." Vivien lowered the cup without taking a drink. "I keep thinking she's going to walk through the door, but she's not. I have to keep reminding myself that she's never going to walk through the door again." She swallowed hard and turned her attention to the garden beyond the window. She looked sad and tired and so very small in his old coat. "I keep thinking of her dying all alone," she said just above a whisper.

"She wasn't alone. My mother was with her."

"What?" Her gaze returned to his. "Nonnie was here?"

"Not here. They were at home." He wondered how much she knew about her mother's death. Judging by the V pulling her brows together, he'd guess not much. "In the carriage house."

"Momma moved out of the carriage house."

He shook his head. "I don't believe she ever moved out."

"I bought her this house two years ago," she spoke as if Henry was a bit slow. "We bought furniture. She had a party and served crab puffs and little weenies." She pointed out the window to the muddy flowerbed where she'd been digging. "We drank Rose Imperial, and the cork flew into the impatiens. It was so hot, Marta Southerland lost her mind and showed up without her Spanx. Momma was horrified."

"Is that what you were doing in the mud? I thought maybe you were searching for lost Confederate treasure."

"It's more valuable to me than lost treasure." Vivien stared at the man across the table. The man with deep brown eyes and dark hair that he frequently pushed off his forehead. He bore a resemblance to the boy she'd once known, only this older version of Henry was bigger and better-looking than she remembered. Maybe he wasn't as big a jerk as she recalled, either. He'd picked her up from the mud and practically carried her into the house. The younger Henry would have just folded his arms across his chest and frowned down at her like she was stealing his precious dirt.

"All I do know is that since I've been back in Charleston, Macy Jane has lived in the carriage house."

He'd made her tea and given her his coat. The seemingly thoughtful man across from her was unlike the boy she'd known. Or perhaps he was just being nice out of respect for her mother. The reason didn't matter. Vivien was grateful to be dry and warm. She'd arrived in Charleston without so much as a cardigan. She'd forgotten her underwear, too, and imagined they were still in a heap where she'd thrown them on her bed. At the moment, though, she had more important concerns than going commando or whether or not Henry had changed or was still a contemptuous jerk. She raised her hands from inside his big coat and rubbed her temples. "What was she doing in the carriage house with your mother?"

"They were tweeting."

Vivien's hands fell to the table and a few drops of tea sloshed over the side of the pink teacup. "Did you say they were tweeting?"

"More like feuding, with the United Daughters of the Confederacy." He shrugged one shoulder. "Something about a shrimp-and-grits recipe. I tried not to listen to either one of them."

"What? Daughters of the Confederacy?"

"The Georgia chapter, I believe."

"Wait! My momma died from a twitter war? With the Georgia United Daughters of the Confederacy? Over shrimp and grits? In the carriage house with Nonnie?" The more he explained, the more baffling it all sounded. Like platform sneakers. Or twerking. Or algebra.

"I don't know precisely what they were doing when Macy Jane passed. I wasn't there. Mother called me right after she called the ambulance and I drove over." His solemn eyes stared back at her and his voice lowered, "By the time I got to the carriage house, your momma was on her way to the hospital."

Vivien might not like Nonnie, but she was relieved and thankful that her mother hadn't been alone.

"We weren't too far behind the ambulance, but Macy Jane was gone by the time we got to the emergency room."

Vivien hooked her finger through the cup handle and raised the tea to her lips. She took a sip and swallowed past the grief rising up her throat. "How did my momma die? What happened?"

"I don't know. Mother said they were sitting at

the kitchen table and Macy Jane just fell from her chair."

Her hand shook as she lowered the cup and tears stung the backs of her eyes. She didn't want to cry. Not now. Later when she was alone she would think about her momma falling from a chair. "The medical examiner is supposed to call me when . . ." she couldn't finish her sentence. She covered her face with her hands and her voice trailed off. She could do this. Her momma needed Vivien to take care of her one last time. But it was hard. So hard. She counted backward from ten, like she'd been taught by her acting teacher. She imagined herself fading into character. Fading into the role of a strong woman who controlled her emotions. She tried to invasion Hillary Clinton, Condoleezza Rice, and Ruth Bader Ginsburg. A strangled sob escaped her lips and she sucked in a breath. Her momma was a good person. It wasn't fair that she died and bad people lived. People like Charles Manson and the BTK killer and Nonnie Whitley-Shuler.

"Let me take you to the Harborview, Vivien."

She felt the weight of his big hand on her shoulder. "I want to go home." She wiped her eyes and looked up at Henry. Up past the mud on his wide chest to his dark eyes beneath darker brows. "I need to go the carriage house."

"Is your suitcase upstairs?"

"Yes." She stood and Henry's hand fell to his

side. She never thought she'd ever have a reason to step foot on Whitley-Shuler property again.

"I'll get it." He pointed toward the garden. "I'm parked in back."

Vivien carried her saucer and teacup to the sink. She remembered buying the cups and saucers for her mother's housewarming party. She rinsed the teapot and set it in the sink to dry. The coat fell from one shoulder and she pulled it tight around her as she moved across the kitchen. Again she caught the scent of his jacket. The thick canvas material had a woodsy top note, a full-bodied middle like wind across warm skin, and an undertone of something definitely swampy. She grabbed her hairbrush and phone from the table. With her thumb, she checked for messages. She had twenty texts and thirty-three e-mails, and ten missed phone calls. None of them from the coroner.

Sunlight broke through the clouds and poured through the drawing-room windows. It cast irregular shadows across the hardwood floor and covered furniture. She slipped her phone into her purse sitting on the sheet protecting the sofa. How did a person plan a funeral? The only funeral that she really remembered was Mamaw Roz's. She'd been fifteen and remembered going with her momma to pick out a casket and order flowers. Everything else was a blur.

Did a person just Google mortuaries? Her

momma had been Episcopalian. Did that make a difference when it came to funeral arrangements and cemetery plots? And what about food? Funeral food was big in the South.

There was so much to do that she didn't know where to begin, and taking care of her momma wasn't something she could push on Sarah. Sarah could run out and buy panties and bras for Vivien. Her momma's funeral was too personal. Something only Vivien could do. Like when she'd been a kid and her momma would depend on her whenever she'd fall into her one of her sad depressions.

Dust tickled her nose and she sneezed. The townhouse was a mess, and her gaze took in the hole above the torn-out fireplace mantel. She'd bought her momma this house, and now it was a wreck. Instead of the pink house where her mother could live happy, it was a real disaster area. Anger bubbled up like lava, and she let it roll through her because it felt a lot better than the burning grief scorching her heart. Her mother had been notoriously gullible, especially when it came to men. It would have been incredibly easy for a crook to convince her that the house needed renovation. A swindler who preyed on vulnerable women. Vulnerable women who owned historic houses that had to have each and every restoration approved, then checked and reapproved by the historical society or preservation society or whatever the heck they called themselves. Vivien looked around at the sanded floor and wiring hanging from an outlet, and her temper rose to thermal nuclear. Every step had to pass inspection and be approved, and a shady contractor could conceivably make this project take years.

"The rain stopped," Henry said as he walked into the room.

She turned to watch him move through the variegated shadows. Sunlight passed over his hard shoulders and through his dark hair. He held her Louis Vuitton suitcase in one hand and her muddy dress and black straw hat in the other. The strapless bra and panties she'd worn earlier were soaked through with rain, and she'd shoved them into a nylon pocket in the pull along.

"Are you ready?"

Instead of answering, she pointed at the missing mantle. "This house was inspected just two years ago. What the heck happened?"

"The flashing pulled away from the chimney." With his free hand he pointed to the ceiling, then lowered his finger to the hole in the wall. "Water ran down the brickwork and caused rot in the lathing boards and plaster."

"Who said?"

"An inspector for one." He dropped his hand and returned his gaze to hers. "A general contractor and journeyman for another."

A skeptical frown pulled at her mouth and she folded her arms beneath the big coat. "Water created all that?" She pointed her chin at the wrecked wall.

"Water is the most destructive force on earth," he said as he walked across the room to the French doors. The sun once again dipped behind clouds and washed the drawing room with deeper shades of gray.

What did he know about home renovation? He was a stockbroker or money manager or something or other to do with banking. Not exactly a job that had anything whatsoever to do with slinging a hammer. "Momma was way too gullible and obviously let some con artist in here to destroy the place." She grabbed her red handbag and followed behind him. "Crooks who prey on vulnerable women should be run over by a bus." For good measure she added, "Then shot."

"That's harsh."

"Momma believed everyone and could be talked into anything. Clearly, some sneaky bastard took advantage of her trusting nature."

"No one took advantage of Macy Jane."

"How do you know?"

He opened the doors and looked across his shoulder at her. The sun broke free of the clouds and he flashed a bright smile. As if he was a heroic caricature, she could swear she saw a twinkle on his right incisor. "I'm the sneaky bastard who destroyed the place."

— Chapter 4 —

The Diary of Vivien Leigh Rochet
Keep out! Do NOT read under Penalty of Death!!

Dear Diary,
  Donny Ray Keever is the CUTEST boy in school. He sits behind me in math and pokes the back of my chair with his binder. He asked me if I had an extra pencil he could borrow. I told him he could keep it. He said, "Thanks." I think he likes me. ☺

Dear Diary,
  Proof!!! Spence Whitley-Shuler is stupid! He chews gum that is so hot it burns your mouth. I always thought Spence was dumb. He smiles at me and laughs like he thinks he's funny. He's not funny. His jokes aren't funny. I think he's slow in the head. Why else would he chew hot gum that burns your tongue?

Dear Diary
It's official!! I love Donny Ray Keever! His hair is golden blond and his eyes are turquoise azure topaz. He's sooo handsome. Sooo super hot. I told him I was getting braces on my teeth next week. He said, "Cool." <u>Cool</u> is the coolest word.

Dear Diary,
I don't think I'm ever going to get a bra. I measured myself today. No change since last time. ☹

Dear Diary
The Mantis accused me of eating some of the petit fours for her stupid garden party. She had a dozen boxes of them delivered this morning. They looked like tiny purple presents with lacy green bows. She said someone ate half a box. She's so stupid. Someone ate a whole box!! I laughed and laughed, but then I got sick. I barfed purple and green in my closet. Momma found out and got mad. She said she was fixin' to wear me out, but she didn't. She did make me clean up the barf. ☹ ☹

Dear Diary,

No Fair! I told Momma I want a Tamagotchi, but she said maybe for my birthday. My birthday is two months away!! All the Tamagotchis will be gone by then. Every kid in the world will have one but me! And Momma might forget. Like when she gets sad and forgets that I don't like macaroni and cheese all the time. Or like the time I was a lamb in the Christmas program. Momma made my costume and we practiced my part: "baa—baa. Behold —baa baa." I got to sit right next to the baby Jesus, but Momma forgot and went to see <u>Titanic</u> with stupid Chuck instead. I cried but Mamaw Roz took me for ice cream.

Dear Diary,

Death to Danny Ray! He said I was fat and the only reason I go to Charleston Day School is because Momma gets financial aid. I almost cried but I didn't. I made my eyes stay dry and I told him I could do something about my weight if I wanted, but he couldn't do anything about his ugly face. When I got home, I told Momma and she said some people feel so bad about them-selves that they have to make other folks feel bad right along with them. She said men are no good and I'm beautiful. But she's my momma and has to say that. I put my head in her lap and she rubbed my back as I cried it out. I don't want ice cream anymore. ☹

Things I Don't Want To Do List

1. Eat ice cream
2. Clean the Mantis lair
3. Clean anything
4. Run in school
5. Math

— Chapter 5 —

Vivien dreamed she was on the set of a film she knew nothing about and in which she didn't want to participate. No matter how much she protested, everyone insisted she play her role. Each time the director said, "Action," the crew stared at her, expecting her to know what to do. She'd always had a gift for memorizing her lines but she'd never been given a script. She liked to break down a scene and know her part before she stepped in front of the camera, but she didn't know her part. Improvisation made her freeze and her insides felt stuck in ice.

She woke once and, for several terrifying seconds, she didn't recognize her surroundings. Then the sharp edges of grief cut into her heart as her gaze took in the shape of her mother's old white dressing table and the outlines of perfume bottles and the snow globe she'd made in the third grade out of a Mason jar and glitter. She buried her nose in her mother's pillow and breathed in the scent of flowery shampoo. When she closed her eyes again, she dreamed of soft loving hands and pink magnolias. She dreamed of Mamaw Roz and her house in Summerville, where she'd spent Christmases and Thanksgivings and where she stayed when her mother fell into depression.

The next time Vivien opened her eyes, sunlight was streaming through the exterior shutters and lacy sheers. The sound of someone moving around in the kitchen downstairs drifted through the open crack in the bedroom door. Last night, she'd texted Sarah the address of the carriage house and location of the hidden key. She thought about getting up, but turned on her side and adjusted the pillow instead. She didn't want to get up. She didn't want to face the day. She didn't want to face what lay beyond the bedroom door. She only wanted to stay in the comfort of her momma's bed. In between the caresses of Momma's soft sheets, where she'd often slept after a bad dream or childhood scare. Her eyes drifted shut and the heavy weight of sorrow pulled her toward a peaceful dream.

"It's time to get up, girl."

Voice recognition stabbed Vivien's sleep, and for several horrifying heartbeats, her peaceful dream turned into a nightmare, much like Dorothy happily skipping down the yellow brick road only to have the Wicked Witch of the West appear in a poof of black smoke and ruin her good time. Her eyes opened and her nightmare was confirmed. Only this witch was blonde and lived in the South.

"I've made you tea and toast." Nonnie Whitley-Shuler stood in the doorway, dressed in a yellow silk blouse and floral scarf tied around her neck.

Her ever-present pearls, yellowed with age and worn by generations of Shuler women, hung around her neck. Nonnie's pearls were a badge of honor and prestige. She loved to tell the story of how her great-grandmother had hidden her momma's pearls in "Grandfather Edward's nappy" when a "swarm of Yankees" had ransacked the family plantation, Whitley Hall.

"I'm not hungry," Vivien croaked.

"You have to eat." Nonnie's blonde hair curled about her shoulders and long face. She'd never been a beautiful woman, but she'd always done the most with what God had given her. "I'm not going to have people say I let you starve."

As always, Nonnie barked and everyone was expected to obey. Vivien sat up and swung her feet out of bed. Not because she'd been ordered, but because no matter how appealing, she couldn't stay in bed forever. Along with underwear and bras, she'd forgotten to pack a funeral dress.

"You look more like your momma in person than you do in movies."

She didn't know if that was meant as a compliment or not, but she took it as one. "Thank you, Ms. Nonnie." She shuffled to the end of the bed and pulled on her mother's kimono robe over her short pajamas. Her cell phone sat on the dressing table and she grabbed it before following Nonnie into the narrow hall, past the closed door of her old bedroom, and down the stairs.

The three original carriage doors had been replaced with arched windows long ago, and she squinted as they passed through the blocky light stretching across area rugs and worn furniture. Vivien checked for messages and missed calls on her phone as she walked into the kitchen behind Nonnie. There was nothing from the medical examiner's office yet, and she set the phone on the oak tabletop where she'd eaten most of her meals as a child.

"Henry told me you were here when my momma passed."

"Yes." A bowl of strawberries sat in the middle of the pedestal table and the older woman carried two small plates of toast to the table. "Would you like jam? I believe Macy Jane made peach again this year."

"No, thank you." She slid into a spindle-back chair.

"I'll have a spot of marmalade."

Yes. Vivien remembered Nonnie's precise "spot of marmalade" and watched her dab the orange preserve at the corner of her toast. Just like always.

Vivien curled her hand around a delicate blue cup and brought it to her lips. Warm tea flowed into her mouth and the taste of sugar on her tongue filled her with visceral memories, sweet and comforting. Since moving away, she'd had to break herself of the sugar habit. As a result, she'd had to give up tea because no matter her physical address, she was still a Southerner. Tea without sugar just wasn't done. Or at least not talked about in polite society. Like French kissing your first cousin.

"Henry tells me you have an assistant traveling with you." Nonnie took her seat across from Vivien and placed a linen napkin in her lap.

"Yes. Sarah should be here anytime." And Vivien had a list of things she needed her assistant to do for her this morning. First, find a Starbucks and a triple grande latte, nonfat, no foam, with two packs of Truvia. Second, shop for panties and bras. Before she'd gone to bed last, she'd washed her underwear and hung them to dry over a laundry basket. Just like when she'd been a teen and in charge of herself.

"Have you heard from the coroner's office?"

Vivien glanced at her phone and returned the cup to the saucer. "Not yet." She surreptitiously slid her napkin to her lap like she was ten years old again. "I need to know what happened to Momma."

Nonnie's long, thin fingers picked up her toast. "Eat first. You're too thin."

That coming from the woman who counted every calorie before she put it in her mouth might be laughable if Vivien was in the mood to laugh. "I'm not a child anymore."

"Yes. I know." She took a bite, and only after she swallowed and touched the napkin to the corners of her lips did she add, "Macy Jane would never rest in peace if I let her girl faint from hunger."

Vivien resisted the urge to shove her food in her face or stick her tongue out. She was thirty years old but Nonnie made her feel like a kid again. "Do you know why Momma didn't live in the row house?"

"She liked this house better."

"This house isn't hers. It belongs to you." Vivien raised the toast to her mouth and took a bite. She didn't realize how hungry she was until she sank her teeth into thick whole wheat and tasted the melted butter.

"This house belongs to your mother. It's in her name." Nonnie's wide green eyes looked across at Vivien as she dabbed preserve on her toast.

A chunk of wheat got stuck in Vivien's throat and she washed it down with tea. Nonnie had given her mother the carriage house? She would have been less surprised if she'd learned Nonnie gave her staunch Episcopalian soul to the devil, which might actually have happened, now that she thought of it. "Since when?"

"Quite a long time. I guess it belongs to you now." The older woman took a small bite as if that wasn't shocking news.

"Why didn't she tell me?" Vivien was beginning to suspect there were a lot of things her mother didn't tell her.

"I assumed you knew. She certainly called the carriage house her home."

Yes, but Vivien had always thought she meant "home" as in where they resided. Her mother had always dreamed of moving away. She'd had fantasies about living in exotic places. She'd wanted a Candy-Button row house of her very own. She'd wanted their own backyard were Vivien could climb trees without someone complaining about broken branches. "What else hasn't my mother told me?" she asked more to herself as she took another bite.

"I couldn't say. Trying to follow Macy Jane's thoughts was often like trying to watch the flight of a butterfly. A beautiful butterfly, drifting from one flower to the next." That was true enough and a surprisingly nice way for Nonnie to describe her mother. Then she totally blew it with, "That's why you were such a hoyden."

Hoyden? Who even used that word anymore? Sixty-something-year-old, uptight, tight-ass women, that's who. Bless her heart. "'By day she was healthy and hoydenish, a veritable dynamo, by night a beautiful enchantress.'" Vivien grabbed a strawberry and bit it in half.

Nonnie lifted a brow. "If you know enough about Zelda Fitzgerald to quote what people said about her, you also know that she was diagnosed with schizophrenia and died in a mental hospital."

Yes. Vivien knew all that. She also knew that

Zelda had bouts of manic genius that inspired her to write beautiful prose. "Don't you think I was made for you?" She quoted. "I feel like you had me ordered and I was delivered to you—to be worn. I want you to wear me like a watch-chain or buttonhole bouquet—to the world."

"Impressive."

Vivien could recall most lines of dialogue from any role she'd ever played. "I was cast as Zelda in *The Last Flapper* one summer in a small theater on South Sepulveda." Vivien shrugged, took her last bite of strawberry, and put the stem on her plate. "I think it was more likely that Zelda was bipolar rather than schizophrenic. And I suspect that, like then as now, treatment didn't help everyone. At least not one hundred percent."

The two women looked across the table at each other with a shared history and awareness. Viewing Nonnie through the eyes of an adult, she seemed less intimidating. Almost human. Like Henry yesterday, she was being thoughtful. Vivien chalked it up to Nonnie's regard for her mother and perhaps the same shock they all felt. "Momma seemed to struggle less the last few years."

"I think you're right." Nonnie took a bite of toast and washed it down with her tea before she asked, "Are you worried you'll develop Macy Jane's illness?"

Not that the reason behind Nonnie's concern

mattered. Vivien was just grateful. "Now that I'm thirty, I don't worry about it as much. Each time I get a little too happy, it does cross my mind, though." The cell phone next to Vivien's plate vibrated and she picked it up. Her chest squeezed even as every other part of her body went numb. She glanced at Nonnie, then pressed the "connect" button. "Hello." Vivien looked at her hand gripping the table's edge and listened as the medical examiner explained that her mother had died from a myocardial infarction caused by a pulmonary embolism. He used words like *deep vein thrombosis* and *right ventricle failure* and *acute vascular obstruction*. Vivien said yes and no and felt numbed by the information coming at her. Likely, there'd been no signs or symptoms. Once it traveled to her heart, there had been nothing that could have been done to save her. Not even if she'd been in the hospital.

Vivien's world narrowed and turned dark and blurry around the edges and she could think of only one last question to ask: "Did my momma suffer?"

"No," the medical examiner assured her. "It happened very fast."

She pressed "disconnect," then looked across the table. "Momma died from a blood clot in her heart," she said, and for the first time that Vivien could recall, Nonnie's composure slipped. Her strength, both elegant and stern, drained from her stiff shoulders and she actually put her elbows on the table.

"How did she get a blood clot in her heart?"

"The medical examiner said it came from her thigh." And for the first time that she could recall, she saw the Mantis as a person capable of real human feelings. "Did she seem tired lately?"

"No." Nonnie folded her arms on the table.

"Worked up?" Vivien took a sip of tea. "Henry mentioned something about a Twitter war." Of all things.

"That." Nonnie waved a hand. "She was naturally offended by the Georgia UDC's ridiculous claim that they serve the best shrimp and grits at their annual fundraising event in Savannah. She corrected our Georgia sisters using the Twitter, but she wasn't worked up. She was more excited about scrapbook paper and stencils being on sale at the Walmart." Nonnie sat back in her chair. "I got up to pour another glass of merlot and I heard a thump. I turned around and Macy Jane was on the floor." Anguish pinched the corners of her eyes and her pointed chin quivered. "I tried to wake her up. I don't know CPR and felt so helpless."

"The medical examiner said there was nothing anyone could have done." Vivien watched Nonnie battle with her emotions. "Even if she'd been in the hospital."

The older woman nodded once and cleared her

throat. Like a door slamming shut, control won out and she was all business once more. "Did your momma ever mention her preference in funeral arrangements?"

"She was fifty. What healthy, fifty-year-old woman talks about funeral preferences?" Now it was Vivien's turn for her chin to quiver. She was an actress but couldn't pull herself together like Nonnie. The tighter she held her emotions inside, the more they leaked out. "I have no idea what she would have preferred or where to start."

"Well, I think Macy Jane would want to be laid out at Stuhr's, with her service at St. Phillips Episcopal."

Vivien nodded. Stuhr's took care of politicians and distinguished families alike. She heard the front door open and close and breathed a sigh of relief when Sarah walked into the kitchen.

"How are you doing this morning?" Sarah asked as she breezed into the kitchen with her phone to one ear, her computer notebook in the crook of her arm, and a Starbucks triple grande, nonfat, no foam, latte in her free hand.

"Thank God." Vivien stood and took the coffee from her assistant. "You read my mind." She'd had several assistants in the past few years and Sarah's ability to know what Vivien needed without constant urging was just one of the reasons she put up with some of Sarah's immature antics.

"Did you get any rest?"

"I managed a little sleep," she said as Sarah air kissed her cheek.

"Good." Sarah looked rested and fresh and totally L.A. with her tousled blonde curls, super skinny jeans, and bandage crop top. Chunky bracelets circled one wrist and an orange leather tote hung from one elbow. "I put together your schedule for the next few weeks, and Randall Hoffman's secretary confirmed your lunch for the twelfth."

"That's this Friday." Randall Hoffman was an Academy Award–winning director and production of his latest period drama was set to start next month. The actress originally cast in the lead role had dropped out, and Vivien wanted that part. She *needed* that part to show her acting versatility. Today was Monday. How many days usually passed between death and the funeral? She'd never dealt with anything like this before and honestly had no idea.

"And Friday morning is your table read for *Psychic Detectives.*"

Psychic Detectives was a hit HBO series and she couldn't pull out now. Not when she was due on the set to start filming in a week. "Okay." She could be in L.A. Friday, then back to Charleston after the table read. "We can have Momma's funeral any day but Friday."

Sarah pulled two packs of Truvia from her tote and handed them over. "You have your second audition for the Steven Soderbergh film on Thursday."

"You'll have to reschedule the audition." Vivien retraced her steps. "Sarah, this is Mrs. Whitley-Shuler. Nonnie, my assistant, Sarah."

"Nice to meet you," Sarah said and returned her attention to her cellphone.

"The pleasure is mine." The pearl-wearing matriarch towered over the two of them like she was a queen. Slight displeasure appeared on her angular face.

Vivien carefully opened her latte and set it on the table. She tore open the white and green packets and dumped the artificial sweetener into her coffee. She didn't know what bee had climbed into Nonnie's bonnet, but she did recognize the pinch at the corners of her lips.

"The *Enquirer* called your publicist regarding the Christian Forsyth rumor." Sarah's thumb busily scrolled the screen of her cell phone as Vivien stirred her coffee. "She gave him a 'no comment.'" Sarah was good at her job. Very little fell through the cracks, but at the moment, every word she uttered felt like another twist of Vivien's already tight emotions. "*People* will feature you wearing the black-and-gold Dolce and Gabbana in their Red Carpet Spotlight next month, and they want a short Q and A about that special night." She paused and Vivien fought the urge to grab the phone and throw it. With each item on her schedule, her anxiety rose. It was too much. It was just all too much. "We haven't nailed down an exact date for your *Tonight Show* appearance. We're waiting to see if they'll reschedule to fit your calendar. Your landscapers broke the Venetian urn next to your cabaña and . . ." She paused as her thumb scrolled lower.

"Good gravy, sweetheart," Nonnie said as she took the phone from Sarah's hand and dropped it in the tote. "Vivien is grieving her momma. Can't all that wait?"

Taken aback, Sarah's gaze darted from Vivien to Nonnie then back again. Poor Sarah. Before she'd come to work for Vivien, she'd dealt with a few difficult actresses and a wild pop princess, but she'd never met anyone like the Mantis. "What?"

For the first time in Vivien's life, she was grateful for Ms. Eleanor Whitley-Shuler, direct descendent of Colonel John C. Whitley, secessionist and aristocrat. "Just tell everyone I have a family emergency and I don't know when I'll be back. Reschedule everything for the next two weeks." She took a breath and let it out slowly. "I don't give a darn about the dang urn."

Sarah's lips drew tight. "You start shooting *Psychic Detectives* on the nineteenth."

"Okay." She'd rack up some serious frequent flyer miles before she'd settled everything here. "There's so much that needs to be done here." Vivien knew she was asking a lot, but it couldn't be helped. "But we should be able to get a lot done within the next two weeks."

"We? Two weeks? You want me here for the next two weeks?" Sarah's lips drew tighter and she shook her head. "There is no way I can be gone for two weeks, Vivien. I can't leave Patrick alone for that long."

Vivien raised her coffee to her lips and took a sip. This was a perfect example of Sarah's immature antics. "My momma just passed and you're worried about your cheating boyfriend?"

"He's not a cheater. You don't know him."

Vivien laughed without humor and couldn't believe she was having this conversation in her dead momma's kitchen. She'd known a lot of pretty boys like Patrick. Out-of-work actors, supported by lame jobs and gullible girls. She used to be one of those girls. "I know he's a parasite who uses women with low expectations and can't be trusted." Which just proved that smart women like Sarah, and like herself, too, could be dumb when it came to men. "I need you here with me." This day had started off crappy and the last thing she needed was a total shit storm between her and Sarah. Especially in front of Nonnie.

Again Vivien heard the front door open and close and within in seconds, Henry appeared behind her assistant. Great, the second to the last thing she needed was another Whitley-Shuler spectator. "You have to stay."

"I can't."

Henry balanced a big white cake in one hand and pushed his sunglasses to the top of his head with the other. He stopped in the doorway and his gaze met Vivien's over the top of Sarah's blonde head. "I need to finish my morning Starbucks before I can deal with this," she said as her hand found the front of her robe to make sure it was closed. At the moment, Vivien had bigger problems than Henry's sudden appearance, and she returned her attention to her assistant. "We forgot to pack underwear, and I don't have a dress. You need to find me a black dress."

"I need Patrick."

"I need underwear."

"I can't stay."

"I can't walk into the mall and buy a dress, Sarah. Not without security."

"I won't lose Patrick."

"You should. He's a loser."

"Ladies," Nonnie interrupted. "I'll make sure you get clothing, Vivien."

Vivien looked into Sarah's determined face and knew she was leaving, with or without her job. "Fine." Sarah could be a pain in the butt, but she was a good assistant, for the most part. It would take months to find and train someone new. Someone loyal who she could trust not to leak information about her private life to the tabloids. "Go home and work from L.A. It will probably be easier anyway." Vivien could manage by herself. She hadn't made her own appointments, called a car service, or carried her own bags in years, but she was certainly capable.

"Thank you." Sarah quickly fished her phone from her tote and promptly ordered the cab that had just dropped her off to return. "I'll grab my stuff and book my flight while I'm on the way to the airport." She disconnected and adjusted the notebook in the crook of her arm. "Patrick loves me," she said in the way women had of excusing men while trying to convince themselves as well as everyone else. "He's a really good guy."

"He's a man skank. He'll sleep with your Spanish neighbor, your Korean best friend, and the Russian girl around the block like he's a foreign-relations operative. Then if you make a name for yourself, he'll sell a story about you to the *Enquirer*." Vivien waved her hand across the air in front of her. It wouldn't even matter if the story was true. "Go."

Sarah turned and almost collided with the three-layer coconut cake Henry held in his hands.

"Whoa there." Henry fought to balance the glass plate in front of his chest. A few slivers of coconut fell to the floor, and just when it looked like he might win, the cake tipped and fell into his black polo shirt. "Damn."

"Sorry." Sarah sucked white frosting off the side of her hand and breezed past him.

He looked down at the cake lying against his shirt then brought his gaze back to Vivien. "She must belong to you."

"Yes. I'm sorry." Vivien lowered her hands to the silk belt of her robe and once again made sure it was still closed around her. "She's young and thinks she's in love."

Nonnie stepped forward and took the cake from Henry's hands and carried it to the table. "Youth is no excuse for bad manners. She wasn't raised right."

Henry stared down at the patch of white frosting and coconut on his shirt. "Ms. Jeffers was just dropping off her cake as I pulled in the driveway." He looked up. "She said she'll be bringing over a chicken-and-rice casserole as soon as it thaws."

"Wait." Vivien pointed to the floor. "She's not bringing it here, right?"

"Etta's going to crow about being the first on the scene with her condolence cake, and she'll naturally expect to see it at the reception next to Louisa Deering's Twinkie loaf just to show off." Nonnie sighed and put one long finger to her bottom lip as she studied the lopsided cake. "For Christmas, Louisa made a wreath out of those little cocktail weenies. Bless her heart."

"Ms. Jeffers isn't bringing her casserole to this house. Right?" Vivien repeated herself. She'd been to a handful of funerals growing up, and she clearly recalled table after table weighted down with every conceivable kind of casserole and salad concoction. The last thing she needed to deal with was Cherry Coke Jell-O.

"No. This kitchen is too small for bereavement offerings."

Just as Vivien thought, a ton of funeral food was headed her way.

"I'll call Etta and have her tell the ladies at St. Phillip's to come to the front of the big house." The top layer of the cake slid off and broke into several pieces. "Well, there is nothing that can be done for that cake now. I'll tell Etta we couldn't help ourselves and ate it up."

Nonnie was going to lie? The woman who'd always demanded Vivien tell the truth or receive some sort of punishment? Vivien opened her mouth and, before she thought better of it, said, " 'Lies make baby Jesus cry.' "

Nonnie's head whipped around and her wide eyes narrowed. "Little white lies, told in loving kindness, are God's tender mercies."

"Where's that in the Bible?"

Henry's deep chuckle made both women turn their attention on him. Amusement shined in his deep brown eyes as he walked to the counter and pulled a paper towel from the roll. "Some shit never changes."

"Henry! I did not send you to the best schools in the country for you to express yourself with common vulgarities."

"Pardon my common vulgarities." Henry looked down and wiped thick frosting and coconut from his shirt. "With all the bossing and sassing, it sounds like old times around here." He glanced up and recognized the displeasure in his mother's gaze before he turned his attention to Vivien. It didn't look like old times, though. Vivien was no longer the plump little girl who stuck her tongue out at people when she thought they weren't looking. All grown up and gorgeous, she made him think of interesting places she could stick her tongue.

"No one is bossing anyone around, Henry Thomas. I'm offering gentle guidance. I don't know where you get your ideas." His mother carried two plates of half-eaten toast to the counter. "I'll go call the parish rector and make him aware of Macy Jane's passing. I'm sure we can get in to see him today."

"Today?" Vivien looked overwhelmed and anxious and gorgeous. Her hair still sleep tousled and her thin little body wrapped in silk. He'd noticed how skinny she was last night. He'd noticed other changes in her, too. Like losing her accent. Which was a real shame. Henry truly did love sweet words spilling like honey from a Southern girl's lips.

"It has to be done before we make arrangements with Stuhr's. You'll need to choose a time and day and Eucharistic ministers."

"Oh." Vivien's green eyes rounded a little and she shook her head. A length of her dark hair fell forward and she pushed it back. "I don't know anything about planning a funeral or Eucharistic ministers."

"That's because you didn't spend enough time in the community of Christ contemplating sin and mortality. I'll make a call to St. Phillip's and make the appointment to see Father Dinsmore," said the woman who claimed she wasn't bossy.

Henry threw the paper towel away as his mother walked from the kitchen. "There she goes. The arbiter of sin and mortality."

"For once in my life, I'm sort of grateful Nonnie is so high and mighty and bossy." Vivien glanced across at him and her green eyes widened. "Oh, sorry to talk about your momma like that."

Once again, she'd managed to sound sincere. "High and mighty and bossy describes her fairly well."

Vivien moved a few steps to the table and grabbed a Starbucks coffee cup. "Never thought I'd live to hear a lie come from her mouth." From the side, she looked so thin he could slip her through a mail slot.

"You mean 'God's tender mercies?' " He grabbed a couple of forks from a drawer and moved toward her. "Mother can justify anything and doggedly stick to it. It's how she wins most arguments." He stabbed a small chunk of broken cake and held the fork out for her. Vivien looked at the fork but didn't take it.

"It's been a long time since I had coconut funeral cake." He took her free hand and placed the handle in her palm. "Don't make me eat this alone." He stabbed another piece and stuck it in his mouth.

She looked at the fork in her hand then up at him as a frown pulled at the corners of her full lips. "I'm not a fan of cake."

He swallowed and stabbed another piece. "Since when? I recall one of Mother's garden parties and the theft of those fussy little cakes she serves."

"Must have been Spence."

He took a bite and chuckled. "A lot of things got blamed on Spence, but he didn't like those sissy cakes any more than I did."

"I don't remember that." She took a drink of her coffee and a small smile curved her mouth. "If I did borrow Nonnie's garden party petit fours—"

"—Darlin'," he interrupted, "you can't *borrow* something that you don't plan to return."

Her smile grew and warm, bubbly laughter spilled from her lips like she was filled with sunshine and champagne.

"Well if I did, *accidently,* take a few of your momma's petit fours, it was because y'all were out of ice cream." She set the fork on the table without taking a bite. "You'll have to excuse me, Mr. Whitley-Shuler. If I'm not ready by the time Nonnie comes back, she'll snatch me bald headed," she said, her accent back in full force and dripping with Southern honey.

— Chapter 6 —

The next twenty-four hours were a kaleidoscope of panic and exhaustion, fear and grief, tumbling and turning and sliding one over the other, changing color and shape but always creating the same unreal images. Sharp and dull at the same time, Vivien's sorrow was a constant in her heart and soul.

If not for Nonnie, Vivien wasn't sure how she would have gotten though the day. The Mantis had been surprisingly helpful, showing glimpses of tenderness and emotion in between domineering commands. She sat beside Vivien as she chose funeral music at St. Phillips and toured the coffin room at Stuhr's. Nonnie knew how many limousines and which hearse they should use. When it came to cemeteries, Nonnie insisted that only Mount Pleasant Memorial Gardens would do. They chose a burial plot not far from former governor James Edwards. Nonnie wrote down the names of the six pallbearers who would carry Macy Jane's white casket, and she knew exactly which florist to call to arrange the flowers. But Nonnie wasn't family. Vivien was family, and she and her momma had always taken care of each other. It was Vivien's responsibility to take care of the intimate details for her mother this one last time.

It was her responsibility alone to write her momma's obituary, and later that night as her panties once again dried in the laundry room, she grabbed the laptop her mother had used to feud with the United Daughters of the Confederacy and wrote. Vivien was an actress, not a writer, and it took her most of the night to end up with something long enough to take up three-quarters of a page in the *Post and Courier*. When she was through, she hit "send" and closed the laptop.

If still alive, she knew her mother would feign modesty and toss in a bit of humility, but she'd secretly be very pleased with her own obituary. In keeping with the Southern tradition of embellishment, and her own momma's lifelong aversion to a flat-out lie, Vivien stretched the truth just to the point of snapping like a rubber band. She wrote that Macy Jane was loved by many for her free (unpredictable) spirit, imaginative (dreamed of exotic places) mind, artistic (painted tables) ability, and award-winning (won third place for her peach jam once) culinary skills.

The last paragraph, she didn't have to stretch anything. She wrote about her mother's kind heart and gentle soul, and that she would be missed greatly. She mentioned family members who had preceded her mother in death, and the handful who still lived in various parts of the country, but she did not mention herself by name. The funeral service was about Macy Jane Rochet, not Vivien Leigh Rochet, and the last thing she wanted was to turn the day into a *Raffle* fan fair.

It was also Vivien's lone responsibility to choose her momma's burial clothes. When she woke the next morning, she laid out the pink silk dress her momma had worn at her housewarming party. She pulled a garment bag from the closet and added a pair of Christian Louboutin pumps her mother had only worn inside because she didn't want to scratch the red bottoms. She added the thirteen-millimeter Mikimoto pearls and matching earrings she'd given her mother for Christmas five years ago, and because her momma wouldn't be caught dead without shape wear, Vivien included her thigh-length Spanx.

She packed everything and hugged the pink dress to her chest one last time. The scent of her momma's perfume lingered on the silk Peter Pan collar, but she refused to give in to tears. She'd spent most of yesterday crying, and if she started, she was afraid she wouldn't be able to stop. If she broke down, she wouldn't be able to get back up.

Once everything was ready for Stuhr's, she showered and pulled a vintage Rolling Stones T-shirt over her one strapless bra. She wore black jeans and leather sandals and very little makeup. She picked up the garment bag before she headed out the front door. She moved along the cobblestone path toward the back of the big house and remembered the many times she'd hid in the boxwood or rose-covered gazebo and eavesdropped on Nonnie's conversations, or climbed the live oak and dropped acorns on Spence and his friends.

It had been twelve years since she'd set foot inside the Whitley-Shuler house, but as soon as she stepped inside she could see that nothing had really changed in the enormous Greek revival. It still smelled of old wood and paste wax, mixed with a slight scent of musty fabric and restored wallpaper. It still felt like a museum with family portraits and paintings, marble statues and Duncan Phyfe furniture.

Vivien found Nonnie in the double parlor, the pocket doors open and the ornate room in the process of being cleaned and polished for the reception the day after tomorrow. Blue and gold period rugs matched the heavy silk drapes, swathing the floor windows just as Vivien remembered. The French doors were open to the piazza that wrapped around the house, and Nonnie stood in front of an ornate marble fireplace, tall and lean in a navy-blue suit with brass buttons. She looked like a general, directing a crew that had already begun to set up extra tables and chairs for the funeral reception. Everyone in the room seemed to snap to attention at her command. Everyone but the one man who stood with his elbow on the mantel's edge, displeasure pulling at his brow. He'd rolled the sleeves of his blue-and-white-striped dress shirt up his forearms and a silver watch circled his wrist. His fingers tapped the marble mantel as he watched his mother point and direct. Then she turned toward him and pointed toward the ceiling. He shook his head, clearly not happy with the orders his mother issued his way. The last time Vivien'd seen Henry, he'd stood in her own momma's kitchen, frosting on his shirt and laughing about stolen petit fours. She couldn't recall if she'd ever heard Henry laugh before. Ever. He'd certainly never called her "darlin'," and for a moment or two, they had been just a man and a woman. Standing in a kitchen sharing a laugh. She'd forgotten their past and that she'd called him Butt Head Henry.

"I'm not your employee," he told Nonnie as Vivien walked toward them. "I'm only here to pick up grandmother's extension leaves for you." He pointed toward a dining table with big claw feet shoved against the far wall. "I don't think you realize what it's going to take to get those damn things ready in two days."

"I appreciate it, son, but right now I need you to go up into the attic and look around for your grandmother Shuler's wedding silver. I need the chrysanthemum cake plate." She gestured with her hands. "It's about yea big, by yea big. It's heavy and tacky beyond words."

Vivien remembered the chrysanthemum silver. She'd polished it enough times that the pattern was imprinted in her brain. She set the garment bag on a horsehair settee and interrupted Nonnie's diatribe on the Shulers' tacky taste. "Excuse me." When the older woman turned toward her she said, "I have Momma's clothes ready."

"Good." Nonnie nodded. "I'll have someone take them to Stuhr's for you."

Which brought Vivien to her second problem of the day. "I need to shop for some things." From behind his mother's left shoulder, Henry's dark gaze met hers and the lines creasing his forehead rose as if he'd looked up and was surprised to see her. "When I left L.A., I forgot to pack a dress."

One corner of his mouth lifted as if she wasn't an altogether unpleasant surprise. In the past two days, Henry had smiled at her more than in her entire life. She turned her attention to Nonnie, away from the confusion of Henry's smiles. "Sarah isn't here to pick something up for me." The last time Vivien had tried to shop like a regular person, a crowd of photographers had camped outside of Dior on Rodeo, waiting for her. Within minutes, the crowd grew bigger, the paparazzi more intense, trapping her inside. Before security could disperse the spectators, a Japanese tourist got mowed down by Paris Hilton's pink Bentley. Thank goodness the tourist survived, but Vivien had been horrified by the whole experience. She'd learned her lesson about walking around like a normal person. "I don't want to attract attention while I'm in Charleston." Her gaze rose to Henry's face as she said, "Sarah usually calls ahead of time so the store manager can get security in place before my arrival."

He shook his head. "I doubt you'll need security."

Maybe he was right. This was Charleston. Very few people knew she was in town. If anyone recognized her, they'd probably think she was just some random woman who resembled Vivien Rochet, a plain and less attractive version, of course.

"I'll call Berlin's." Nonnie pulled a cell phone from the pocket of her blazer and dialed the number. She relayed Vivien's problem and concern, then she placed a hand over the phone and said, "Ellen's checking to see if they still have the black Armani."

Vivien knew exactly where Berlin's was located. As a kid, she and her momma had window-shopped at the exclusive clothier at King and Broad. They'd talked about the day they would be rich enough to walk through the doors and buy designer dresses and frivolous hats, but like all the other things they'd dreamed about, they'd never done it. Now they would never get the chance. "Is Momma's car in the big garage?"

"That car doesn't run. Henry will drive you," Nonnie volunteered her son like he was a chauffeur service, then turned her attention to the voice on the phone. "Oh that's great."

Vivien glanced at Henry and the aggravation chasing away his slight smile. As a boy, he'd often been kind of scary and intense. As a man, he looked more dark and broody than scary, like Heathcliff or Mr. Darcy or Joe Manganiello.

"I'll take a cab," Vivien said rather than risk Henry getting stormy or pensive or going were-wolf on her.

"I'll drop you off at Berlin's," he offered but he didn't sound happy about it.

"Yes, that's right." Nonnie paused and looked at Vivien. "What size are you, dear?"

"Zero."

Zero. Zero wasn't a size. It was nothing. Zip zilch zippo. Diddly-squat. It was a goose egg, a bagel, a rolling doughnut. It wasn't the size of a woman. Or least it shouldn't be the size of a woman.

Henry sat in a black-and-white chair, leaning forward with his forearms on his thighs, and pretending to read the fashion magazine in his hands. He sat near the rear of Berlin's and he couldn't quite figure out how he'd landed the job of Vivien's chauffer and personal bodyguard. He'd meant to just drop her off and be on his way, but she'd sat in his truck staring at the storefront instead of opening the door. She'd fussed with her big sunglasses and the ball cap he'd lent her, clearly nervous. He'd been thinking of a way to shove her out the door when he heard himself offer to wait for her inside the shop. He supposed it was the Southerner in him, but if he'd known Vivien would take more than ten or fifteen minutes, he would have bitten his tongue off rather than take on the job.

Hell, he already had a job. One that did not include Vivien Rochet trying on dresses and studying herself from different angles in a three-sided mirror. At the moment, his latest job waited in his shop for him to finish. He'd built the curved kitchen island of cherrywood and steel, and he needed to add drawers and pulls before he had his guys install it in a penthouse on Prioleau Street.

"I'm almost done. I promise."

Henry lifted his gaze from an article on "beach hair." Vivien moved from a dressing room, breezing past him toward the floor-length mirrors. The back of his skull pinched his brain. He recognized that dress. It was the first one she'd tried on an hour ago. If he'd had a gun, or a knife, or a hammer, he might have put himself out of his misery.

Once again, he watched Vivien study the dress clinging to the slight curves of her body. She turned from side to side and placed a palm on her flat stomach. With her free hand, she lifted her hair off her long neck and shoulders as if she'd never seen herself in that particular dress. Like she hadn't noticed the way it cupped her small breasts and cute little butt, or the way the black material rested across her white shoulders.

"This dress does fit beautifully on you," a saleswoman told her as she got down on one knee and fussed at the hem. "I think it just needs to be taken up an inch."

"I think you're right." Vivien tilted her head to the side. "And with the Manolo peep toes, I won't look so short and stocky."

Stocky? She was either kidding or one of those annoying women who dug for compliments. She dropped her hair and slid both of her hands down her side to her behind. If she asked if the dress made her butt looked big, he didn't trust himself not to choke her. He'd almost forgotten that she was a spoiled movie star who thought people lived to serve her and couldn't get a morning latte without an assistant. There had been a time in his life when he'd been as thoughtless. When his ego had driven him to win at all costs and put his needs above those around him.

"I'll wait for you outside," he said as he stood.

From within the three mirrors, three Viviens lifted their gazes from the hem of her dress. Her green eyes sought his image over her shoulder. "I'll hurry," she said.

One Vivien was bad enough. Three Viviens were two too many. She was aggravating and annoying and so outrageously beautiful, she turned him off and on like he was a light switch. He tossed the magazine on the chair and walked by rows of designer clothes hanging from racks bolted to the old brick walls. He moved out the glass doors and into the heat and humidity of the oldest part of the Holy City. Traffic congested the corner of King and Broad, adding a layer of exhaust to the hot, muggy air. He'd rather choke on soupy fumes than watch Vivien grab her behind again.

He shoved a shoulder into the side of the building and pulled his cell phone and sunglasses from his breast pocket. He had a real life and a real job and didn't have time to babysit a spoiled actress or read beach-hair tips from a fashion magazine. He answered e-mails and text messages from suppliers and clients and checked to make sure his request for final approval on a renovation in the French Quarter was on the Board of Architectural Review's agenda.

After ten minutes, Vivien had yet to appear and he checked on some beat-up tech stocks while he waited. Trading was no longer his full-time job, but he did keep a peripheral eye on the market. At the height of his trading days in New York, he'd invested in news-driven stocks and the sectors in play. These days he managed the limited partner-ship and hedge fund he'd created with his mother and brother several years ago. The fund was just one piece of their family's investment portfolio, and he made sure it made more money than it lost. Now that banking and finance wasn't his full-time job, he could relax and even enjoy playing the market. Now that it wasn't his job, he could focus on what he really loved. The job he would have gravitated toward naturally, if he'd ever been given the choice.

For as long as he could recall, he'd had an intense interest in the warm grains and smooth textures of exotic woods. He'd loved to envision different and unusual uses for different and unusual hardwoods. He'd always had a natural vision for spatial design, even before he'd known there was such a thing.

The front door to Berlin's finally swung open and Vivien strolled outside, once again wearing her jeans and T-shirt and his Clemson baseball hat. She carried her red purse but nothing else.

"Where's your dress?" he asked. She'd tried on enough to pick at least one.

"It's being altered right now." She dug in her purse and pulled out her sunglasses. "We need to come back in an hour."

"What?"

"Since the ladies were sweet enough to have their seamstress get to work on the hem right away"—she paused and shoved her big sunglasses on her face—"the least I could do was tell them we'd wait."

"We?" He felt the corner of his eye twitch.

"Oh." She glanced around at the traffic, both vehicle and pedestrians, then looked up at him through the dark lenses. "Am I keeping you from something?" she asked as if he just naturally had all day to wait on her.

He'd like to leave her stranded, but of course he hadn't been raised to abandon women. "What do you propose *we* do for an hour?"

"I need to go to Bits of Lace." She looked behind her as if she expected someone to jump out at her. "The ladies in Berlin's said it's down the street."

He was sorry he'd asked. "The underwear store?"

She nodded and the shadow from the baseball cap's bill slid across the seam of pink lips. "I think I should call and tell them I'm coming in." Once more she dug in her purse and this time pulled out her cellphone. "I'll have to Google them to get the number."

"Why?" he asked, suspicious of her motives. His mother had called Berlin's and they'd put together an entire rack of clothes just for her. He wasn't about to watch her try on a trunkload of panties for an hour. From behind his sunglasses, he let his gaze slide to her lips. Damn. He felt like a light switch again, and it didn't seem to matter that he didn't want to get turned on.

"The store should probably have warning in case they want to get security in place first."

He looked up into her eyes. The first flicker of desire was snubbed out. Thank God. "I don't think anyone will recognize you." If he needed any more proof that she was full of herself, calling a small underwear store and wanting security was it. "Hell, princess, I hardly recognize you and I've known you for years."

Worry wrinkled her brow. "Are you sure?"

"I'm sure you're being paranoid." He took a few steps down King toward the underwear store but stopped when she didn't follow. "Isn't it this way?" He waved in the general direction of Bits of Lace. There was a sports pub near the store and he could grab a beer while he waited.

"We can't walk."

"It's only about four or five blocks."

"If things get crazy, your car will be too far away."

Crazy? It was possible that someone might recognize her, but he seriously doubted people would go crazy. Then he thought of her crazy *Raffle* fans. They were weird. "We'll drive," he said, and changed direction toward his truck, even though he did think her pampered ass was overreacting. He doubted her fans knew she was in Charleston, and it was unlikely that someone dressed in some goofy leather and chain-mail costume would pop up in an underwear store.

Henry drove the few blocks and found a parking space across the street from Bits of Lace. While Vivien shopped for bras, he relaxed at the King Street Grille next door. He picked a table near the front, and at that time of day, the place was empty except for three couples sitting at different tables and a group of young guys at the bar. ESPN offered commentary on the Rangers/Cubs game on the television overhead, and he kicked back and looked at the menu. He couldn't decide between pork sliders or nachos and ordered both along with a bottle of Palmetto porter. After spending the past hour in a women's clothing store, sitting on fussy furniture, and flipping through chick magazines, watching sports and drinking dark beer felt like coming home after an aggravating trip for an annoying employer. His shoulders relaxed and tension drained from his joints. Sitting in the sports bar instead of standing in a lingerie boutique while Vivien looked at panties felt like a reprieve from a firing squad. From the smart-mouthed girl who'd grown into a beautiful woman, and the troubling reaction that he hadn't expected and didn't want.

The waitress delivered his beer and he took a drink of the stout porter. Instead of sitting in a pub, still troubled by his physical reaction to Vivien, he should be at his shop, working on the cherrywood island or drafting a bid for the new medical complex in North Charleston. No matter the brand of little French blazers his mother had always dressed him in as a child, no matter the exclusive boarding schools or Princeton degree, working with wood was in his DNA. Like his father, Henry loved the smell and touch of wood beneath his hands. Even as a kid, he'd loved crafting something from his imagination.

He sucked foam from the corner of his mouth and set the glass on the table.

Henry had always done what had been expected of him. Except for when what was expected had almost killed him. He'd walked away from his white-collar career and never been happier. His mother considered his custom millwork a waste of his education. She didn't see a journeyman as a proper job for a Whitley-Shuler, and he wasn't at all surprised that she'd volunteered him to drive Vivien around as if he had nothing better to do. Nor was he surprised that Vivien was pushing and testing his patience just like when she'd been a kid.

So when Vivien walked through the sports pub's doors fifteen minutes after he'd ordered a beer, he had to admit that he was surprised. He'd expected her to take at least another hour just to annoy him.

"I shopped as quick as possible," she said, almost breathless, as if she'd run from one rack of bras to the next. She set her bag and purse in the chair across from him. "I don't think I've ever shopped that quick."

Now she was quick. When it didn't matter. When they still had half an hour to kill before they returned to Berlin's, and he was kicked back with a beer and some of his favorite bar food. He raised a hand and got the waitress's attention. "What can I order for you to drink?" he asked as she slid into the chair next to him.

"I'd love a mojito." She left her sunglasses on her face like she was a member of the CIA. "Thank you."

He gave the waitress Vivien's drink order and asked for a second plate. "How'd it go? Any of your fans jump out from behind shelves of panties and ask for an autograph?"

She laughed and again he was reminded of sunshine and honey. Of whiskey in a teacup that warmed a man up from the inside out. "No. I worried about nothing." She shook her head and the sunlight pouring in through the large windows slid across her smooth cheek. Her dark hair stuck out the back of the baseball cap and brushed the back of her T-shirt. "Thank goodness."

"You're too uptight." She was all smooth skin and shiny hair and working him like a light switch again.

"Me?" Her mouth dropped and she sucked in a shocked breath. "You were born uptight, Henry."

She was probably right about that, but he wasn't

ever going to admit it. Vivien's drink and extra plate arrived and she slid three paltry nachos onto her plate.

"I'm not the one who is so uptight I won't remove my sunglasses. Inside a bar."

"I don't want to draw attention."

"Your sunglasses draw attention." He took a drink of his beer. "If people stare at you, darlin', it's probably because they think you're hiding a black eye. God, they probably think I gave it to you."

"Woman beater." She laughed and pulled the glasses from her face. She set them on the table and pursed her lips around her mojito straw. "You're so uptight, you can't even walk into a lingerie store." She paused to take a bite of one chip. "You're probably one of those guys who's afraid that being surrounded by display bins filled with panties will suck out all your testosterone."

"My testosterone is not affected by panties." In fact, he was very fond of the sight of lacy panties on a woman. Especially if she was trying to suck out his testosterone.

She shook her head and tried not to smile. "I remember one summer when you pitched a conniption over my and Momma's clean under-wear hanging on the clothesline."

He remembered that because he'd been traumatized by the sight of all those granny panties flapping in the breeze. "You two strung

97

your clothesline in front of the carriage house."

"We didn't have a backyard." She shrugged and finished off her measly chip.

"I was fourteen and my friends from school were heading up that day." He wondered if she still wore big silky underwear. Somehow, he doubted it.

"You could have just taken the laundry down instead of freaking out."

He doubted he'd freaked out. "I didn't want to touch y'all's grann . . . ah, laundry."

"You haven't changed. You're still all uptight and fussy." She took a drink and swallowed.

"I've never been uptight and fussy." More like annoyed and provoked.

"I think you're scared that all those panties will touch you and will shrivel you up like a raisin."

He raised a brow. "Nothing ever shrivels me like a raisin." Was he really talking about his balls? With Vivien Rochet? "I'm good that way."

"The proof is in the pudding, as my mamaw used to say." She reached for her shopping bag and set it on the table in front of him. "Prove it."

"I'm not sticking my hand in there."

"It's not a bag of snakes, Henry." She reached for a chip. "Go ahead."

"I'm not your assistant. You can't order me around."

"Scared?"

"Stop, Vivien." She was pushing him. Provoking

him and, by the sparkle in her eyes, she a
having fun doing it, too.

"I double-dog dare you, Henry."

Behind her pretty face, he could almost see
the little girl who'd rummaged through his
closet, then dared him to call her a thief. The
chubby little kid who stuck her tongue out at him
when no one else was looking. "You can't double-
dog dare before you dare and double dare."

"I'm not playing around." Her gaze narrowed
and she shook her head. "I'm going straight to
the double dog."

"You're ridiculous." He put the bag in his lap
and kept his gaze locked with hers as he reached
inside. Silk and lace touched the tips of his
fingers and he pulled out a blue bra. A flimsy,
see-through bra. He held it up by one strap and
studied the tiny purple flowers before he
dropped it back into the sack.

"How do you feel?"

"Not a bit shriveled." And getting less shriveled
by the second. He handed her the bag of bras
and panties and glanced at the Tag Heuer on his
wrist. "We should get going." He stood and dug
his wallet out of his back pocket.

"Thank you, Henry."

Before he'd found her in Macy Jane's muddy
garden, he didn't think he'd ever heard
"thank you" pass her lips. "For what? You
didn't eat much." He tossed two twenties on the

table then stuffed his wallet into his back pocket.

"For driving me around today when you didn't want to." She grabbed her purse and sunglasses. "And for making me laugh and forget for just a few minutes why I'm here."

He looked down into her green eyes and the laughter fading from her gaze. "You're welcome, Vivien Leigh." She slid the sunglasses on her face and he put his hand in the small of her back. As they crossed the street, he tried to recall exactly when he'd last put his hands on a woman's bra and panties. It had probably been a few months ago. A few months' worth of pent-up lust explained why the sight of Vivien in a black dress, the touch of a blue bra, and the warmth of her back against the palm of his hand made him think about sex. He opened the passenger door of his truck for Vivien, then moved to the driver's side. He definitely had to do something about the dismal state of his sex life. The problem was, he wanted more than just sex. He was thirty-five and had been in two serious relationships. Both women had left him when they'd figured out that he hadn't been serious enough to put a ring on it. It wasn't that he was opposed to marriage, he just hadn't ever been ready.

Cool air from the truck's vents brushed across his forearms as he drove Vivien back to Berlin's. He thought of the single women he'd dated since he'd been back in Charleston. Most had been smart and attractive women. A few had even earned his mother's stamp of approval, but he wasn't Spence. He didn't need Nonnie to approve of the women in his life.

He pulled the truck next to the curb in front of Berlin's and Vivien ran in to grab her dress. His brother had married a bona fide St. Cecilia debutante. Nonnie had been beyond thrilled to have a daughter-in-law, like herself, who'd been presented at the ultra-exclusive St. Cecilia ball held every November. Spence had done what had been expected. He'd married "true Southern," but look where it got him. In the middle of a brutal divorce and chasing the pain away with booze and women. Henry was different. He wasn't looking for a pedigree. He was looking for a woman that he would love forever. That he *wanted* to love forever.

After he dropped Vivien off at the carriage house, he pointed his truck toward his small home on John's Island. The size of the house and the fact that it was only six years old had appealed to him almost as much as the large shop located out back. Before moving into the fifteen-hundred-square-foot house, he'd torn out several walls and made the kitchen, dining room, and living room all one larger space. He'd converted one bedroom into an office and he'd torn out the wall between the other two to make his master suite. The whole house could fit in his mother's bedroom, but he loved it.

Orange streaks splashed across the sky by the

time Henry pulled his truck into his driveway and parked next to the garage in back. Even before he opened the door to his shop, he could smell freshly cut wood and sanding dust. He unlocked the door and flipped on the lights. Besides fresh wood, the building also held the scents of stain and varnish and was filled with molding and millwork machinery. His shoes kicked up a thin layer of sawdust covering the floor as he made his way to the kitchen island he'd fabricated for the penthouse in town. He ran his hand across the gleaming wood as he continued to the clamp table holding the spines and seat of a chair. It matched two others as well as the maplewood table he'd been building for Macy Jane. Now it belonged to Vivien. He'd have to ask her what she wanted done with it.

He thought of Vivien in her hat and sunglasses, all paranoid as if crazed fans were hiding around every corner. As if she might be recognized when in reality, no one had given her a second glance.

The cell phone rang in his shirt pocket, and he looked at the number a second before hitting the talk button. "What's up, Spence? Are you back in town?"

"Yeah," his brother answered. "I got home about an hour ago."

For the past week, Spence had been blowing off steam on a fishing boat in the Florida Keys. "Did you catch anything?"

"Nothing to brag about. I heard about Macy Jane." Spence paused before he added, "That's damn sad. She was a nice lady."

"Yes she was."

"I heard you took Vivien shopping today."

He bent down and picked up a bar clamp someone had left on the floor. "You must have been talking to Mother."

"No. Rowley Davidson just sent me a text. His wife, Lottie, went to school with Vivien, and she showed him something on the Internet."

Henry walked toward the clamp rack and placed it in the row where it belonged. "Exactly what does Rowley Davidson's wife, Lottie, have to do with me?"

"He sent me an Internet link to one of those gossip sites." Spence laughed. "You should take a look."

"Why?"

"Just do it." Again Spence laughed like there was some sort of hilarity going on. "I'm saying good-bye now so I can send you the link."

Spence hung up, and less than a minute later, Henry received his brother's text. He touched the link with his thumb and waited. A red and black site popped up—along with a photograph of Henry sitting next to Vivien at the King Street Grille. She had a nacho in one hand. He had her bright blue bra dangling from one finger. The cutline read: Unidentified man fondles Vivien Rochet's bra.

— Chapter 7 —

Dear Diary,
I got a pain in my chest yesterday. I'm sure I'm going to need a bra any day now. ☺

Dear Diary,
Yesterday I was cleaning the inside of Henry's closet. It's terribly dusty, ha-ha! I found one of those wood boxes he's always making with hidden drawers. The last one I found wasn't very tricky and I found an old watch in one and a tiny jade elephant in the other. I really wanted that elephant, but I was afraid he'd know it was gone. This time he thought he was extra tricky and made the box with a puzzle top. I'm still trying to figure it out, but I'll get it open. Henry Whitley-Shuler will never outsmart Vivien Leigh Rochet!

Dear Diary,
Hip Hop Hooray!!! Momma said I can take hip-hop and ballet class because we're Episcopalian now. We were First

Baptist and dancing is a sin if you're Baptist. Drinking alcohol, too. Nonnie took me and Momma to St. Phillip's, and the Episcopalians said I have to get baptized to wash away all my sins, but I'm only thirteen (in three months) and I don't think I'm done with sinning yet. I said I want to wait until I'm twenty-five. That way I don't have to worry for a while yet about going to hell if I tell a lie, and the Episcopalians will have lots more sins they can wash away. Nonnie frowned like Cruella de Vil and Momma said, "Don't make me call Santa on you, Vivien Leigh!" I don't believe in Santa, so that doesn't worry me anymore.

Dear Diary,
  Curses, Josephine!!! Tropical Storm Josephine knocked down a tree on our power line. No TV for two days!!!! Nonnie said ocean water got in the Shuler house at Hilton Head. ☺ Storms always make me think of my daddy and I get sad. ☹ He died before I was born and before he could marry Momma. I think that's why Momma can never find a boyfriend that sticks. She's still sad about Daddy. Momma

showed me an old newspaper article about Daddy and Hurricane Kate sinking his schooner. He and his whole family loved to sail and were rescuing Cubans, kind of like that Elian kid a few years ago, when Hurricane Kate happened. I got sad reading about it. Daddy never got to see me, but Momma said he'd wrap me up in sweet if he'd lived. I don't know. Sometimes I act up and make people mad. Sometimes I'm not sorry when I say I am.

Dear Diary,

HELL'S BELLS AND HEAVENS TO BETSY!!! I got Henry's puzzle box open. It was filled with a wood pipe, two keys, and letters from a girl named Tracy Lynn Fortner. I think her family has a town named after them. At first the letters were so boring that I almost fell asleep then I choked and swallowed the gum I stole from Spence. The letters were all mushy about how much she missed Henry when he was away at school and how much she loooooved him and loooooved talking to him on the phone. Ugh!! Then she wrote that she was really afraid and that her parents were going to be disappointed and humiliated because she failed a test. At first I thought she was buggin' because she'd failed a math test or maybe gym class. But NO!! She said she took three E.P.T. tests. Henry got a baby on Tracy Lynn Fortner! Then she wrote that she didn't want to see Henry anymore when he was home. She said it was too painful, and she told him not to call or write or talk about it to anyone. Did Henry have a baby? Where is it? I can't ask about it or tell anyone because I'll get in trouble for snooping in Henry's stuff. It's a pickle, but when I really think about it, I wouldn't tell anyway. Some stuff hurts people and shouldn't be talked about. Like Momma's sadness. I don't like it when kids at school talk about Momma's sadness.

Things I Want To Know List

1. My daddy's people
2. When I get to wear a bra
3. If I'll get Momma's sadness
4. What I will be when I grow up
5. If gum really stays in your stomach forever

— Chapter 8 —

The funeral service for Macy Jane Rochet took place at St. Phillip's Episcopal Church. The parish rector, Father John Dinsmore, clothed in his white vestments and aided by an equally impressively dressed verger, delivered the liturgy for the burial of the dead. Secretly pleased that the church was filled to capacity and the mourners would hear his deep, compelling voice, he praised Macy Jane for her love of God and dedication to the community of Christ.

Vivien hadn't known her mother to have so many friends but, as Vivien was learning, there was quite a bit she'd never known. Quite a bit Macy Jane had kept from her. Quite a bit she'd have to sort out, later. When she had time and space to think and breathe. When she was finally alone and could curl up in a ball.

When Father Dinsmore praised Sister Macy Jane's love and devotion to Jesus, Vivien almost smiled. Whether it was, "Jesus hates ugly," or "Lies make baby Jesus cry," or "You can worry or vex—or insert any verb—Jesus right off of his cross," Jesus had always been big in her momma's life.

Vivien sat in the front pew, surrounded by more

than a hundred people, but she'd never felt so alone in her life. Not even as a kid, singled out for being different. She wore a sleeveless black dress and her grandmother's pearls. The princess-length necklace was nowhere near the same quality as the Mikimoto pearls Vivien had given to her mother, but the sentimental value was beyond measure.

She'd combed her hair into a loose bun at the nape of her neck and wore her mother's black pillbox hat with the netting pulled over her face. She'd brushed waterproof mascara on her lashes and red smudgeproof lipstick on her mouth. Nonnie sat on one side of Vivien and her uncle Richie and his wife, Kathy, sat on the other. Just a few feet away, Macy Jane's white casket gleamed beneath the chandeliers, and Vivien was grateful that the Episcopal Church required a closed casket. She didn't think she could hold herself together if she had to look at her momma once more, wearing her pink dress and holding prayer beads in her hands folded across her abdomen.

The worst part was over. At least she hoped it was the worst part. Earlier, she'd done her duty and sat by the open casket while mourners poured in for the viewing. Except for the lipstick that was a shade too orange, her momma looked like she always looked. Like she was asleep and would open her eyes and sit up, and Vivien had had to hold herself tight so she wouldn't jump up and run out of the room. She'd had to hold herself together when she wanted to tear off her own skin, rip out her own aching heart, or wail like Marta Southerland when she'd approached the casket.

Vivien had held it together during the viewing and during the long funeral. At the conclusion of the service, Henry and Spence and four other pallbearers carried the casket out of St. Phillip's and to a silver hearse parked at the curb. Across from the church, a large group of boys and teenage girls, middle-aged women and men, stood behind a security barrier guarded by the four big men. In light of the TMZ internet post, Sarah had arranged a security detail to make sure the funeral wasn't disrupted, but the gathering across the street was solemn. They simply raised one hand in the air above their heads, Zahara West's rebel brand drawn on their palms. The salute was a sign of respect taken from the Raffle trilogy, and the sight of her fans gave her pause before she dipped inside the silver limo and sat next to Nonnie. Across from her sat her momma's only brother, Richie, and his wife, Kathy, watching the Raffle fans as if they were about to rush the car. Vivien wasn't all that surprised to see them. Thanks to TMZ, they knew she was in Charleston. Someone had caught her eating at the sports pub, but the image of her blue bra dangling from Henry's finger almost made it worth it. She wondered if he'd seen the

110

picture. Did he still think she was just paranoid?

The funeral procession wove through the Holy City toward Mt. Pleasant Cemetery. Vivien forced herself to engage her uncle and Kathy in small talk, even as Kathy eyed Mamaw's pearls around Vivien's neck. It had never been a secret that Kathy thought Macy Jane got everything after Mamaw's death. She believed that Richie got slighted and had refused to accept that there'd been little to get. Her momma had always said that death made some people "too tacky for words. Kathy is from the North. We have to pray for her." Vivien didn't care where the woman was from, she just never felt like praying for a woman who'd said bad things about her mother, nor for Uncle Richie, who'd never quite forgiven his sister for her mental illness and the chaos it had created in the family.

After several minutes of "yes" and "no" answers, Vivien turned her gaze and looked out the tinted windows. Small clusters of Raffle fans gathered along the route and stood with palms raised on the side of the road.

"Who are those people?" Nonnie wanted to know.

"Fans of the Raffle books and movies."

"What in the devil are they doing?"

"Showing respect for Momma."

"Well, they're not even bothering to hide their crazy."

Vivien didn't think they were crazy, at least not all of them. She appreciated her fans, but some of them were certifiably crazy. Last year, a man dressed as Evil Commander Rath had tried to break into her house and she'd had to beef up security. Most were normal, respectful people but she did worry that some might show up at the cemetery and cause a distraction just by being there.

As the limo pulled to a stop at the grave site, Vivien was relieved not to see anyone standing among the headstones with Zahara West's symbol on their raised palm.

The pallbearers poured out of the second limousine, then carried the white casket to the site. Nonnie, Vivien, Richie, and Kathy sat in the chairs provided by the funeral home. Henry and Spence stood directly behind them as Father Dinsmore conducted the committal service. The soles of Vivien's peep-toe pumps were planted on the grass turf while her fingers twisted her white hankie. She'd thought the viewing had been the worst part.

She'd been wrong. Nonnie placed her hand on Vivien's and gave her a gentle squeeze. The older woman's touch of unexpected kindness sent Vivien over the edge, and she could no longer hold back her grief. From behind her sunglasses, tears fell from her lids and a sob escaped her lips. What was she going to do without her momma?

Henry rested a hand on her shoulder, and he spoke next to her right ear. "You can do this, Vivien." His warm breath seeped through the netting of her veil and brushed the side of her throat. "You're going to be okay." With him standing so close, she almost believed him. He squeezed her shoulder and the warmth of his touch gave her strength at the moment she needed it most. His thumb brushed the back of her neck before he straightened and dropped his hand, and she felt the absence of his strength.

The graveside service was blessedly short, and a confusion of emotions tumbled inside her stomach as she climbed back into the limo and rode away, leaving her mother behind. She felt relief that the funeral was over and guilt that she felt relief. Her momma was gone, and Vivien was completely alone now. Anxiety crawled across her skin and she made herself take slow, even breaths. Her momma would soon be in the ground.

By the time Vivien made it to the reception in Nonnie's double parlor, her head pounded and her throat hurt from trying to breathe past her tumble of grief and anxiety.

Vivien raised the black netting from her face and made her way to the bar as Richie and Kathy joined the line of mourners at the tables groaning under the weight of funeral food. She'd managed to pour a glass of wine before her momma's friends closed in on her to express their sorrow and give condolences. Everyone wanted to give her a hug and weep on her neck and let her know they'd pray for her. Vivien wasn't opposed to anyone praying for her, she just wondered if the prayers would be sincere, or more in the vein of the disingenuous, "She's too big for her britches. I'm going to pray for her."

A plate of food appeared beside her on the bar, filled with cherry-and-Coca-Cola salad, cheese mousse, and ham. A few minutes later, someone added corn loaf. After that another added anchovy-stuffed eggs and rosemary potatoes. The faces and names before her became a blur. For an hour, she received touches and hugs and yet felt so alone in the world.

"Macy Jane was a wonderful lady," one of her mother's many church friends praised, while another said, "the service was real lovely," all approved of her momma's "big funeral."

"So much classier than Richard Green's service last week," one of the Episcopal ladies said, and they nodded in agreement.

"After the liturgy, his wife, Lucy, popped up beside the prayer table and sang their favorite song." The woman's lips pinched. "Sixty-Minute Man."

"Filthy," they all agreed.

"Shocking."

"Inappropriate."

"I'm going to pray for her."

After another fifteen minutes of gossip and grief, Vivien excused herself to use the bathroom. She pressed a cool washcloth to her face and wondered if anyone would notice if she escaped to the carriage house for a nap. Of course sneaking away wasn't a choice, and she reapplied her red lipstick, preparing for the long day ahead of her. When she returned, well-wishers had scattered about the room, and she moved to the bar once more and the plate of food. Someone had added a piece of Louisa Deering's Twinkie loaf, bless her heart. She poured a glass of Pinot Grigio because the day had been long and was going to get longer. She raised the glass to her lips and glanced through the original-glass windows. Henry and Nonnie stood in the backyard under the wisteria arbor. The late-afternoon sunlight bounced off the lenses of Henry's sunglasses and the single button of his black suit jacket. He raised his hand to the top of his head and the bottom of his jacket rose up his hips. Nonnie shook her head and he dropped his hands to her slim shoulders. Nonnie put a hand to her lips and Henry pulled her into his arms and patted her back. He looked more the parent than child, and Vivien would not have believed it if she hadn't see them with her own eyes.

"Vivien?"

She turned toward the sound of her name and

it took her several moments to recognize the cute round face framed by light blonde hair. "Lottie Bingham?"

"It's Davidson now." Her old friend grinned and pulled her into a tight hug. "Lordy, there's nothing to you anymore."

Weight was one of Vivien's least favorite topics. Throughout her life, people had either called her fat or skinny. They'd either tried to restrict her fattening food or yelled at her to eat a cheese-burger. She pulled back and looked up into Lottie's big blue eyes. "How have you been?"

"Real good." Lottie dropped her arms and took a step back.

"Rowley and I heard about your momma as soon as we got back from Dollywood. I'm so sorry, Viv."

Dollywood. Too funny. "Thank you."

"You look like your movies. Well, except for the one where you were a hooker."

Vivien laughed. *The Stroll.* She'd chosen the role as her *Pretty Woman* to break herself out of the sci-fi mold. It had worked, sort of. The R-rated movie had been universally panned by critics and nominated for a Razzie. She didn't think the movie was as "bad as a cheap hooker." After multiple script changes, "a turkey of a film stuffed with filler," was somewhat accurate. "What have you been up to since high school?"

"I went to the University of South Carolina and met my husband, Rowley." She paused and pointed to a redheaded man talking to Spence on the veranda. "We have two girls, Franny Joe and Belinda," she added.

A lot of Southern women were married and on their third child by the time they reached thirty. If she'd stayed in Charleston, she was sure she'd have a husband and a kid or two by now. Just one more reason why she was glad she'd left town at the age of nineteen. Vivien wasn't opposed to marriage, but she'd been raised by a single mother in the backyard of a single woman. She didn't know a lot about marriage, but she liked the idea of falling in love and sharing her life. Of finding a man who had her back and wasn't intimidated by her success. She'd like to give it a try someday, but there were a couple of problems blocking that path.

First, Vivien didn't trust men.

As a kid, she'd watched men use and lie to her mother, and her own love life wasn't much better by comparison. In the past, she'd dated bums and users who'd sold stories about her to the tabloids. Horrible stories that made her wary and distrust-ful of anyone outside the business. There was a reason why actresses and actors dated each other. A tacit agreement that neither would sell stories in fear of having their own story sold.

Second, Vivien didn't really like dating actors.

Yes they were pretty to look at, but she didn't find them very interesting. She was an actress. She knew the business. She lived and breathed it every day, but it was one of the last things she wanted to talk about when she went home at night. She'd much rather talk with people who lived outside the Hollywood bubble. People who didn't say things like, "When I was on set last week . . ." or drop names "At Sundance this year, Bob threw a party that . . ." or complain about their privileged lives "I ordered kale chips on my rider! Where are my freaking kale chips?" Vivien had to admit that she was privileged too, but she was often bored by the same conversations from the same people who'd forgotten that they hadn't always been so fortunate. Vivien hadn't forgotten. On those rare occasion when she did, she reminded herself that she and her mother had cleaned house for the privileged. The house in which she now stood in her Armani dress and six-hundred-dollar shoes.

Vivien chatted with her old friend about their days at Charleston Day School and refilled their wine glasses. The two of them stood at one end of the bar, as Lottie caught her up on various classmates. She raised the wine to her lips and, over the top of her glass, her gaze landed on Henry, standing within a circle of men, drinking hard liquor, and laughing at something. He'd taken off his black suit jacket and looked handsome in his white dress shirt and black tie. Henry had called her "darlin' " yesterday. That made it two times now.

"And no one's seen hide nor hair of Caroline Mundy since forever. I suspect that's because she went from debutante to doublewide."

A tall blonde with killer curves joined the circle of men and slid her arm around Henry. He tilted his head to one side and gave her a killer smile. Vivien wondered if he called the woman "darlin'."

"Do you remember Jenny Alexander?"

Vivien thought a moment and returned her attention to her friend. "Brunette? Pants so tight you could see her religion?"

"That's the one. Her brother Paul married one of the Randall girls. They had three kids, and one day he just up and decides he's a lesbian. Like Bruce Jenner deciding he's Caitlyn." Lottie gasped. "Do you know the Kardashians?"

Vivien caught herself before she rolled her eyes. "I met Khloe at the Moschino fashion show in Milan, but no." She looked toward the circle of men. Henry was gone and so was the blonde. "I don't know the Kardashians." Khloe seemed perfectly nice and Vivien did not begrudge any of them their success. She just wasn't a fan of scripted reality.

After several more minutes of listening to her

friend, she excused herself to say good-bye to her uncle and Kathy. The two were driving back to Texas and wanted to make it as far as Atlanta before they stopped for the night. She walked them to the door, where Richie gave her a surprisingly warm hug and an invitation to visit them anytime. He might have even been sincere. She hoped so because he was the only family she had left. Kathy gave her a pat on the shoulder and Vivien watched them walk across the veranda and down the steps. She looked beyond her relatives to the sidewalk across the street. A small group stood near the curb and Vivien moved back into the house. Their hands weren't raised and they weren't in costume. More than likely they were just tourists gawking at one of Charleston's most beautiful and historic mansions. Maybe she was just being paranoid, but she didn't want the public to know where she was staying in Charleston. Her momma's carriage house had absolutely no security and flimsy locks. That had to change if she was going to stay there while she settled her mother's affairs. She had to leave for L.A. in the morning, but she'd call Sarah later and see if she could manage to have a security company take care of it while she was gone. While she was in Charleston taking care of her mother's affairs, she needed to feel safe.

When she returned to the parlor, she chatted

with Gavin Whitley and ate the strawberries and watermelon someone had set in a bowl next to her plate. It had been a long time since she'd seen Gavin, but she recognized him immediately. He was the male version of his sister. Better-looking because the Whitley genes were better suited for a man. He was tall, blond, and blue-eyed like Spence, but there wasn't a bit of Henry's dark broody looks in Gavin Whitley.

Two hours into the reception, Vivien's feet hurt and she was so tired she was almost groggy. She was talked and hugged out, but she knew she couldn't leave yet. She poured another glass of wine and found a blue-striped settee next to the open French doors. The small couch wasn't all that comfortable, but it was out of the way. A nice breeze touched her face and she closed her eyes. She breathed the fresh air deep into her lungs and dreamed of climbing into her momma's bed.

"How are you holding up, Vivien?"

Vivien opened her eyes and looked up at Spence Whitley-Shuler. Other than a quick hello and thank-you earlier, she hadn't seen or spoken to Spence in years. He'd lost his suit jacket and had loosened his tie. "Tired."

"You did a good job with your momma's funeral." He sat beside her on the small couch. "Macy Jane would have liked it."

"Thanks." He took her hand in his and squeezed her fingers.

"You're as pretty in person as you are in your movies."

If she didn't know better, she'd think she'd fallen into an alternative universe. One where the Whitley-Shulers were nice to her, called her "darlin'," and squeezed her hand.

"If you need to," he paused to pat his shoulder, "you can cry it out right here."

"Are you flirting with me, Spence Whitley-Shuler?"

"Of course," he admitted through his jovial smile. "I'm a bit offended that you had to ask." He didn't look offended at all.

"Where's your wife?"

"Underneath Hardy Townsend, I imagine." He laughed at her surprise. "We're almost divorced. She's marrying Hardy as soon as the ink is dry on the divorce papers."

"Oh. Sorry. I didn't know."

He shrugged. "She'll be better off. We married for the wrong reasons."

"What reasons?"

"Her daddy and my mother thought it was a wonderful idea."

Of course Nonnie had picked Spence's wife. No doubt, she'd pick Henry's, too.

Spence hit her with his elbow. "And it didn't hurt that her feet are always in the shade. If you know what I mean."

Vivien laughed and felt some of the day's

tension ease the back of her neck. Perhaps because she'd known Spence as the Whitley-Shuler who smiled and laughed easily, she felt comfortable with him. The kind of comfortable she'd never felt around Henry. "Next time, choose a wife for more than her bra size."

"No next time." He shook his head even as he grinned. "Have you seen that photo of Henry holding up your bra?"

"Yes." She bit the corner of her mouth to keep from laughing. "Has Henry seen it?"

"That blue bra hanging off your finger was the funniest damn thing I've seen in a real long while."

Henry moved his gaze from Hoyt Colicut's smiling eyes to his brother and Vivien. "Don't ou have something better to do than surf gossip sites on the Internet?" Spence chuckled and Vivien gave him a smile that lit up her pretty face. Henry thought of her tears at her mother's grave, and the grief she could no longer hold inside. The sound of her breaking heart had almost broken his.

"Not when my boss is on TMZ 'fondling' Vivien Rochet's bra."

Henry returned his attention to his employee and younger apprentice. The photo was on just about every tabloid site, and a dozen or so people had mentioned "that bra photo" throughout the day. Hoyt making it a dozen and one. "Don't you have a wife and new baby waiting for you at home?"

"Yeah. Before I go, I wanted to ask you if I should keep working on Miss Macy Jane's table."

"It's almost done, but there's no hurry." Not that there ever had been a rush. Macy Jane had designed the pineapple pedestal table but never planned on using it. Henry and Hoyt talked about the plans for a renovation on Lamboll and by the time Hoyt left, the mourners had dwindled to a few dozen of Macy Jane's friends and members of her church.

Henry walked to the old oak bar and poured a shot of bourbon over ice cubes in a lowball glass. He raised his free hand to the tension in the back of his neck as the sound of laughter spilled through the thinning crowd like sunshine and honey. He didn't have to turn around to determine the source of the laughter. He knew.

"I don't like that."

Henry looked across his shoulder at his mother. He didn't have to ask what she meant. He knew that, too. "It's harmless."

"You know your brother lately."

Yes, Henry knew Spence was behaving like a prison escapee, determined to experience all he'd missed before he got caught and was locked back up.

"It would be a disaster if those two became involved."

Henry raised his glass. "You're assuming Vivien wants to get involved with Spence. She's got her issues, but I don't think she'll fall for Spence's shenanigans."

"Grief can make people behave in regrettable ways. When my momma died, your uncle Gavin was so distraught, he just fell in bed with a waitress from the Golden Skillet."

"No one just falls in bed. You make it sound like an accident."

"Well, all I know is that his wife was so beside herself she considered getting a tattoo out of spite and rebellion."

"I wouldn't worry about Vivien. She's leaving in the morning." The bourbon warmed the back of his throat as he swallowed.

"That still leaves tonight."

Henry turned and looked beyond his mother to Spence and Vivien, seated on the empire settee across the room. She put her hand on Spence's shoulder and gave him a little push. His brother grinned like he'd won the Lotto. Again the sound of laugher spilled from Vivien's lips. Red lips that had preoccupied Henry's head with thoughts of pressing his mouth to hers through that damn black netting.

Nonnie put her hand on Henry's forearm. "You have to do something."

Henry pulled his gaze from Vivien's mouth and pretty face, once more lit up with laughter. "What do you think I can do about it?"

"You have to distract her. Charm her so she won't be interested in Spence."

"What?" He scoffed. "What makes you think I can charm her at all?" He wasn't sure she even liked him any better now than when they'd been kids.

"You're just like your father." A blonde brow rose up her forehead. "You can charm anyone if you put your mind to it."

His father. She wasn't talking about Fredrickk Shuler. He looked into his mother's insistent green eyes and searched for the woman who'd cried in the backyard. The woman who had a soft core surrounded by a steel shell. "Don't ask me to do something so underhanded."

"I'm not asking you to seduce the girl." She folded her arms beneath her breasts. "Just spend time with her until she leaves."

Once again, it was up to him to protect his family from his mother's secrets. Most of the time, he filled his role without question. He was the oldest and responsible for holding it all together and making sure there were no fractures, but this was too much. This time what his mother asked of him felt sleazy, no matter the reason. He took a drink and filled his mouth with the hard liquor. Sometime he disliked his mother almost as much as he loved her.

"You owe me twenty bucks."

"I do?" Vivien put her hand on her chest. "For what?"

"*The Stroll*," Spence answered. "I watched the whole movie. I figure you also owe me two hours of my life that I can never get back. Ten dollars an hour should cover it."

"The film wasn't that bad."

He raised a brow. "It was up for a Razzie."

She was surprised he'd paid such close attention to her career. "Yes." She laughed and held up one finger. "But it didn't win."

"Well, it made the Worst Film Ever Made list."

"That's not true." She took a drink of her wine. "You always were a big fat liar, Spence."

"Me? You were a bigger liar than me."

That was probably true. "I'm sure you lied more."

"Remember the time we all thought you broke your leg?"

"No."

"You wrecked your bike in the driveway and you laid out there screaming your head off and holding your leg. I think you were probably nine or ten."

She wrecked on her bike a lot.

"Tears were pouring down your cheeks. You tried to stand up several times but kept falling down again in a pathetic little heap." He chuckled.

"Even Henry was convinced you were really hurt. Macy Jane was frantic and Mother volunteered to drive y'all to the emergency room."

It was coming back to her.

"Then like that," he paused to snap his fingers, "you stopped wailing and cocked your head to the side. Your ears perked up at the sound of an ice-cream truck driving past the front of the house. Then you were off like a shot, running across the backyard yelling, 'Wait for me, Mr. Koolie.' "

Yeah, she remembered that day. "I was a regular on his route." And a loyal customer. "Even now, I crave a Sno Kap whenever I hear 'Little Brown Jug.' "

Spencer patted her leg just above her knee. "You were always a great actress." His fingers brushed her leg. "And pretty as a September peach."

"Spence." She put her hand over his to keep it from wandering any farther up her thigh. "I think of you as a brother."

"I'm not your brother."

"I know, but it still feels creepy."

"Think of me as a kissing cousin until it doesn't feel creepy anymore." He laughed and was so nonthreatening she smiled. "A third cousin twice removed."

"Hello brother." Vivien and Spence looked up at the sound of Henry's voice. "Mother needs to talk to you." His gaze moved from Vivien's face to his brother.

Spencer frowned and took a drink from his glass. "What does she need to talk to me about?"

"I couldn't tell you."

Spencer patted Vivien's knee. "Don't run off. We need to catch up some more."

Henry watched his brother walk away then turned back to Vivien. His eyes looked into hers, as sharp as black diamonds, and his lips were compressed in a firm line. He was the exact opposite of his brother in every way. "Come with me," he said and held out his hand. Then his gaze softened and the corners of his mouth curved into a warm smile.

"Why?" She'd been around plenty of actors who could learn a thing or two about turning on the charm from Henry.

"Because you look exhausted and need a break."

That was true. She needed a long break in her momma's bed. She slid her hand into his, feeling rough calluses against her palm as she rose. He had the hands of a blue-collar man, yet he'd been raised to sit behind a desk while manual workers did his bidding. "I need to tell everyone good-bye."

"They'll understand." He moved his rough palm to the middle of her back and escorted her through the kitchen and out the back door.

Even when she was in four-inch heels, he was

still several inches taller than her. Vivien assumed they were walking to the carriage house, but instead they moved toward a row of parked cars and stopped next to a deep blue Mercedes Roadster. "Am I going somewhere?"

"I thought you might like a little fresh air."

While Spence's touch had felt like a brother's, Henry's did not. His warm hand resting in the middle of her back heated up her skin through her dress.

Maybe it was the stress of her mother's funeral. The exhaustion of standing strong and the gnawing fear that she was totally alone, but she wanted to give in. She wanted to curl into Henry's solid chest and fall asleep on someone who was stronger than she was, but that was absolutely a bad idea. She wasn't thinking straight if she thought Henry Whitley-Shuler was a comfortable place for Vivien Rochet to land.

Henry slid a pair of Ray Bans on his face and gave her that beautiful smile she'd seen the other day. The one filled with charm and a flash of white teeth. "I double-dog dare you."

— Chapter 9 —

Henry pulled the Roadster into the two-car garage next to his truck, hit the control button, and shut the door behind him. Next to him, Vivien reclined in her seat, her eyes closed behind her sunglasses. Her breasts rose gently in sleep and her black dress had slid up her bare thighs. Once they'd slipped out of the city, he'd put the top down and she'd quickly fallen asleep. Somewhere over Wappoo Creek, the hat lifted on the breeze and he would have bet money that it was going to fly off her head, but it didn't. The thing was obviously fastened to her hair with pins that could withstand a hurricane.

He cut the engine and, for a few moments, he watched her steady breath as she slept. He'd done the right thing. The necessary thing, like always, but he didn't feel any better now about putting distance between Vivien and Spence than he had when he'd walked up to her and extended his hand. He'd watched Vivien and Spence laughing and joking and had planned to do absolutely nothing. Then his brother slid his hand on her knee, and he'd known he didn't have a choice.

"Vivien." He touched her arm, her smooth skin cool to the touch. This time doing the necessary thing not only felt like a burden, it was complete torture. "Time to wake up, darlin'."

Her eyes fluttered open and she turned her head to look at him. Confusion furrowed her brow and creased her fair forehead. "Are we home?"

"Yes. My home."

"What?" She sat up straight and glanced around the garage. Her hat finally gave up and fell to one side. "Where am I?"

"My house on John's Island."

Her head whipped around and she put a hand to her hat. "Why are we here?"

Because his mother wanted her as far away from Spence as possible. "Like I said, I thought you could use a break."

"I have to go back."

Henry opened his door and stepped into the dimly lit garage. "You don't have to do anything."

Her gaze followed him as he moved around the front of the car. "I have to thank people who brought funeral food to Momma's reception."

"Are you a masochist?" He opened her car door. "No."

"Then why would you want to sit in Mother's parlor until all the church ladies are talked out?"

The corners of her mouth twisted up as she turned and placed one foot on the concrete floor. Her dress slipped farther up her smooth thighs and his gaze followed. For one moment, his brain froze in anticipation of a flash of her underwear. "I can't just up and leave without so much as a good-bye." Her second foot joined the first and she stood.

"Why not?" He shut the door behind her and figured he had his mother to thank for making him feel as if he was back in school, dying to see a girl's panties. Dying even more to see her out of them.

"I don't want people to say I have the manners of a savage."

There would be no removing Vivien's underwear. That wasn't in the plan. "Do you really care?"

"Of course." She put her chin on her chest and slid her fingers beneath her hat.

Her answer was a surprise. As a child, she'd behaved as if she didn't care what anyone thought, especially if their last name was Whitley-Shuler. He was a little disappointed that she cared now.

She pulled pins from her hair and added, "Nonnie has been helpful with everything, and I just don't feel right leaving her to clean up." The black hat came off in her hands and she raised her gaze to his.

His mother never "cleaned up" anything. She always had hired help. Vivien knew that. "Are you kidding?"

"Do you always grill your guests with a dozen questions before you uncork the wine?"

"Not usually." He chuckled and turned toward

the back door. "But I do have one more question."

"What?"

"Red or white?"

"White when it's so damn hot outside."

He held the door open for her. "I have a really good French chardonnay."

"I'm not a wine snob," she said as she moved past him. The top of her head barely reached his nose as she brushed past, and he breathed in a faint trace of flowers and fresh air caught in her hair. He shut the door behind them and led the way through the laundry room to the kitchen. The heels of her shoes tapped across the kitchen floor, and he couldn't help but wonder what she thought of his modest home. It was a far cry from the estate where he'd been raised, and the Tribeca apartment he'd rented in Lower Manhattan, but he felt more comfortable here than any place he'd ever lived. It was his. A reflection of the man he was now and nothing like the man who'd once blazed through life like his ass was on fire because it was expected of him.

Henry opened his refrigerator and pulled out a bottle of wine. He set it on the granite top of the island that separated the living room and kitchen. Before he'd moved into the home, he'd torn down walls and eliminated negative space. It was simple and small. A far cry from the complicated and enormous life he'd led for the first thirty years.

He twisted the corkscrew and his gaze followed Vivien as she walked to the fireplace. Her head tipped back as she looked up at the abstract painting above the mantel. "I bought that from a local artist," he said as he pulled the cork from the bottle. "It's called Holy City." Free-form shapes and swirls of purple and blue paint depicted imagery of churches and bright yellow crosses.

"That looks like St. Michael's," she said and pointed to a white, watery image in the center.

"It is." He poured two glasses of wine, then shrugged out of his suit jacket. He hung it on the back of a kitchen chair and pulled his tie from around his neck before he grabbed the glasses off the island and walked toward Vivien. Patches of evening sun poured through the windows and pinpricks of light spun across the rim of the glass he handed her. "St. Mary's is near the left corner." He pointed to the left side of the painting.

She looked across her shoulder at him. "Who's the artist?"

"Constance Abernathy." He took a drink, and the rich spicy wine lingered in his mouth after he swallowed. His gaze moved from Vivien's beautiful green eyes to her pretty red mouth.

"You know her?"

"Yes. In fact, she was at Macy Jane's memorial." Even though he'd been around Vivien for several days now, it was still somewhat a shock to stand so close to her and see how much she'd changed from the chubby little brat he'd known.

"Tall? Blonde?"

He turned his attention back to the painting. "Yes." It was an even bigger a shock to have the woman whose bikini poster hung on the walls of teenage boys around the world, casually drinking wine in his living room. Her strange fans would be camped out, hands in air, across the street if they knew she was here. Only they didn't. Henry was the only person on this planet and the next who knew Vivien Rochet stood in his small home, looking as sexy as hell.

"Girlfriend?" She took a drink and walked to the overstuffed sofa. "Henry?"

"What?"

"Is she your girlfriend?"

"Who?"

"Constance, the artist."

Lord, her red lips were a distraction. "Used to be." He pointed his chin upward and unbuttoned the collar at his throat.

"Do you care if I take off my shoes?" she asked, but didn't bother to wait for permission. He didn't blame her. With her presence in his house, he couldn't seem to keep his two thoughts together long enough to answer. Well, at least not two appropriate thoughts. He'd have to do something about that. Maybe remind himself that she was a selfish diva who complained about making her own coffee. Then she moaned and wiggled her toes, and he didn't care if she demanded a Starbucks be built in her backyard.

She immediately lost five inches in height. "How long have you lived here?" She set her glass on the end table and raised her hands to the back of her head. The black hem of her dress rose an inch up her white thighs as she pulled the pins from her twisted bun. A deeper, sexier moan escaped her lips and wrapped around his chest as she shook her head. Her unbound hair fell down her back, and the warmth squeezing his chest got hot and shot straight to his groin.

"Henry?"

"What?"

"I asked you a question."

"Pardon me. I didn't hear you."

"I like your place." She reached for her wine and sunk into the couch. "How long have you lived here?"

"About two years." He sat on the opposite end of the couch, as far away as possible. Unfortunately it was a small sofa to accommodate the space. "I bought it shortly after I moved back, but I did major renovation before I moved in." She crossed her legs and he kept his gaze pinned on her face instead of her black dress sliding up her thighs. "I knocked down walls and pretty much gutted the place." He pointed to the double patio doors made of low-e solar glass and hard maple. "The exterior doors are on pivots instead of hinges."

Vivien listened to Henry as he talked about the doors and windows he'd replaced in his cozy little house. The size, as well as the modern construction, surprised her. She pictured him on a plantation somewhere. In riding breeches, shiny boots, and cut-away jacket. Lord of the manor.

"I made the doors of Burma teak and—"

"You made the doors?"

He paused and his lips compressed as if he was insulted. "Of course, Vivien. I made the doors in my shop. I laid the cork flooring in the kitchen and set the cork wall bricks, too. It's what I do for a living."

Shop. Henry Whitley-Shuler had a shop. That was almost too incredible to be believed. Like if he said he had a Harley and was a Hell's Angel. She looked at the kitchen floor a few feet away. What had looked to her like penny shaped tiles were even slices of corks. "You had to drink a lot of wine to make that floor."

"I didn't drink all that wine."

The couch was deep and her feet didn't touch the floor. They kind of stuck out like a kid and she pulled her legs beneath her. Sitting there on Handsome Henry's comfy couch, staring into his brown eyes, she felt comfy. "You didn't slice all those corks in your Little Shop of Horrors?"

"No, Vivien."

She noticed that when he was annoyed with her, he flattened her name. She tried not to laugh, but she didn't try all that hard.

"What?"

"I just can't imagine you in a 'shop.' Last I heard, you lived in New York. Momma told me you worked on Wall Street or something like that."

"Yeah. Something like that," he said and tried not to smile, but he didn't try all that hard, either. And when Henry tried not to smile, his eyes smoldered and an irresistible little tug curved the corners of his mouth. "I traded in my big desk with a great view of the Hudson for a table saw."

"I can't imagine Nonnie was too happy about that." She took a last sip of her wine. "Didn't you go to Pepperdine?"

"Princeton." He rose from the couch to grab the bottle off the kitchen island. He refilled her glass and set the bottle on the end table. "And no. Mother wasn't happy at first but she's come around. Sort of." He returned to his seat on the couch and his eyes watched her over the top of his glass as he took a drink. "To her credit, she'd rather see me alive than dead."

Vivien paused in the act of raising her wine. "She'd rather see you alive than dead? What does that mean?"

"It means I had to change my life." He shrugged one shoulder. "A little over two years ago, I was sitting at my desk in my twenty-sixth-floor office, reviewing the basket of stocks I was following when I got a sudden sharp pain in my chest. I stood up, and that's the last thing I remember until I woke up in St. Luke's emergency room. I had what the doc called a Monday-morning heart attack due to stress."

"Henry." She raised a hand to her chest. "I didn't know that." He'd been thirty-three. Three years older than she was now. "Are you okay?"

"I'm good. I saw several cardiologists and they all told me the same thing. Get the stress out of my life, or risk a second heart attack. I didn't have to be told twice." He chuckled without humor.

"When I'm under stress, I break out really bad." When she was under a lot of stress, she also missed a period or two and her hair fell out. "But I can't *die* from zits." She thought a moment. "Although last year someone took a picture of me leaving my dermatologist's office with a belligerent pimple on my chin. It made the front page of *Star* magazine. I was embarrassed but not surprised." The fuzzy glow of fine chardonnay warmed her stomach and spread across her skin. She was a lightweight when it came to alcohol and tended to get real chatty. Like now, so she should probably slow down before she fell face-first into the sofa and started snoring. It had been a long day, a long several days. "It's been a stressful week. I'll probably need microdermabrasion and a wig and a picture of my bald head will end up in a tabloid with some made-up story about a cancer scare." Vivien turned until her back rested against the arm of the couch, and she stretched her legs on the cushions as far as possible without sticking her feet in Henry's lap. "Did you see the blue bra photo?"

"What?"

"The blue bra photo."

"Yes." A nice shade of red crept up from behind his white collar and flushed the side of his neck.

Vivien cleared her throat to keep from laughing. "It's going to be in *Star* magazine." Usually it wasn't funny, but Henry holding up that blue bra, after he'd called her paranoid, was hysterical. "It's going to be in the 'normal or not' pages." The red creeping up his neck reached his ear and she put her hand to her lips to keep her laughter inside.

"You were always a good actress." He took a drink. "I almost believed you."

"I'm not acting." She cleared her throat. "*Star* always pays for the worst possible photos for that section. They love pictures with Jack Nicholson picking his nose, Lindsay Lohan stumbling out of a bar, or the trifecta of terrible, Kirstie Alley walking out of a grocery store, eating a doughnut, and pushing a shopping cart filled with Cheetos and toilet paper. So all things considered, it could have been a lot worse than you waving around my demi bra."

"I wasn't waving it around." He frowned at her like when she used to break something and lie about it. "You dared me to hold up that bra."

"*Au contraire*, Henry. I dared you to touch the underwear." As a kid she'd loved to push and poke Henry. As an adult, she couldn't recall if provoking him had ever been this much fun. "I never said to pull out my bra and *fondle* it."

"Stop, Vivien."

"The picture will probably end up on the front page of the *Enquirer*," she said as if she hadn't heard him. "They pay a lot of money for a photo of me eating something." The laughter she'd struggled to keep inside erupted into a fit of giggles. "You're famous."

He drained his wine. "God almighty."

She noticed the empty glass in his hand. "No more wine for you?"

"I have to take you back to the carriage house."

"Right now?" She didn't want to leave now. She wanted to stay in Henry's cozy house where she didn't have to think of the world outside the walls. Maybe she shouldn't have poked the beast.

"Not yet." He stood, and for the second time that day, held out a hand for her. "I have something to show you."

"Am I gonna want to see it?"

"Darlin', you're going to be amazed."

If it was his penis, she didn't want to be amazed. She didn't want to know anything about Henry

Whitley-Shuler's penis. She didn't even want to think about it, but the more she tried not to think about it, the more impossible it was *not* to think about it. Like not thinking of pink elephants or the Stay Puft Marshmallow Man.

He helped her to her feet then dropped her hand. "You'll need your shoes."

Or Henry Whitley-Shuler's amazing penis. Vivien tried to step into one pump, then the other. She wobbled and almost fell. The wine sloshed and she set it on the coffee table. Her feet were in full revolt and wouldn't be crammed back into her five-inch peep toes. "My feet are mad and won't go in my shoes." There was nothing like a little pain to shove thoughts of Henry from her brain.

He dipped his head and looked into her eyes. "Are you okay?"

She was definitely tipsy. "Are you asking me if I'm drunk?"

"Of course not. I would never ask a lady if she's drunk." He moved toward the kitchen and asked over his shoulder, "But are you?"

"Maybe a tad tipsy."

He chuckled. "I have some flip-flops by the back door that you can wear."

"Where are we going?"

"You'll see." He set his glass on the island as he passed and grabbed a bottle of water out of the refrigerator.

She moved toward the back doors and slipped her feet into a pair of big leather flip-flops. "I can't picture you as a flip-flop guy."

He pushed one side of the doors and it opened on pivots several inches from the frame. "Why not? Spence and I spent our summers mostly barefoot at Hilton Head."

The swampy night air settled on her skin as they stepped outside and moved across pavers to a building larger than his house. "Slow down. I can't walk fast and keep these on my feet." He adjusted his stride and her shoulder bumped into him.

He pushed her arm with his elbow. "Do you think any of your weird Raffle fans are going to pop out from behind the trees and salute you?"

"I never call them weird. I call them dedicated," she said as they walked side by side. "Raffle fans pay my bills. Although I do get some very weird mail, and they do have a tendency to pop up in unexpected places."

"Like the side of the road?" He glanced down at her. "Showing their respect and allegiance to Zahara West?"

"Yes." She paused and looked up at him, the porch light lit him from behind and settled in his dark hair. "Don't tell me you saw the movies?"

He grinned. "The books were better."

She guessed she shouldn't be surprised, but she was. She'd never figured him for a dystopia fan.

He continued across the driveway and she followed. "But you looked damn good in your metal-and-leather bikini."

"I hated that bikini. It had to be taped on and my skin got raw. I broke out in a heat rash." She scrunched her toes to get a tighter grip on the flip-flops. "The leather cat suit wasn't much better. It took three hours to get stitched into it. And the sweat . . ." She must be drunk if she was talking about sweat. "I mean glow. We filmed the 'Moons of Fontana' scenes in Yuma, in a hundred-and-three-degree heat. The glow was disgusting."

"You're totally blowing my leather bikini fantasy." He opened the door to a dark building and reached his hand inside to flip on the lights.

She glanced up at him out of the corners of her eyes and bit her lip. Henry had a leather bikini fantasy. She didn't know how she felt about that. A little shocked that he'd admit it, and a little flattered, too. She walked into the open building filled with big saws and sanders and huge God-knew-what. He moved in front of her and her gaze slid from his dark hair brushing the collar of his white shirt to the crisp pleat centered between his broad shoulders. Her gaze slid to his behind and she wondered what he'd do if she slid her hands into his pants pockets.

"Watch your step." He put his hand on the small of her back and steered her around a stack of molding.

The shop smelled of freshly cut wood, varnishes, and a slight tinge of oil. The warmth of his palm seeped through her dress and heated her spine.

"Macy Jane asked me to make her a dining-room table and chairs for the row house." He handed her the bottle of water and pulled a tarp from a long table made of dark wood.

She unscrewed the cap and took a long drink. "You made this?"

He took the bottle from her and raised it to his lips. "Yes, Vivien."

"Momma had you make a table for a house she never planned to live in?" For a short time, she'd relaxed enough to let her grief ebb like low tide. While she and Henry had talked about his life and stress and her bra, she'd almost forgotten the sadness of the day. The hole in her heart and the ache in her soul.

"She talked a lot about moving into the row house." He sucked a drop of water from the corner of his mouth then handed the bottle back to her. "But I think she liked to talk about moving more than she really wanted to move."

That was her momma, all right. Making empty plans.

"She found some tall pineapple candlesticks in an antique store and brought them to me for 'inspiration.' I don't make ornate furniture and, if she hadn't been your momma, I would have run in the other direction as fast as possible. I restore elaborate furniture for clients, but fabricating cumbersome, overly-elaborate tables isn't something I do here. It's not something I *want* to do."

"Did you mention that to momma?" She raised the water and put her lips where his mouth had just been on the bottle.

He chuckled. "I tried, but each time I tried to talk her out of such a heavy dust collector, she added something even more ornate. Another inlay or lion's paws, so I avoided talking to her about it." He got down on one knee and pointed to the pedestals. "I found a guy in Virginia to carve the pineapples and put them on the lion's-paw base. Hoyt's been busy staining all those nooks and crannies."

The pineapple represented warmth and hospitality and her momma loved the symbol of welcome. Vivien lowered the bottle. Or, she mentally corrected herself, *had* loved the symbol. The grief she'd felt since Saturday night rushed at her like a gust of wind, filled with shards of pain and sorrow. She'd managed to hold her emotions at bay through her momma's viewing and church service. She'd locked down her panic at the graveside and the reception afterward, but it suddenly broke free and rushed up from within the pit of her soul. It stabbed her heart and pierced the backs of her eyes without warning.

"It's made of African maple with Rhodesian teak veneer inlays." He stood and brushed sawdust from the knee of his navy-blue pants. He looked over her head and pointed. "The chairs are an original prototype I constructed for her last year."

Tears blurred Vivien's vision and she pressed her lips together to keep a sob from escaping. It was the pineapple table her momma would never see. The long emotional day. The wine that made her relaxed and unable to hold back the pain that was swamping her like a rowboat in a hurricane.

"The knuckle joints are—"

She raised her fingertips to her mouth to keep her pain inside. Her mother was gone and was never coming back. No more phone calls and her momma's soft, "Hey baby girl," on the other end. No more hugs or kisses on her cheek. No more seeing her happy face and smiling eyes when she was in a sparkling mood. No more wild fantasies she never intended to live.

"Vivien?"

The last memory of her mother's face was in a casket. With her lips painted a tinge too orange.

"Vivien? Are you okay?"

"No." She looked up at Henry, a blur of dark eyes and hair. Anguish cut her insides to shreds and clawed at her stomach. She grasped the black dress over her abdomen with her free hand. "It's not fair." She sounded like a child but she didn't care. It wasn't fair. The world was full of people who deserved to die. Her momma didn't deserve to die at fifty years old.

"I know."

She shook her head and brushed her tears from her cheeks. "No you don't. You still have your mo—mma. And—and Spence. I'm alone. For-ever."

"Please don't cry, Vivien."

"You ca-can call Nonnie." She swallowed and her sob came out as a sort of croak. "I have no—no one."

"Sure you do."

"No, Henry. I don't. Sh-he was all I had." She brushed away her tears and groaned as he pulled her against the comfort of his solid chest. As if it was the most natural thing in the world, she wrapped her arms around his waist. She didn't question it. Didn't wonder how she had come to rest her cheek on his white broadcloth shirt. He smelled like his hunting coat, minus the swamp. Woodsy and fresh; warm skin and cotton heated her cheek and his heart pounded beneath her ear.

"It'll be okay." He rubbed his hand up and down her back. "I'm here. My mother will always welcome you, and Spence will . . ." His fingers brushed her hair from the side of her face. "I'm here for you."

"It's not the same." Her life would never be the same. "She'll never see her grand—nd."

Her chest caved in and she tried to breath past the pain. "She'll never see her grandchildren," she got out. "My children will nev—ver know her."

"Vivien . . ."

"I left her at the cemetery so she could be put in the ground. I—I can't get that out of my head."

"You're breaking my heart." He hugged her even closer, pulling her inside where she felt safe and protected. Growing up, she'd had to protect herself. These days she had bodyguards to keep her safe. There was no one to grab her and give her what she didn't even know she wanted most.

"What can I do?" Henry spoke into the top of her head. "I don't know what to do to help you."

Until now. Vivien pulled back and looked up at him. Up into his handsome face so close to her own. His intense gaze was in conflict with his comforting voice and soothing touch. Slowly he lowered his face and his brown eyes locked with hers.

"Vivien." Her name was a whisper. A soft breath against her lips that sent shivers down her spine. "I'll do anything for you."

For the third or fourth time that day, Vivien stood shocked to her core. Stunned by Henry Whitley-Shuler. He wasn't looking at her like she was a pesky girl, nor did he appear to want to shake her. No, he looked like a man who wanted to do something entirely different with his hands.

And she wanted him to. She wanted him to

touch her and give her something else to think about besides her mother. She wanted him to give her what she hadn't known she needed until he'd touched her.

He brushed his mouth across hers, lingering for a few breathtaking moments. "Tell me what you want." His lips pressed into hers, not quite a kiss and entirely too short. "Ask anything."

She sucked in a breath as her heart pounded in her chest. She wanted him to kiss her and make her breath stop in her chest. To use his strong hands and make her forget the pain ripping at her heart, she wanted him to kiss her all over and take control, but she didn't want him to make her ask. "Henry," she whispered and rose onto the balls of her feet. She looked into his deep brown eyes and swallowed hard. She'd never been the kind of girl to *ask* anyone for anything. "Just kiss me."

A rough groan brushed her mouth as one of his arms clamped across her back, pulling her even tighter against him. His free hand cradled the back of her head, and he kissed her long and slow, giving her what she demanded. Even as he lit a tingly little fire in the pit of her stomach, he never lost control. Just when she would have pushed it—pushed him—he pushed away and his hands fell to his sides. "Let's get you home."

— Chapter 10 —

The Diary of Vivien Leigh Rochet
Keep out! Do NOT read
under Penalty of Death!!

Dear Diary,
 I got the part!! Drama club is putting on <u>Little Shop of Horrors</u> and I'm playing Audrey!! The real Audrey, not the plant. I tried out and got the role. I was so nervous because I had to sing. I didn't know if I could do it, but Momma bought me the movie and I watched it over and over on the VCR until I learned all the songs and dialogue. I watched it even more than I watch <u>Clueless</u>, the best movie ever made. Loraine Monroe-Barney thought she was going to get the part because she's really popular and a cheerleader. Everyone in school thought she was going to get the part because her great-granddaddy has a county somewhere named after him, or some such. I was soooooo nervous. I couldn't sleep

or hardly eat. Momma says I can worry Jesus off his cross, but I couldn't help it. This is the BEST day of my life.
☺ ☺ ☺

Dear Diary,
  I'm definitely going to need a bra soon. Momma said not to rush it. She said the girls in our family are late bloomers, and when we do finally bloom, we're likely to have small blossoms. I don't care. I just want to wear a bra like all the other girls in school.

Dear Diary,
  Good news is Momma got rid of Stupid Chuck. Bad news is she got a new boyfriend, Booker. He has brown teeth and smells like beer. I call him Booger and Momma says I'm just being ugly. Mamaw Roz said not to get worked up about Booger 'cause he'll be gone faster than green grass through a goose. Uck!!

Dear Diary,
  Henry and Spence came home for summer break. Momma and I took Spence a present because it was his birthday. He's a year older than me,

but he's really weird. Momma says I just don't recognize happiness when I see it. Whatever. He's just not right. Henry came late to the party and he brought a girl with him. He's sixteen and can drive and isn't as ugly as he used to be. The girl had red hair and pretty white skin and works at Piggly Wiggly. After the party, I heard Nonnie tell him that the girl was the worst kind of strumpet. He said, "You're wrong, Mother. She's the best kind of strumpet." I think Henry was talking about S.E.X. Nonnie got mad and stormed out of the kitchen like the Wicked Witch of the West. I laughed because Henry is usually her flying monkey. He said that I need to stop listening to other people's business. I said that he needs to kiss my go-to-hell. Momma said we both need Jesus.

Dear Diary,
  The kids at school say Momma's crazy. I try to say she's not, but deep down, I know they're right. She came to pick me up from school once with her dress inside out and her hair was sticking up. I was so embarrassed my stomach hurt. Then I felt really bad and cried because

I was embarrassed of my momma. She can't help it. Last week, she painted the living room yellow. She stayed awake all night, and when I got up for school, she was laughing and talk-talk-talking like she does in her happy moods. She said she'd drive me to school, but I grabbed a Pop-Tart and ran out of the house before she could find her purse. The Pop-Tart made my stomach hurt.

Dear Diary,

I LOVE ACTING!! My drama teacher said I'm "gifted" (in a good way), and I played Audrey better than any other student she's ever taught. Momma said I need to reach for the stars, and she took me to the kids' theater and signed me up for acting classes once a week. Someday the world will know VIVIEN LEIGH ROCHET!!

Things I Want To Be List

1. An actress—duh
2. Actress-double duh
3. Actress-triple duh
4. Skinny
5. Momma with five kids

— Chapter 11 —

Vivien shoved one foot into her peep-toe pump and looked across her shoulder at Henry, standing in his kitchen, thumbing through messages on his cell phone as if he hadn't just kissed her.

"Shake your tail feathers," he ordered without looking up.

After he'd kissed her, he'd practically shoved her out of his shop, and she was still reeling from running behind him across the yard. Or maybe she was still reeling from his crazy-wonderful kiss that left her wanting more. He'd pulled her close, then pushed her away, putting more than physical distance between them. "Why are you cranky?"

"I'm never cranky, Vivien." He'd said her name. A clear sign that he was cranky.

"You were born cranky." Her other foot refused to slide into her shoe and she gave up.

"You were born a pain in the ass."

With one shoe on and one off, she limped to the kitchen. "You didn't think so a few minutes ago." He didn't respond. "You kissed me like you were trying to see if I still have my tonsils." Which was probably a stretch.

He glanced at her out of the corners of his eyes then returned his attention to his phone. "Don't blow what happened out of proportion," he said as if the kiss changed nothing between them.

Still slightly off balance, she folded her arms beneath her breasts. "I'm not blowing anything out of proportion, Henry." The kiss had made her want him. Want Henry Whitley-Shuler, and that changed everything.

"Let it go, Vivien."

Not a chance. "Admit it, Henry."

He sighed and turned toward her. "What do you want to hear? That if you weren't drunk, I would have tossed you on your momma's pineapple table, pushed your dress up and your panties down."

Oh. His words settled in the pit of her stomach and made her mouth dry. He'd been thinking *that?* "I thought I was a pain in the ass."

"You are." He raised a hand and pushed her hair behind her ear. "You drive me insane with your pretty face and sassy mouth and the way your cute bottom looks in that dress. You purposely try to provoke me until I lose control."

"If you'd lost control, I'd be on my momma's table. Remember?" His palm slid from her ear to the side of her neck. She liked his rough hands on her skin and she turned her face into his palm. "I'm not drunk, Henry." She glanced up and recognized the look in his eyes: that hard searching gaze as if he could see inside her brain and read the truth. She kissed his palm and his lids dropped to half-mast and his eyes softened and warmed. She'd never seen desire in Henry's eyes, unless it had been the desire to wring her neck. This desire poured through her, heating up thousands of little nerve endings and settling between her thighs.

He hesitated for one awful second before he lowered his face once more. This kiss started as a soft whisper of desire. It was a gentle intake of breath and a rush of longing. It was warm sunshine on the darkest day of her life.

Vivien was thirty and had kissed a lot of men, both on and off the screen. Men who'd tried to seduce her with charm and money and power. She thought she'd experienced it all, but this was different. New. This was desire and longing, held in check by a gossamer thread, and more seductive than all the charm and money and power in the world. This was seduction that tightened her breasts. It forced a gasp from her lungs and a shudder in her chest. Henry took advantage of her parted lips, and Vivien didn't hesitate to welcome his warm tongue inside her mouth.

With her head tilted back, she slipped one hand to the back of his head and touched the fine strands of his hair with the tips of her fingers. She kicked off her one shoe and rose on her toes, sliding up his chest and kissing him hard. She wanted to push him into losing control.

Henry pulled back and his eyes were almost black and filled with a passion she felt in her knees. His breath rushed from his lungs as he dipped his head for more, filling her with hot little tingles that rushed through her veins.

He slid one hand to the back of her neck and the other to her bottom. His fingers curled in her hair, and he pulled her closer. Everywhere his chest and hips brushed against her, the volatile sparks raced through her and hit a flash point in the center of her chest. His erection pressed into her thighs and passion seared her insides, scorching her skin and making her feel like she'd touched lightning. It burned her up from the inside out and she pulled back to look up into his dark gaze and hunger looking back at her. "Henry," she whispered, and raised her fingertips to her lips, half expecting to feel burned.

He breathed in deeply through his nose and looked up at the ceiling. "If you want me to take you home, tell me right now," he said, but he didn't drop his hands. He returned his gaze to hers. "Before I let you make me completely insane."

Well aware that she was playing with fire, she slid her hands up his hard chest to the sides of his neck. She'd touched lightning, and she liked it.

In the distance, the soft sounds of nightfall faded as desire took over and she lifted her mouth to his. In an instant, the once soft kiss turned voracious.

Slick and feeding with a passion that was far too big to hold back. She wanted Henry and it somehow felt right that she should have him.

Her hands moved to the front of his shirt and her fingers worked the buttons until it lay open to her touch. Then her hands were on him, touching his warm skin and hard shoulders. Combing her fingers through his chest hair and pressing her palm against his tight belly.

So intent on the feeling of his muscles beneath her hand, she didn't realize Henry had unzipped her dress until he pulled back long enough to push it from her shoulders. The black Armani fell to her feet in a dark pool, followed by her bra.

Henry shrugged out of his shirt, then he pulled her against his hard chest. Her tight nipples raked his warm skin and felt so good she shivered.

"Damn," he said, his voice strained as he stepped back to look at her. His heavy-lidded gaze poured over her from the top of her head, past her face and shoulders, downward to her breasts and black panties. "Look at you," he said just above a whisper. "All grown up and perfect." His fingers brushed the tips of her sensitive nipples.

She moaned and slid her palm over his flat stomach and let her fingers follow his dark happy trail to the button closing the waistband of his pants. He'd dressed left of his zipper and she pressed her hand against him, the heat of his erection warming the wool material.

He sucked in a breath between his teeth and grabbed her waist. He lifted her onto the cold granite island and spread his fingers wide along her ribs as he looked at her. His gaze touched her breasts and belly and thighs. Then he slid his hands to the backs of her shoulders, arching her back and bringing her breasts close to his face.

His breath whispered across her aching nipple just before he softly sucked her inside his hot wet mouth. Vivien moaned and planted her palms behind her. His cheeks drew inward as he created a delicious suction. One hand slid from her back, down her belly, and he pulled her panties from her and dropped them beside her dress. Her breath stopped in anticipation of his touch. Then he gave it to her and air rushed from her lungs and her head fell back.

"You're wet, Vivien Leigh." His rough voice vibrated against her breast as he stroked her slick flesh. He caressed her like a man who knew exactly how to make a woman feel good. She didn't have to give him directions and it would have been so easy just to succumb right there. To let him stroke her to orgasm. It wouldn't have taken much more and she'd be gone, but she didn't want to orgasm by herself on a cold slab of granite. She wanted him to come with her.

"Stop," she said and grabbed his wrist. He slid his wet hand up her stomach to her breast, and his fingers played with her, spreading moisture across her nipple. He followed with his mouth, and a sound of deep male pleasure rumbled deep in his throat, primal and possessive and pushing her so close to the edge she feared she would orgasm with nothing more than his mouth on her breast.

"Stop, Henry."

He leaned his head back and looked at her. His gaze totally gone with passion. "I'm not taking you home."

"I don't want you to take me home." She licked her dry lips. "Take your pants off and take me to bed."

His pants hit the floor practically before the words left her mouth. Blue-and-white-striped boxers followed and she barely got a glimpse of his impressive erection before he lifted her. She wrapped her legs around his waist and the length of his hot velvet penis pressed into her crotch and behind.

She brought her face to his and his tongue ravished her mouth as they moved from the living room down the hall to his dark bedroom. Light from the windows spilled across the big bed, and he gently laid her across the deep blue quilt. Her arms felt empty and she raised herself on her elbows as he opened a drawer of his nightstand. As he rolled a thin condom over the plump head of his penis, he watched her, his lids heavy and his eyes shining with pent-up hunger. Then he covered her, warm skin and hard body, wrapping her in a possessive embrace. The head of his erection touched her, smooth and hard and incredibly hot. He slid halfway inside, felt the taut resistance and took her face in his hands. He kissed her gently as he withdrew then pushed a little farther inside.

She sucked in a breath, his breath, as he pulled out almost completely only to bury himself deep inside. A rough groan tore through his chest and echoed in her ears.

She wrapped one leg around his back. "Henry," she whispered as he began to move, setting a perfect rhythm of pleasure. "That feels good."

With his face just above hers he asked, "Tell me how good."

Every cell in her body was focused on the thrust of his hips, and she tried to think past the pleasure slicing though her body and twisting her insides into fiery knots. His black gaze was a turbulent meld of rampant lust and tempered restraint and she managed a "Real good," before she gave in completely to desire. Over and over, harder and more intense, he thrust into her. His breath brushed her cheek as he drove her farther up the bed, pushing her closer and closer to the edge. She was little more than pure lust and raw abandon, and he owned her body in that moment. She didn't care, as long as he didn't stop. "Henry," she cried out as she moved with him. Deeper. Hotter. So close. "If you stop I'll kill you!" Her heart pounded in her ears and her breath rushed from her lungs. She cried out . . . something . . . as a white-hot orgasm flashed like lightning from the tip of her toes to the top of her head.

She heard her name torn from his throat as he joined her in a climax that lasted forever but was much too short.

Neither of them moved and were incapable of saying anything for what seemed like a long time. Not until their breathing slowed and their heart rates returned to normal.

"Jesus, Vivien." He buried his face in the crook of her neck. "That one was ripped from the pit of my soul."

She knew what he meant. "I felt it in my toes. I think I got a cramp in my foot."

Henry lifted his face and smiled, very satisfied that he'd caused her pain. He kissed her shoulder, then withdrew from her, moving from the bed to the bathroom. Variegated shadows slid across his the muscles of his back and hard butt. "Don't go anywhere," he said over his shoulder just before he disappeared into the bathroom. Even if she wanted to leave, they both knew she had no way to "go anywhere."

Cool air brushed across Vivien's heated skin. She took care of herself, working and toning her body, but she wasn't totally comfortable lying on Henry's bed with nothing but a smile. Vivien slipped beneath the covers, and she sighed as the smooth sheets slid across her skin. Henry had good sheets and she'd come to appreciate a high thread count.

The toilet flushed in the next room and she looked toward the bathroom door. Henry walked toward her, naked and beautiful within the light falling across the bedroom. Looking at him, at his dark hair and handsome face, his lean body and long stride, a warm little glow stirred unexpectedly in her chest. The feeling both confused and scared the daylights out of her.

"What are your plans?" Henry asked as he slid between the sheets.

She sat up. "Did you want me to go?" She should probably go.

"No, Vivien." He wrapped an arm around her stomach and dragged her right back down. Several streams of weak light slipped between the shutters and shone in his black hair and across his tan cheek.

Afterglow. The crazy feeling had to be due to afterglow. "You want me to stay?"

He lay beside her and easily situated her until her back was against his chest. "I want you to stay," he said next to her ear. The warmth of his chest and cup of his pelvis heated her spine and bare behind. "Is that a problem?" His fingers brushed across her shoulder, tracing an invisible line that raised her sensitive skin.

Afterglow that felt like sparkles inside. "No." Now that she knew the cause of her crazy feeling, she relaxed and snuggled her bottom against his crotch. She settled into a warm comfortable spoon with Henry, and the easiness of it all surprised her. Like her mother, she didn't have the best track record with men. Unlike her mother, she was normally long gone before they broke her heart.

She'd just had sex with Scary Henry. His bed was the last place on earth she'd ever thought she'd find herself naked, and she should be freaking out. She should be trying to figure a way to get the hell out of there with the least amount of embarrassment. She should be getting dressed and on her way out the door to avoid the 8 a.m. walk of shame.

Henry's skillful touch slid down her arm and she felt it all over her body. Pleasure climbed her spine, and she settled firmly against his groin as a whole new round of desire chased the sparkly tingles across her skin.

Henry poured a cup of coffee and his gaze fell on Vivien's empty wineglass on his coffee table. He stood in his kitchen wearing jeans, a wrinkled T-shirt, and the flip-flops Vivien had worn the night before. The clock on the coffeemaker indicated that it was eight fifteen. Vivien would be gone by now, cruising at 35,000 feet, some-where between South Carolina and California.

A burnt bagel popped up from his toaster and he lathered it up with cream cheese. He'd only caught a few hours of sleep before he'd had to wake Vivien earlier. She'd been warm and comfy, curled up next to him as if she belonged in his arms and in his bed. She'd fallen asleep first, and he'd watched the rise and fall of her small breasts and her pale face surrounded by all that dark hair. She was thin—perhaps too thin—but her muscles were toned and her skin smooth. The stress lines he'd noticed all week in her forehead were smooth and she looked as if she'd finally found some peace. Her sleep had been deep, her breath even as if she trusted him to keep her warm and safe, but Henry was the last person she should trust.

It had still been dark when he'd driven her to the carriage house to grab her suitcase before her 6-a.m. flight. She'd eaten an apple and washed it down with strong coffee and they'd chatted about the weather and which airline served the best breakfast in first class. They'd talked about Macy Jane's funeral, but as if by tacit agreement, neither spoke of the night before. As Vivien quickly changed her clothes, Henry had kept an eye on the big house. He'd half expected his mother's bedroom to be ablaze with light as she awaited Vivien's return. If she'd been awake and seen his car pull up to the townhouse, his cellphone would have started ringing and his mother's severely displeased voice would demand to know why he'd brought Vivien home so late, or early in the morning rather. If she suspected anything, she definitely would have had something to say about it by now, but his cell hadn't so such as beeped with a text and there hadn't been so much as a lamp burning in the big house. He hadn't spoken with his mother since he'd left her house yesterday. She was the last person he wanted to speak to now. Henry took a big bite and washed it down with coffee. From the moment Vivien had walked into his house last night—no, the moment she'd slid into his car, he'd fought an impulse to touch her and pull her against his chest. He'd fought it as she'd unpinned her hair and shook her head, letting loose the scent of wild flowers. He'd succeeded in fighting it even as she'd sat on his couch, her bare legs stretched out on the beige cushions, laughing and trying to rile him up. Then she'd cried for her momma, her green eyes filling with tears and pain, her voice breaking, and he'd lost the fight. He'd given into his impulse to pull Vivien against him when he should have stepped away.

Hell, he *had* stepped away. He'd stepped away and put the distance from his kitchen to the couch between them. He'd tried to ignore her as she'd poked and provoked him, like when she'd been a kid and it had been a game to her. She wasn't a child now, but her poking and provoking had still been a game. A sexually charged game that he hadn't wanted to play but couldn't resist. A game that had big consequences for them both.

Once she'd pushed him into admitting that he'd wanted to toss her on her momma's pineapple table and pull her panties down, the sexual charge sizzling between them caught a spark and shot straight to his groin. Then she'd turned her face into his hand and the last threads of control turned to ash. She'd kissed his palm and looked up at him, a full-grown woman's desire shining in her beautiful eyes and he hadn't been able to recall a single reason why he shouldn't jump on her like a duck on a June bug. He'd kissed her and touched her and danced the razor's edge. Right and wrong hadn't mattered, silenced by the taste of her lips and the need pounding between his legs.

Henry took another bite of his bagel and washed it down with a gulp of coffee. Vivien's mouth had tasted of Chateau Montelena, of pear and honey. Henry had always been a sucker for good wine on soft lips. Her slick tongue had played with his, and her breathy little moans urged him on, making him want to hear more, filling his head with the sound of her ultimate pleasure.

Henry grabbed his coffee and headed to his bedroom.

I'm not drunk, she'd said. If not drunk, then she'd been tipsy. And vulnerable. Henry set his coffee on his dresser and walked into the bathroom. Vulnerable and grieving, but that hadn't stopped him from tossing her on his counter and eating her up like a dessert buffet.

He pulled his T-shirt off over his head and stepped out of his jeans. Warm water rained down from the ceiling as he turned on the six heads and stepped into the shower.

He wasn't proud of his behavior. He hadn't been raised to take advantage of drunk, grieving women. Henry tipped his head back, and let the water pour over his face. He thought of Vivien's face when he'd been buried deep inside her. Intense and totally mindless to anything but him and the hot, sexual pleasure he pumped into her.

"If you stop I'll kill you," she'd hollered unnecessarily. He'd been mindless at that point, too. Mindless to anything but her tight body milking every last drop of pleasure from him.

Even now, he couldn't quite wrap his head around the night before. He'd had sex with Vivien. Good sex. If she hadn't fallen asleep so soundly, he would have had sex with her again. The kind that was hot and sweaty. The kind that could never happen again.

He blamed his mother. If Nonnie hadn't insisted that he do something about Spence's hand on Vivien's thigh, she wouldn't have been in his house last night.

Once again, his mother's paranoia had surfaced and she'd expected him to fix everything. That was him. Henry the fix-it man. He was the oldest male and head of the family, the person to make sure that all inconvenient skeletons remain tightly locked in the Whitley-Shuler closet.

He tipped his head forward and let the water rain down his back, waiting for the tension to ease between his shoulders.

So many secrets and scandals to keep hidden. His and Tracy Lynn's. Nonnie and Fredrickk's. Macy Jane and Vivien's. He was tired of it all. Tired of the intertwined lies and secrets that began thirty-five years ago with Nonnie and Fredrickk Shuler and the biological father Henry had never known.

He'd first discovered that Fredrickk wasn't his biological father in the fifth grade when his school class had learned about genetics. They matched blood types and mapped inherited traits. He learned that he got his earlobes from his mother and hairline from his grandfather Whitley. He learned that he had type B blood, while Fredrickk and his mother had type O.

He recalled sitting in science class, studying his charts and graphs. He remembered his teacher, Mr. Roy, standing by his desk pointing to his mother's and Fredrickk's blood types. Then he remembered the man's voice had trailed off as his finger stopped at Henry's blood type.

"This can't be right. You must have confused your parent's blood types."

"Yeah," he'd said, but he knew there wasn't any

confusion. When he'd called his mother and asked about blood types for his class, she'd told him that both she and Fredrickk had type O. He remembered because she'd told him that they'd been real popular at the annual St. Cecilia blood drive because people with type O were universal donors.

Sitting in that biology class, he'd just been a kid, but it hadn't taken him long to figure it out. It was impossible for type O parents to have a B child. He remembered feeling as if someone had punched him in the chest even as his ten-year-old brain refused to understand what it meant.

The warm water did little to ease Henry's tension and he reached for a bar of soap. He lathered a washcloth and scrubbed his face and body. His mother had lied to him. Fredrickk lied, too, but he'd already been dead for four years when Henry had stared at the paper that changed his life.

His mother had lied to him. Ironically, she'd been caught in her lie when she'd told the truth It had never occurred to Nonnie to lie about blood type. If she'd known, she would have lied about that, too.

When he'd questioned Nonnie, she hadn't wanted to talk about it and had told him to let it go. Some things were best left alone, but of course he hadn't let it go. He'd pushed until his mother had begrudgingly told him that she'd been three months pregnant when she married Fredrickk

Shuler. His biological father was a man named Frank Olivier, a journeyman hired to restore the cabinets at the family plantation, Whitley Hall. His mother was twenty-five and had taken one look at Frank's dark eyes and handsome face, and she'd instantly fallen for the thirty-year-old. His mother, who'd never seemed to put a foot wrong or breach society rules, had been wildly attracted to Frank and addicted to their secret affair. She'd loved Frank, but love wasn't enough. Women with Nonnie's blue blood certainly didn't marry blue-collar men.

Ever.

Henry shut off the water and reached for a towel. Some things hadn't changed in Southern society. Young women with old names did not get pregnant out of wedlock and they certainly didn't marry unsuitable men. Nonnie's great-grandfather, grandfather, and father had all belonged to the holiest of the holy, the St. Cecilia Society. Nonnie had made her debut at the exclusive St. Cecilia ball. She'd worn a white gown and gloves and her father had presented her to society when she was seventeen. Being a Southern debutante had been very important to Nonnie, and instead of telling Frank she was pregnant with his child, she'd made an "arrangement" with Fredrickk Shuler, ten years her senior. The Shuler name was even older than the Whitleys' and just as respected.

Luckily for his mother, the Shulers lacked the one thing Nonnie had in abundance. Like a lot of old Southern gentry, they had short arms and long pockets. Land rich but cash poor. Fredrickk had been in desperate need of money, and Nonnie had been in desperate need of a "respectable" husband like Fredrickk who overlooked her expanding waist on their wedding day.

The thick towel soaked up droplets sliding down Henry's back, and he wrapped it around his waist. His memory of Fredrickk was faded, but he did recall riding in his Lincoln and sailing the two-man dinghy in Harbor Town. He'd never met Frank, but he'd hired a private detective when he'd turned twenty-one. He learned that a few years after Frank left South Carolina, he'd been killed in a motorcycle accident. He hadn't married or had children—except for Henry.

The sheets on the king-size bed were still rumpled from the night before and Henry dropped his towel to the floor. The day Nonnie had told him about his father had also been the day he was put in charge of guarding the family secrets. Whether or not he wanted the burden hadn't mattered. It had been placed on his ten-year-old shoulders, and he'd never opened his mouth to anyone.

Not even Spence.

Henry opened a dresser drawer and grabbed a pair of clean boxers. Scandals and drama and guarding secrets brought his thoughts back around to Vivien, her pretty face, and warm body as she slept next to him. Guilt chomped at the back of his neck as he dressed. He'd had hot sex with a beautiful woman. He liked hot sex with beautiful women. Sex with beautiful women took up slots one, two, and three on his list of favorite things to do. If Vivien were any other woman on the planet, he'd try like hell to get her naked and filling up any and all spots on his favorite things to do.

He stepped into his boxers, then pulled on a pair of jeans. Vivien wasn't just any woman. She was the one woman he never should have touched. For several good reasons, she was the one woman he could never touch again. No matter how much he wanted to kiss her north and her south. Too bad he hadn't remembered that last night.

He'd only brought Vivien home to keep her from Spence and his brother's roaming hands. If his mother knew he'd let his own hands roam all over Vivien, she'd pitch a shit fit. Not that his mother's fits regulated his life. Even if he'd given his mother a thought last night, he still would have gone ahead and stripped Vivien naked. He just didn't want to hear about it from a self-righteous hypocrite.

Henry looked at his phone and the one missed call from Hoyt. Somehow he'd managed to avoid a self-righteous bullet.

— Chapter 12 —

"I'm not your servant and I'm not your lover." Vivien read her dialogue out loud as she sat at an oblong table in the HBO production office off Santa Monica Boulevard. Across the table, the head writer for *Phychic Detectives* scribbled notes on the script. Vivien would star in a guest role, playing a woman named Jenny Mumsford, the wife of Reverend Enoch Mumsford. The role had initially attracted Vivien because she'd never played a woman like Jenny. A woman who had the gift of telekinesis, like Stephen King's Carrie. Enoch is abusive and has convinced Jenny that her powers come from Satan. In the last scene, Jenny gets revenge on the reverend in a spectacular bloodbath.

"I am everything," the actor who played her husband and antagonist read. "I am your God."

"Jenny hesitates as if to say something," the scriptwriter read. "But he is the only thing keeping her from eternal damnation. Close scene on Jenny's defeated profile."

Vivien made a note on her script and placed her pen on the table. Shooting the first scene of her story line was set to start in a week. That gave her five days to figure out what she wanted to do with her mother's estate.

As the director and writers talked about the setup for Jenny's second scene, Vivien's mind wandered to Charleston and everything that waited for her there. She had so much to do, and it felt just as overwhelming today as it had five days ago. Her grief and heartache felt just as raw as the day Henry found her digging in her momma's flower bed, searching for a champagne cork.

Henry. Henry Whitley-Shuler. She'd had sex with him last night. She'd woke in his bed and arms and it all seemed so unreal. He'd kissed her and she'd kissed him right back. One unreal kiss had led to more kissing and touching and getting naked. Vivien had never been the kind of girl to throw caution to the wind and hop in a man's bed unless she was in a relationship. Something she and Henry definitely were *not*. Jumping in Henry's bed the day of her mother's funeral had been inappropriate, scandalous, and just plain mind-blowing. And impulsive. Vivien didn't like impulsive. Impulsive got her in trouble. She liked to make a plan and stick to it.

Perhaps it had been the stress of the day and the constant grief slicing her heart, but she certainly hadn't even given a token resistance to Henry's touch on her arms and his kiss on her neck. In fact, she'd pretty much goaded him into it. Like when they'd been kids and she'd provoked him just to see his reaction. Only this time he hadn't scowled or called her a brat or threatened to kill her. This time he'd stripped her naked and she'd threatened to kill *him* if he stopped.

The memory made heat rise up her face and burn her cheeks. Who knew uptight Henry could kiss a woman and make her feel like she'd been struck by lightning? Who knew uptight Henry could make her come all undone?

After the table read, Vivien met with Randall Hoffman at Bouchon and discussed the starring role in his period drama based on the life of Dorothy Parker. Vivien wanted that part, along with every other actress in town. It would not only show her acting range, but an Academy Award–winning director usually meant Academy nominations for acting, too. Not only would starring in a Randall Hoffman film add more prestige to her résumé, it was essential when she started her own production company. Something she very much wanted to do in the future.

Following the lunch, Vivien drove to her house in Beverly Hills. She slowed her BMW as she passed through the gates and pulled into the garage of her Mediterranean-inspired house. Her meeting with Randall Hoffman had gone well. She was fairly certain she'd charmed the pants off him, but he wouldn't make a decision until he met with the casting director. She'd known that in advance, of course, but waiting added stress on top of stress to her life. She wished she had a feeling one way or the other if he was going to cast her.

Exhaustion weighed on her shoulders and burned her eyes as she parked in the garage and took the elevator up to the second floor. Was it really just this morning that she'd caught a flight to L.A.? Really just this morning that Henry had woke her from a deep sleep and made sure she caught her 6-a.m. flight? Was she really catching a 6-a.m. flight right back to Charleston tomorrow?

Vivien had been jet-lagged many times. She'd flown into thirteen cities in twenty-five days, sometimes more, to promote her latest film. She'd answer the same questions thirty times a day, and her brain would just shut down at some point.

This exhaustion was different, it was a mind, body, *and* soul. She'd love to just collapse and take a long nap, but it wasn't possible. She had too much to do and if she laid down, she knew she wouldn't get back up until the next morning.

Some moments after Vivien got home, Sarah arrived and helped her pack several suitcases. This time they made sure she packed enough underwear and bras.

"How was the funeral?" her assistant asked.

"Difficult." Thank God she'd had Nonnie's help or she wasn't sure she would have been able to manage everything on her own. Besides her shocking behavior with Henry, the biggest surprise of the past week was the discovery that Nonnie was actually human with a real, beating heart. As a kid, she'd blamed the woman for most things that had gone wrong in her life. As an adult, she'd joined with her in common grief. Her momma had always called Nonnie family, and while Vivien would not go that far, perhaps they could be friends.

"How's Patrick?" The man skank.

"Fine." Sarah looked away, but not before Vivien saw the tension in the corners of her blue eyes. "I think you'll need the new Balenciaga wedges," she said as she disappeared into the closet, the subject of Patrick closed.

Vivien folded a red cardigan and put it in the suitcase. Who was she to judge? She'd certainly dated her share of men like Patrick. Men who couldn't be trusted out of her sight. Men she'd had to worry and wonder about and lose good sleep over. She thought of the last guy she'd trusted, Kyle Martin, aka surfer dude. She'd met him on an audition for a Neil Marshall horror flick. He'd had sun-bleached hair and bronzed skin stretched over hard muscles. He'd been the first to say "I love you," and by then, she'd fallen for him, too. The relationship had been fun and easy and they both wanted the same things in life. They'd never fought or even argued, and if she'd question him about the days he'd go missing, he'd smile and change the subject and she'd let him because he'd never given her reason not to trust him. When she'd left to begin filming the first Raffle movie, she'd been secure in her ten-month relationship. He'd kissed her good-bye. Told her that he loved her and not to worry about him. He'd known of the lying, cheating men in her past, and he'd promised that he'd never hurt her.

When she'd been given the part of Zahara West, he'd been genuinely supportive. They'd both known how much her life would change but they'd promised each other that it wouldn't change *them*. She loved and trusted Kyle—right up until the day a friend texted her while she'd been camped out in a Guatemalan rain forest to inform her that she'd seen Kyle's profile on Match.com. From the ruins of an ancient city, Vivien plugged into the World Wide Web and discovered her "boyfriend" was seeking women twenty to twenty-five within a hundred-mile radius of Los Angeles. He liked "hiking" and "hanging ten in Half Moon Bay." He preferred "tall, curvy blondes" and his idea of a "great date" was "taking a special lady on a Sturgis run."

If Vivien hadn't looked at the fifteen photos he'd provided (one of which had been taken at a friend's wedding and he'd conveniently cropped Vivien out), she would not have recognized him by what he'd written. Kyle surfed, but he certainly never surfed the big waves at Mavericks, and he didn't even have a bicycle, let alone a Harley. She wasn't tall or blonde or curvy or any of the things he'd written that he wanted. She'd been stunned and numb, as if someone had taken over her body and she was living in an alternate universe. One that was the exact opposite of her life, like Alice in *Through the Looking Glass*.

Who are you? she'd wondered as she'd stared at his dating-site photos. *Have I ever known you? Was everything a lie? The time you taught me to surf and the white daisies you bought because they're my favorite? When we laughed our heads off at silly movies, was that a lie? Who are you, Kyle Martin?*

God she didn't recognize the man on Match.com. Didn't know him, but she found out what kind of man he was after she broke up with him and he sold a story to the tabloids. An untrue story of a supposed eating disorder that made her crazy and bitchy and impossible. The whole thing had been hurtful and humiliating and the beginning of the anorexia rumors that still plagued her. Vivien knew she was thin. She had to watch everything she ate. It was part of her job. One of the unwritten rules in Hollywood. When a costume designer made clothes in a size zero, an actress didn't have to be told to lose weight. Vivien had given up French fries, pizza, and ice cream, but she wasn't anorexic. She wasn't crazy or bitchy or impossible, like Kyle had said. He'd sold her out for a few bucks and his name in a headline. She'd thought he'd cared about her. He'd told her he loved her. Obviously that had been a lie. Their whole relationship had been one big fat lie, and she'd never had a clue.

"What about the newest Loubs?" Sarah asked from the closet. "Cheetah is hot this season and so versatile."

She really didn't think she'd find herself anywhere in Charleston that required Louboutins with 120-millimeter heels. If she did, she had the Manolos she'd picked up at Berlins. "I don't think so." One of the perks of being Vivien Rochet was the designer shoes and clothes and handbags and beauty products that arrived at her door in hopes that she'd be photographed or mentioned wearing them. She thought of the suede T-straps that made her look like she had legs for days. The image of her legs wrapped around Henry's waist while wearing her do-me Louboutins popped into her head. "But I might need the red open-toes." Her cheeks heated and she changed her mind. "No." But maybe . . . "Yes." She'd been thinking a lot about Henry, and she wondered if he'd been thinking of her.

Sarah stuck her head out of the closet. "What is it?"

"Yes," she answered before she changed her mind again. She grabbed her cell phone and thumbed through her texts. Nothing from Henry and she knew he had her number. Not even a "Hope you made it okay," or "How was your flight?" She tossed the phone on her bed next to her suitcase. She didn't know what made her think he might contact her today, other than they'd had sex the night before.

She'd stripped naked in front of him, but how well did she know Henry? Really? It had been years since she'd seen him. Not since the day he'd threatened to kill her when she'd found the letters in his puzzle box and the condoms in his sock drawer. He'd just turned eighteen.

"The car service should be here at four tomorrow morning," Sarah said as she moved from the closet with an armload of shoes and handful of dresses.

Vivien groaned. It hardly seemed worth it to return to Charleston, but she could get a lot settled in three days. She could make headway packing her mother's things and decide whether to store, donate, or toss. She could take another look at the row house and decide what needed to be done before she could put it on the market. There was no reason to keep it now. She'd ask Henry how much longer before he had the place restored.

She thought of Henry and the day he'd made her tea and given her his smelly coat to wear, and the weird little glow she'd felt in Henry's bed stirred in her chest again. It scared and confused her as much as it had last night, but it made her smile, too. Like Kyle and all the other men in Vivien's past, Henry was probably a cheating man skank. Like previous boyfriends, he probably couldn't be trusted.

A frown pulled her brows together. Why was she even thinking about Henry and trust and boyfriends? He was never going to be her boyfriend. He was scary Henry Whitley-Shuler. Growing up, she'd never trusted him for a second.

Yet, being with him last night had felt different. They were adults now. They were no longer kids butting heads. She was a grown woman. He was a mature man she thought she could trust, but what did she know? She'd fallen in love with a surfer who'd had a secret life on Match.com and then sold a bogus story to the tabloids that was still affecting her life. Clearly, her judgment couldn't be trusted.

"It's hotter than a four-balled tomcat."

The steady creak of an old rocking chair settled in a comfortable, familiar, place in Henry's soul. As boys, he and Spence had spent hours on the veranda, looking out at Charleston Harbor. Nothing more on their minds but identifying various boats sailing the waves as they swatted at mosquitoes. As men, their minds were occupied with weightier issues.

"More like four and three quarter balls." Henry rolled his head to the left and looked at his brother in the chair beside him. Through the humid sludge of a Charleston night, the weak porch light slid across Spence's profile.

"Let's live dangerously. It's hotter than a four-balled tomcat and two naked ladies wrestling in a pepper patch." The ice in Spence's glass rattled as he raised it to his lips.

Henry laughed and turned his gaze to the inky harbor and faint lights of passing boats. As kids, he and Spence had spent a lot of their summers with their grandfather in Hilton Head and been in awe of his bottomless well of Southern expressions and euphemisms. They'd soaked them up like sponges and squeezed them out as needed to make each other laugh. "And it's only June. Next month it's bound to be hotter than a four-balled cat *watching* half a dozen naked ladies wrestle in a pepper patch."

"That surely would be something to watch."

Grandfather Shuler had attempted to teach them the important things in life. Things like hunting and fishing and women. He referred to the four seasons not as summer, spring, winter, and fall, but turkey, fish, deer, and duck. Women were never fat—they "weighed heavy like cream," and a woman's "special parts" were "gumdrops" and "sugar cookies." As a result, Henry and Spence had snickered when offered either.

Henry wiped moisture from his forehead with the back of his hand. They'd just finished a supper of leftover funeral food that Nonnie insisted they come over and help "clean up" with her and the Episcopalian ladies. Neither he nor Spence were great cooks, and eating day-after-funeral ham seemed preferable to a can of soup or a table at a local restaurant. But when it came to "cleaning up" day-old tomato aspic and Gouda cheese grits, he and Spence had escaped to the wraparound veranda and their favorite old rocking chairs. "It's going to be weird not seeing Macy Jane around here anymore." Again the rattle of ice. "I wonder if Vivien plans to move into the carriage house."

"I imagine she'll sell it. Her life is in Hollywood." Just this morning, he'd dropped Vivien off at Charleston International with an airport escort. "She's high maintenance." She was too famous to stand in a ticket line or go through security like regular people. Her fans popping up at Macy Jane's funeral had proven she needed security and handlers and someone to attend to a myriad of important details.

"Sure grew up pretty, though."

"Uh-huh." Last night he'd attended to her important details, to her hard little nipples in his mouth, and his hand in her panties. If she were any other woman he wouldn't mind touching her again. Hell, if she were any other woman, he wouldn't mind taking a close look at her "sugar cookie."

"Where did you take her yesterday?"

"What?" He turned and looked at Spence.

"Where did you take Vivien yesterday after you stole her from me?"

"I didn't steal her."

"I was getting somewhere with her when you moved in."

Henry couldn't tell if Spence was kidding or not. "We just got some fresh air." He raised his glass and changed the subject. "What are your plans for employment?" he said before his favorite aged bourbon passed his lips and filled his mouth with smooth, oaky liquor. Until a few months ago, Spence had worked in the regional office of his former father-in-law, Senator Coleman. "I don't think you'll have any problem getting a job in local government."

"I'm not cut out to be a public servant."

That was news to Henry. He turned his attention to his brother once again. "Since when?"

"Since I graduated from Columbia with a poly sci degree." Spencer took another drink and sucked scotch from his bottom lip. "I hate politicians."

Henry laughed. "Mother has her heart set on calling you Governor."

"Yeah. I know she does, but she also had her heart set on calling you a Wall Street Titan." The sounds of cicadas and crickets and the creak of Spence's rocking chair filled his pause. "I guess she's doomed to disappointments."

"You haven't told her?"

"Not yet."

"Do me a favor and make sure I'm out of town." Practically from birth, Spence's life had been plotted out for him, just as Henry's had. Their mother was going to pitch a fit. "If you're not planning on being Governor Whitley-Shuler, what are your plans?"

"I have few things in mind." He rocked his chair a couple of time then said, "I think I'd like to write a novel."

"A novel?" Henry wouldn't have been more surprised if he'd said he wanted to drive a dog sled. "When did you decide this?"

"Aboard the *One and a Tuna.*"

"The what?"

"The majestic fishing vessel where I battled mighty tarpon in Key West."

Henry laughed. "Now I know you're pulling my leg."

"I'm dead serious. I figure all I need to write like Hemingway is a wooden yacht and a steady supply of mojitos." Spencer sounded a little wistful when he sang, "Wasting away in Margaritaville."

He'd lost it. Mixing up Hemmingway and Buffet. "You gonna blow out your flip-flops and raise six-toed cats?"

"No cats." He rocked the chair for several creaks. "I'm thinking I'll win a Pulitzer for my insightful portrayal of the human condition and sell the film rights to Hollywood."

"Sounds like you have it all planned out." No doubt about it, his brother had lost his fucking mind.

"I'm pulling your leg about portraying the human condition. I'm too big a sinner to preach morality and too superficial to examine the meaning of life." Spencer laughed like he was real funny. "Maybe I'll ask Vivien about writing for Hollywood."

Vivien. Henry was spending too much time thinking about her without his brother bringing up her name.

"When's she due back?"

"Tomorrow."

"What time?"

"Don't know," Henry answered, and he had no intention of finding out. None. Nada. Zippo.

He was back to frowning at her like she'd stolen his basketball and lost it. The first thing Vivien noticed as she walked out of Charleston International the next day, was the downward curve of Henry's mouth. He stood at the curb next to his truck, his emotions hidden behind sunglasses and his unreadable face. "How are you doing?" he asked, as if she were a stranger. As if she hadn't had sex with him. As if she couldn't distinguish the scent of his skin from the smell of hot concrete and car fumes.

"Good." He tossed her Louis Vuitton suitcases

into the back of his truck like they were gym bags. He was as indifferent to her expensive luggage as much as he appeared to be indifferent to her. Clearly he was back to being the Henry she'd known as a child.

No matter how hard she attempted to engage him in conversation, he hardly spoke on the drive from the airport. He dropped her off at the carriage house and set her luggage just inside the door, then he practically burned rubber and squealed his tires in his haste to leave. She might have thought he'd forgotten all about the other night if he hadn't glanced back at her one last time, his gaze clear and unguarded. For several heart-beats, he'd paused by the driver's side door of his truck. His dark eyes locked with hers, and for several hot and intense heartbeats, his gaze had been anything but indifferent.

Henry's moods were too confusing to think about and analyze, and why should she spend her time trying to make sense of him anyway? He wanted to ignore her like he had when they'd been kids. Fine. He probably had a string of women he confused besides her. He probably had a revolving door for a love life, and she needed to focus on the important reasons she was back in Charleston. None of which had anything to do with Butthead Henry.

The inside of the carriage house seemed so empty without her momma. Too quiet and dull.

Vivien kicked off her pumps and walked barefoot up the stairs to her old bedroom. She turned on the palmetto ceiling fan and took a step inside. The slight breeze from the fan disturbed the yellow sheers in her old bedroom, and the plantation shutters locked out the afternoon sun.

Her old twin bed sat in the middle of the room, arranged on the yellow polka-dot area rug she and her mother had found at Rug Masters when Vivien was fifteen. That was the year she'd been into polka dots, and the quilt on her bed matched the canopy and the yellow-and-white paper on the far wall.

Vivien moved into the room that still had all her acting awards pinned to a corkboard. She'd spent a lot of time in this room. Lonely days filled with grand dreams and staring into an old cheval mirror, practicing lines and her smile for when she was famous.

The hardwood floor creaked under her feet as she moved to the closet and opened the door. Her organza prom dress was still there, taking up most of the space inside. The huge skirt had made her look like one of those cakes with a Barbie doll stuck in the top. She'd gone to the prom with Levi Morgan, and he'd ended up drinking too many juleps and passing out in his car. She hadn't minded all that much. She'd been into the dress and the glamour more than she'd been into Levi.

On the shelf above the dress sat boxes and totes filled with her childhood. Everything in the room and the rest of the house had to be looked at and gone through and decisions had to be made. Decisions that only Vivien could make. Looking around, she realized that she'd grossly underestimated the time it would take her to go through everything. There was no way she could settle her momma's affairs before she needed to leave again.

She thought of Nonnie and Henry and, for the first time in years, the idea of spending time in the carriage house didn't make her want to run down the driveway screaming like Heather Langenkamp with Freddie Kruger on her tail. Living across the yard from Nonnie didn't feel like the Nightmare on Elm Street.

The doorbell rang and as if Vivien's thoughts conjured her up, Nonnie stood in the doorway, a covered dish in one hand and Louisa Deering's Twinkie loaf in the other. "We're still cleaning up leftovers from Macy Jane's funeral reception." She shoved the dish at Vivien. "Elsa Jean Packard's Battle of Honey Hill bacon and butter beans."

"Great." Vivien took the dish and tried not to grimace.

"While you were gone, I had new locks put on the doors and all the windows."

"Oh!" Vivien looked at the big shiny deadbolt

on the front door. With everything else on her mind, she'd forgotten to mention new locks to Sarah. "Thank you." She stepped aside and the older woman headed for the kitchen. Nonnie Whitley-Shuler, aka the Mantis, the Wicked Witch, and Cruella de Vil, among others, had given a thought to Vivien and her safety. Such a kind gesture almost brought a tear to her eyes.

"You're welcome. I had them installed in case those people you attract turn up and show their crazy."

— Chapter 13 —

Dear Diary,
  Yeah!!!! I finally get to wear a bra. ☺ I wanted a pink one with foam padding in it. Momma said no. ☹ She said only tacky hussies wear padded bras. I don't think that's true.

Dear Diary,
  Vivien loves Bubba!!! I got a boyfriend. Woohooo!!! His name is Gary but folks call him Bubba. He lives on Tradd Street in a big brick house. Everyone calls him fat, but I told him he's husky. We went to the Battery today and had ice cream. On the way home, he held my hand. At first it was weird and sweaty. Then in was nice. Kind of tingly in my arm and stomach. I think he might have kissed me good-bye, too, but Henry and Spence are home on some kind of school break. They were playing basketball in the driveway and me and Bubba let go of hands really fast. He left really fast, too. It's just like Henry and Spence to ruin my first

date. ☹ Henry said I could do better than a boy who looks like Cartman. Spence laughed and started quoting lines from South Park 'cause Spence is stupid. Bubba does <u>not</u> look like Cartman. He doesn't wear a coat and hat every day. Spence and Henry have been burrs in my ~~butt~~ patootie for years. When I'm rich and famous, I'm going to make them sorry. Especially Henry! ☺

Dear Diary,

Momma took me to her doctor and I had to take a long test. The questions where stuff about how I feel when I'm happy or sad. It was the scariest test ever, but the good news is that I'm not like Momma. The doctor said I have a 7 to 10 percent chance of getting Momma's illness before I'm thirty. Momma was very happy and said that's good. I hope so. I don't want to do crazy stuff like taking apart the washing machine and cleaning each part. Then getting sad because I can't put it back together again.

Dear Diary,

I saved up money and got Va-Vooms

for my bra. They're rubbery and look like crescent rolls. When I put them in my bra, I go from an A cup to a B. Anything bigger and people will notice, like when Hillary Asner came to school in her Bombshell bra. A girl can't just go from an A to a D cup overnight.

Dear Diary,
  Bubba kissed me today!!! It was magic. He pretended that he was reaching a tree branch above my head and he kissed me. I'll remember it for the rest of my life. He said I kissed good for my first time. He's so sweet and I'm lucky to have a boyfriend like Bubba.

Dear Diary,
  Death to Bubba!!! He likes Katelyn Mathers now and won't talk to me. He told everyone at school that Katelyn is a better kisser. He gave her a stuffed dog and a roll of cherry Lifesavers. I tried not to cry, but I did anyway.

Kiss My Patootie List

1. Mantis
2. Henry
3. Spence

4. Bubba
5. Donny Ray
6. Uncle Richie and Kathy

More to come later.

— Chapter 14 —

Henry unlocked the French doors of the pink row house and pushed them open. He couldn't help but recall the last time he'd walked into the courtyard behind him and found Vivien up to her elbows in mud, searching for something. Her bare legs wet from the rain and streaked with dirt. She'd looked small and vulnerable and gorgeous.

That was part of her appeal. Her charisma. The reason men around the world wanted Vivien Rochet.

God help him. He was one of them.

The sound of his boots' heels seemed to bounce off the walls in the silent old home. It had been three days since he'd picked Vivien up from the airport and dropped her off at the carriage house. Three days since he'd looked into her green eyes and seen her confusion. Three days since he'd forced himself to walk away when it would have been so easy to wrap her in his arms instead. Easier still to dip his head and kiss her until she was breathless.

For three days he'd avoided Vivien because he wasn't so sure he could walk away a second time.

The house smelled of old wood and the new plaster he'd used to repair the wall. He didn't know what Vivien planned for the historical house, but whether Vivien kept the house or sold it, the renovation had to be completed and inspected before SFN signed off on the project.

Despite the sluggish heat, there was a slight breeze and he left the doors open to chase away the stale air. He inspected the new plaster, then grabbed a flashlight. He got down on his knees and looked up into the chimney. Years of soot smudged the shoulder of his blue T-shirt and the knees of his Levis.

He shined the beam of light at the old bricks, looking for any sign of water. The night he and Spence had supper with Nonnie and the church ladies, she'd volunteered him to pick Vivien up from the airport when he'd had no intention of putting himself anywhere near temptation. Yet just as he and his brother had been preparing to leave, his mother had volunteered him as some sort of preemptive strike out of fear Spence would make the offer first.

If not his mother, he wouldn't have picked Vivien up at the airport beside a ridiculous pile of overpriced luggage and a beefy security concierge. He wouldn't have stared at her red lips just beneath the dip of her big straw hat. He wouldn't have smelled her perfume and been reminded of the night she'd spent in his bed. Okay, he didn't need her perfume to remind him. His thoughts turned to Vivien whether he wanted them to turn or not.

He slid the beam of light up the flue. He was tired of being the family fix-it-guy. Tired of keeping secrets and the burden of knowing them all. Tired of the guilt.

He slid the light and inspected the bricks on the left. He was almost certain Vivien would sell the house. There really was no reason for her to keep it. She didn't live in Charleston and there was nothing here for her now that her momma was gone. After she packed up the carriage house, there was nothing more for her to do. Everything else could be handled by realtors and brokers. Two weeks, maybe three, and she'd be gone, too.

All he had to do was avoid her like a plague of chiggers.

"Are you looking for Santa?"

The flashlight slipped from his hand and he smacked his head into the bricks. "God *damn!*" he swore.

"Sorry."

He ducked from beneath the chimney and his gaze landed on Vivien's shiny red shoes and bare legs. She wore a black skirt and red blouse and if he looked hard enough, he could see the outline of a red bra. She had a deep green leaf stuck in her hair next to her left ear as if she'd ducked under a tree. He smiled. He couldn't seem to help himself. Must have something to do with the knock to his head.

"I didn't mean to scare you."

"You startled me." He stood and brushed soot from his jeans. "It would take someone bigger than you to scare me."

"I just met with the executor of Momma's estate." She set her purse on the sofa covered in a drop cloth. "Everything was fairly easy. There were no surprises." A frown pulled at her brow. "Except that the carriage house is now mine. I'd have thought she'd leave it to your mother. It was hers before she gave it to Momma."

He didn't correct her. "What are your plans for this house?"

She let out a breath and looked around. A breathy little sound like when he'd kissed her neck and behind her ear, and she'd liked it. "Sell it." She glanced up at the molded ceiling. "It's a beautiful house. Someone should live here that loves it," she said.

His gaze slid down her chin and throat to the top button of her blouse resting between her breasts.

"Someone who likes living in a money pit."

"That someone isn't you, Henry?" He'd kissed her just above that button too.

"No. I prefer modern plumbing and design."

She returned her gaze to his. "When do you think you'll be done with the renovations?"

"Your mother had a real fluid timeline and she kept changing her mind about what she wanted done." He tossed the flashlight next to her purse.

"I have to finish the handrails and crown molding in the master bedroom. I should wrap that up in a week, maybe two." He took several steps toward her before he reminded himself not to. "What do you want to do with the dining-room table and chairs?" He lifted his hand, and his fingers brushed her hair as he pulled the leaf from a soft curl.

"I don't know." She shook her head and her cheek brushed his palm.

"This belongs to you," he said and handed her the leaf.

"Henry?"

He stuck his hands in his pockets before he gave into temptation and ran his fingers through her hair. Vivien was beautiful and he was ridiculously attracted to her. Standing here in the red silky blouse that was almost see-through, and her red shoes that put her lips just beneath his, he fought the temptation to kiss her. To run his hands up and down her back and butt and feel her small hands on him. To catch her soft moan in his mouth, and the taste of desire on his tongue. "Yes?"

She twirled the stem of the leaf between her fingers then looked up at him out of the corners of her green eyes. "I think we should talk about the other night."

"We should forget the other night happened."

A frown pulled her brows together. "Do you think that's possible?"

"Of course."

"Are you going to able to forget?"

Never. "Forget what?"

She tilted her head to one side and he should have recognized the look in her eyes, but he was thinking up his next lie when she said, "Do you really think you can forget lifting me on top of your kitchen island?"

"What kitchen island?" He knew what she was doing. He knew her tricks; he was wise to her pushing and provocations. He also knew he couldn't let her push him into doing something stupid. Like giving in to the desire raging in his pants.

"The granite island where you stripped off my panties and kissed me all over."

"I didn't kiss you all over." There were parts he'd like to kiss. Soft, slick parts that made him so hard he couldn't stop thoughts of putting his mouth there.

Her eyes got a little squinty. "You kissed me all over then carried me to your bed like a caveman."

At the moment he felt like a caveman. Like there was a real thin thread keeping him standing upright instead of bending her over and getting primeval.

She poked him in the chest with her finger. "Don't act like I'm disposable. Like I'm just one more woman in the revolving door of your love life. Like I'm easily forgotten."

He lowered his gaze to her finger on his chest. She was pushing and he was teetering.

"Henry."

He lifted his gaze. Teetering at the edge, stretching the thread close to a perilous snap. "What?"

She smiled, a sexy little tilt at the corners of her red lips. "You remember. I can see it in your eyes."

"What you see is pity. I feel sorry for you on account of you being coyote ugly."

"Are you about to chew your leg off?"

"Thinking about it, yeah."

"I hate it when you do that."

"What?"

Her eyes got serious. "Treat me like I'm doing something bad. It makes me want to poke at you."

"I know." Just a kiss. A kiss wasn't sex. "I know that about you." He lowered his mouth to hers. "I've always known that about you." Her breath hitched in her chest and she kissed him back, soft and passionate like the other night. And just like the first time, the kiss caught fire and turned carnal. Wet and feeding, sucking out reason. Right and wrong, guilt and consequence turned to ash beneath the scorching need racing across his skin and making him so hard he had to lock his knees to keep from falling. He lifted his face. "Stop me before we can't stop."

Her hand slid down his chest to the front of his jeans. "Too late." She brought his mouth back to hers and the thread keeping him from going caveman snapped. She caressed his erection through the denim as his big fingers fumbled with the tiny buttons closing her shirt. He gave up halfway down and pulled the blouse over her head. The skirt fell to the floor without much effort and she stood before him in her red underwear and tall red heels.

"God Vivien," he managed as she pulled at his button fly. "You're killing me with the red bra and panties."

"You like?"

He hooked a finger beneath a red satin strap. "I love."

As she pulled at his belt, he lowered his face to the curve of her neck and opened his mouth against her soft skin. She smelled of flowers and he kissed his way across her shoulder. She slid her fingers beneath his boxers and wrapped her hand around his erection."

"You're hard, Henry." She moved her palm down and brushed her thumb across the head of his penis. "You must have a thing for coyote ugly."

"I have a thing for you." He grabbed her wrists and pinned them behind her. Her back arched and he buried his face in her cleavage. He rubbed his cheek against her breasts and sucked her hard nipples through the slick silky bra. He loved her small breasts. In his hands. Mouth. Against his chest.

"Let go."

He did as she wanted and she reached for the front of his pants. She pulled and unzipped and shoved her hand inside. Her soft palm wrapped around his dick and he nearly lost control. He loved the touch of her soft hands on him. How she let him know how much she wanted him. He'd been with women who'd wanted to be with him because of his last name and family connections. Vivien wanted neither of those things. She wanted him in spite of his name and he wanted her in every barbaric beat of his heart. In the place deep in his soul that made him want to beat his chest and jump on top of his woman.

He spun her around to face the couch. Then he bent her over and she grabbed the back of the colonial sofa. He pushed her panties down her legs and palmed her smooth behind. He pulled a condom from his wallet as his Levis slid down his legs. The belt buckle hit the floor with a thud as he tossed his wallet on the couch. "Spread your feet a little bit for me," he said as his underwear joined his pants and he rolled the condom down his shaft.

Her high red shoes brought her to the perfect level and he slid his hand over her bottom and between her legs. She was wet and ready and moaned deep in her throat as he teased her slick flesh. Her back arched as he positioned himself, and his hands grabbed her around the waist as he slid into the hot pleasure of her body. She was incredibly tight around him, and he pulled almost all the way out before he sank so deep her bottom pushed against his thighs. He leaned forward and kissed the side of her neck. "You feel good, Vivien."

Her response was to push her bottom against him, wanting more. He gave it to her in long powerful thrusts. He drove inside again and again, his pulse pounded in his head, he held himself back until he felt the first tightening pulse of her orgasm. His own orgasm curled and tugged and burned deep in his belly. He wanted more. He wanted her and he thrust hard. A deep guttural moan climbed up his throat as fiery liquid heat surrounded him. The most intense pleasure he'd ever felt in his life ripped through his body and he closed his eyes. It spread fire across his skin, grabbed his insides, and stole his breath. His flesh surrounded by hers. His heart pounded and he could hardly breathe. He should pull out. He couldn't. Not just yet. The condom broke and he was surrounded by paradise. A hot slick paradise that nearly buckled his knees. The last time he'd touched paradise had put him through hell.

If panic had form, it would look like Henry. He yanked his T-shirt over his head, and Vivien looked down at the covered buttons of her red blouse. When he'd crawled out of the fireplace earlier, he'd given her a smile she'd never seen before. Not like the smile he'd given her the day of her mother's funeral. The one filled with megawatt charm and bullshit. The smile he'd given her earlier had touched the corners of his eyes and made her feel as if she was the only woman on the planet, as if she lit up his life when she walked into a room. As if he smiled just for her, but he wasn't smiling at her now.

"Tell me you're on birth control."

Vivien glanced up and left her blouse untucked. "I don't take birth control." It made her gain weight and become bloated and she couldn't fit into her metal bikinis. "I always insist on a condom."

"Shit." He put his hands on the sides of his head like he wanted to crack his skull.

Just moments ago, she'd felt wrapped up in warmth and desire. Now he was distant and cold and looked at her like he used to. As if she'd done something wrong, like breaking his condom on purpose.

"I won't get pregnant."

He looked at her and dropped his hands. "How can you be sure?"

"I have irregular periods. It kind of runs in my family."

"What does that mean?"

"It means that if I wanted to get pregnant, I'd have to buy one of those fertility tests to tell me if I'm ovulating." And she'd have to gain twenty pounds. She'd been told that her history of irregular periods, coupled with her low weight, made it very unlikely for her to conceive. She wanted children. Just not yet. She wanted to get her career established to the point where she could take time between movies, and she wanted to find the right man. She want to get married and do things in order.

"Do we need to buy one of those?"

"No." He looked so relieved she had an urge to punch him. "You don't have to look as if you just escaped death row," she said as she moved past him on her way to the kitchen. A glass sat upside down on the counter and she filled it with water. What was she doing? He was Henry Whitley-Shuler. She raised the glass to her lips and drank. Of course the thought of having a baby with her sent him into a panic. Clearly, he was not the right man for Vivien Rochet.

Henry moved behind her and took the water from her hand. "I haven't had a condom break since I was seventeen." He drained the glass. "I don't ever want to live through that again."

She turned to face him and her annoyance faded. She'd never given a thought to how he'd felt seventeen years ago. She'd just always assumed he was happy about it.

"You never told anyone about Tracy Lynn."

"Of course not."

"Why?" He refilled the glass and handed it to her. "I expected you to."

She shook her head. "I might have been a bratty kid who snooped through your things and called you names, but I was never mean." She took a long drink and sucked water off her bottom lip. "I never intentionally caused anyone pain, and I knew that would be painful for a lot of people." She handed him the glass.

"You're right. It would have hurt a lot of people. Mostly Tracy Lynn and her family."

"Do you ever see her anymore?"

He shook his head. "Never. I heard she married a lawyer and they have three kids and live in Shreveport." He drained the glass and set it on the counter. "I think seeing me would bring up painful memories and hurt her unnecessarily."

"What about you?"

His brow lowered over his serious brown eyes. "What about me?"

"Does the memory cause you pain?"

"More guilt than pain, but yeah." Lines creased his forehead. "I don't like to think about it. I don't like to think about what could have been and how my life would be different." He raised his gaze and looked past her. "It just stirs up the past and nothing can change it anyway."

The last thing she wanted was to stir up guilt and pain from the past. She took his hand and purposely changed the subject. "I noticed that ou don't use Climax Control Trojans these days."

He looked at her and confusion deepened the lines on his forehead. "What?"

"You used to use Climax Control Trojans."

"You remember what kind of condoms I used in high school?"

She chuckled and squeezed his hand. "I didn't know anything about condoms and had no idea what climax control meant. So I researched it."

A bemused smile passed his lips and cleared his forehead. "You researched it?"

"Of course." She put her arms around his neck. "I notice you don't use climax control condoms these days."

"I don't have a control issue these days." He brushed his hand up her arm, leaving tingles on her skin. "I practiced until I got it right."

A single candle flickered on the round kitchen table inside the carriage house. The light overhead was turned low enough that the flame cast wavering light across Henry's face, through his hair, and on the wall behind him.

"I don't know what to do with Momma's collection of Limoges boxes. I didn't realize she had so many." Vivien took a bite of juicy quail Henry had had delivered from one of his favorite restaurants.

"Put them on eBay."

"I can't sell Momma's Limoges." She shook her head and swallowed. "I wish I had family."

"What about the aunt and uncle who came to the funeral?" He cut a few pieces of asparagus.

"Uncle Richie and Kathy?" She reached for a glass of wine. "I don't know." Kathy had always been nasty to her mother, but Vivien might not have a choice. Her family tree had dwindled to a twig. "If I'd ever met my daddy's family this might be easier."

Henry's knife stopped and his gaze lifted to hers.

"But maybe not. Momma always said that the Rochets had very few extended family members and she'd never met them." She raised the glass and took a drink.

He stared at her across the table. "I take it you never tried to find them."

"Through the years, I've thought about hiring someone to find my daddy's family, but Momma never wanted me to reach out. She said it was too painful for her."

Henry lowered his gaze and finished cutting his asparagus. "What about now?"

Vivien shrugged. "I'll think about it, but I don't know." She set the glass by her plate and reached for her fork. "I mean, the Rochets must have known about me. My daddy married Momma three months before Hurricane Kate killed him."

"Hurricane Kate?" Henry stuck a piece of quail in his mouth and chewed for several thoughtful moments. Then he leaned back in his chair. "I've never heard about your father and Hurricane Kate."

No reason he should have, she supposed. "My daddy's name was Jeremiah Rochet and he was killed before I was born. He and his family were on their three-masted schooner when it went down in the Florida straits during Hurricane Kate. Momma wasn't aboard because she was pregnant with me and had morning sickness. Momma says we were blessed by the tears of baby Jesus that day."

"Really?"

She paused to take another bite, then continued with the heartbreaking story of her family. "Pieces of the *Anna Leigh* were found, but the Rochets were lost forever."

"That's a real tragedy." He swirled wine in his glass. "Did your momma tell you how many Rochets were lost at sea?"

"Five. Both my grandparents, my daddy and his two brothers. They were part of the Democracy Movement and routinely rescued Cuban refugees."

"Your family was Cuban?"

"No. They were humanitarians."

His brows made a V in the center of his forehead. "Isn't that something."

"I used to daydream about what my life would be like if Daddy had lived."

"Vastly different, I would imagine." He raised his glass to his lips. "I just can't picture you as a Cuban rescuing humanitarian."

Vivien laughed. "If Daddy had lived, I might

not be the person I am now. I might have been sent off in the Peace Corps, and I wouldn't have started acting and I wouldn't have the life I do today." She looked across the table into his dark eyes, which were watching her like he expected her to do something or say something. She continued, "When I was young, I used to fantasize a lot, but never about carrying water to villages in Africa. I guess I just didn't inherit the humanitarian gene from my Daddy's side." She set her fork on her plate. "My dreams were kind of vague. Except for the part where I got famous, then come back to Charleston and get revenge on anyone who'd done me wrong."

His forehead cleared. "What sort of revenge did you plan for those poor people?"

"I'd tell them to kiss my butt. I remember that I actually wrote a list. I called it the 'kiss my patootie' list."

"Your big dream has come true." He leaned forward and placed his hand over hers. "You're famous and can get your revenge on anyone who was ever mean to you."

"No. I've learned that living well and thriving like a weed is the best revenge." She smiled and turned her hand palm up. "Besides, you were number one on my list."

He laughed and rose to his feet. "I believe you've already told me to kiss your butt a time or two."

"Probably." She stood and he pulled her close, exactly where she wanted to be. "I'm leaving tomorrow."

"I know." He hugged her even closer. "I'll take you to the airport."

"I'd like that." She took him by the hand and led him to her momma's bedroom. That night, his touch seemed less hurried. He took his time and looked into her face as they had sex that felt a little different. That felt like making love. The next morning when he drove her to the airport, she wasn't ready to go.

"When are you coming back?" Henry asked.

She looked across the cab of his truck as he raised a mug of coffee to his mouth. "Saturday." She hoped to see him when she returned. She thought that she probably would but he'd never mentioned anything about a relationship more than sexual.

They'd had a nice few days together. Okay, a few great days. Fabulous days, but that was it. He'd never hinted in anyway of a future for them. "We're both grown-ups," she began, deciding it was best to talk about expectations, or lack of expectations, before she left. "You know you don't owe me anything, Henry."

"Yes, I know."

"I'm going to be flying in and out of town until I get everything settled here." She was a grown woman. She wanted to do the mature thing. The *realistic* thing. "A lot of time we're going to be miles apart, and I just want you to know that I'm perfectly okay with you dating other women."

He glanced at her, then back at the road. "Is that right?"

Of course not! "Yes. As long as I know you're only going to see me when I'm in town."

Again he glanced at her. "Let me see if I'm hearing you right." He pulled the truck to a stop at a red light. "It's fine with you if I have sex with other women while you're out of town."

Hell no! Just the thought of him touching another woman made her feel sick. "Yes." She wanted him to object. To tell her he didn't want anyone but her.

The light changed and he drove through the intersection. "But when you're in town, I'm your exclusive piece of meat."

She wanted . . . Wait. Had he just said, "piece of meat?" He couldn't be serious. "Yes."

"I'm not just meat, Vivien."

He was serious. She recognized his serious scowl creasing his forehead. She raised a hand to trap her laughter behind her fingers.

He glanced at her and an exasperated frown tugged the corners of his mouth. "It's not funny."

Oh but it was. Henry Whitley-Shuler, descendant of southern gentry, former Wall Street trader, current journeyman cabinetmaker.

Man meat.

— Chapter 15 —

Barricades and studio security surrounded two city blocks in downtown Los Angeles. Production trailers clogged a parking lot, and the California sunlight pinwheeled off a row of Airstreams. Outside the silver trailers, the cast of *Psychic Detectives* joked while the crew set up for a long shot.

"I've confirmed your car service for tomorrow at eleven." Sarah sat in the salon chair next to Vivien and scrolled information on her tablet. "You aren't needed on the set until one."

While the hair stylist reglued a widow's peak half way down Vivien's forehead, she read the lines for her second scene that day. Not that she really needed to. Memorizing lines came easy for her. It was staying in character that gave her trouble at times. She sat in the makeup trailer, getting her bad wig and the dark circles under her eyes touched up. Today she would shoot her second scene. Tomorrow her third and final scene, when she'd have black contact lenses in her eyes and a beating heart prostheses beneath her worn dress. She'd stare at her husband, her heart pounding harder and harder as the evil Reverend Mumford exploded in a torrent of blood and gore. She couldn't wait.

Vivien closed her eyes and inhaled a deep breath. She pictured Jenny in her head, and thought about her character's simple objective and the final inciting incident that pushes her to act and unleash her telekinetic ability on her husband. Vivien quieted everything in her head, and thought about abuse and what she knew of PTSD. She thought of hiding from trauma and shielding emotions until they bubbled up. She thought of rough hands . . . and the brush of fingertips waking her in the morning. She thought of the soft, gray light of morning chasing away the night and whispered kisses on her bare shoulder. Her eyes opened and she smiled when she should be frowning. When she thought of Henry, he cleared her head of everything but him. She'd been back in L.A. for three days, and she'd been thinking about him way too often. As a result of all that thinking, she figured out what it was about Henry that made her want to be around him. What it was that made it so easy.

She trusted Henry in a way that just felt natural and easy. There weren't many people she trusted these days. Only three, actually: her assistant, her agent, and her manager and they'd all signed confidentiality agreements. She'd trusted her momma. Her momma never would have hurt her. Her momma never would have lied and told stories about her that weren't true. She never would have sold stories that *were* true. Neither would Henry. His character was too solid to lie and leak and sell out.

"Vivien." A production assistant stuck his head in the door. "We're ready for you."

She looked in the mirror at herself. At her dull, limp wig and pallid skin. *Haggard* came to mind. She stuck the script under one arm and stood. Sarah followed her out the door and into the California sunlight. She walked onto the hot set and handed the script to her assistant.

"Quiet on the set!"

The sound and speed rolled and the clapboard was placed in front of the camera. "Scene fourteen, take one."

"Action," the director yelled and Vivien walked into the parking lot. She stared blankly ahead at a beige Chevy. Jenny's life was one dull task after another of living beneath the thumb of a man who claimed to speak for God. She'd been beaten down to the point of being blank by a man who'd convinced his flock that he was the second coming of Christ. She—*Jesus Christ, Vivien!* popped unexpectedly into her head. *That one was ripped from the pit of my soul.*

"Cut!" Everything stopped and the director said, "Vivien, you just found out your husband cleaned out your bank account and you had to leave the store without your bag of groceries. He is having sex with a fifteen-year-old. You're supposed to look defeated, not suddenly smiling like life is a bowl of cherries."

"Oh." She hadn't even been aware that she was smiling. "Sorry." She retraced her steps.

"Quiet on the set!"

The camera and sound rolled again. The assistant director yelled "mark it," and the slate person put the clapboard in front of the camera. "Scene fourteen, take two."

"Action!"

Vivien took a deep breath and let it out. She stuffed her head with Jenny and her horrible circumstances. She became her character. Meek. Submissive. In fear of her powers and believing Enoch is the only man who can save her from hell. *I'm not your man meat, Vivien.*

"Cut!"

Vivien bit the side of her lip and retraced her steps. It took six more takes before the scene ended with her gazing across the parking lot at her husband and a fresh-faced girl. The young girl who used to be her.

On Vivien's way home from the set, she checked her text messages. Henry's name popped up and she bit her lower lip. *How's work?* Two words. He only wrote two words but that wasn't the point. He'd reached out to her.

She waited until she got home to write back. She didn't want to write too much and give him the impression that she missed him or sat around thinking of him. She typed, *Fine. How's everything with you?* It wasn't until she crawled into her four-poster bed that he texted back. *Muggy as hell here in Charleston. Met a friend for a drink.*

Vivien found the remote and hit a button. Across the room, her flat-screen television rose from a recessed compartment. *The Tonight Show with Jimmy Fallon* flashed on the screen, but she wasn't interested in Jimmy tonight. Henry had met a friend for a drink. Possibly a female friend. Yes, she'd told him he was free to see other women, but she hadn't meant it. He had to know she hadn't meant it.

Right?

They weren't in a relationship. They'd had great sex, but sex wasn't love. Not even when it had felt like making love. He'd said he didn't want to be her man meat, but he hadn't said what he did want to be with her. He'd never talked of any sort of future between them. No, "let's fly off to Mexico this summer" or "bring an extra tooth brush to my house." He'd told her he'd pick her up from the airport. That was it. Not exactly a commitment.

Vivien tossed the remote and curled up on her side. There were plenty of obstacles that stood in the way of them ever becoming a couple. First, they lived thousands of miles apart. Second, he was Henry Whitley-Shuler, Charleston royalty, and just his name gave him entrée into the most exclusive clubs and organizations. She was Vivien Rochet, international movie star. Her name was known around the globe, but her name could never get her into the circle of society that had welcomed Henry at birth. Men like Henry had relationships with young ladies who came from old families with old family names. Not with a girl who came from the carriage house and used to vacuum their carpets. No matter how rich and famous she'd become, men like Henry formed real relationships with women like Constance Abernathy. Former St. Cecilia debutantes, members of the Junior League, and dabblers in the arts.

At the end of the day, fame and fortune and hard work was not enough. She might play fairytale characters in movies, but in real life there was no enchanted wand to turn her into a suitable princess worthy of southern royalty.

At the end of the day, she was not enough and she better remember that before she fell completely in love with Henry.

Vivien's face lit up when she talked about acting and the Dorothy Parker role she hoped to land. Her eyes shined with a spark of life that chased away the sorrow of her mother's passing and the stress of the past week. She looked happy and happy looked good on her.

She'd been home a full week this time, cleaning

and packing up her mother's house. As before, he'd picked her up at the airport, but this time he'd followed her into the carriage house and made love to her on the living-room floor. He still had rug burns to prove it.

"I really want that role," she said as she wrapped her mother's china in newspaper and stuck it in a box. "Every actress in Hollywood has auditioned for it." She grabbed another plate "It's a Meryl." She wore jean shorts and a white T-shirt and sneakers. A Clemson ball cap cast a shadow across her forehead, and her hair was held back by a plain rubber band. There was nothing plain about her.

"A what?"

"The kind of role that wins awards." She looked up, focused and determined like when she'd been a kid. "I want to win an Oscar."

He laughed and set a blender in the donate bin next to an old toaster. "I thought it was just great to be nominated. Isn't that what y'all say?"

"That's crap." She waved a hand in the air. "Everyone wants to win."

Henry thought about his former life, when he'd wanted to win at all cost. When losing hadn't been an option. When he'd been flying high and his heart had beat to the rhythm of the stock market. He understood Vivien's ambition, it just wasn't his life any longer.

"If I'm cast, I'll have a wider range of films on

my resume and grow my brand." She chatted about future parts and the production company she planned to create. "No remakes," she said. "I mean, how many different times and ways do you want to see *The Invisible Man* or *Zorro*? I hate to see big studios suck the life out of Jane Austen or Hitchcock when the originals are such classics and should be left alone." She wrapped one last plate. "But first I need to land that Dorothy Parker role."

"When will you know if you get the part?"

"Soon." Vivien put the last plate in the box then shoved her hands on her hips and glanced about the kitchen. "It looks like an episode of *Hoarders* in here."

Not quite, but there were three bins: keep, donate, and throw away. She'd made headway sorting her mother's personal belongings, but she still had quite a bit to do yet.

"Momma was sentimental. A lot of the time, she couldn't bear to throw away anything. Then there were other times when she cleared the house of clutter and threw away the stuff she hadn't been able to part with the day before." Sadness crept into her eyes and she turned toward the sink. "Her life was a rollercoaster." She washed her hands with a bar of rose-scented soap.

"So was yours." Henry joined her at the sink and took the soap from her hands. "You were forced to live her ups and downs alongside her."

He would smell like roses, but he'd smelled like worse.

"Yeah, but she couldn't help it." She ripped off two paper towels and handed him one. "Most of the time it was okay."

Her green eyes looked into his and he could see that it hadn't been "okay."

"When she was stable, she was a real good momma. She cared for me and loved me and I loved her. Then she'd get hyper manic and stay up for days doing a hundred projects at once." She looked down at her feet, and the bill of her hat blocked his view of her face.

Henry reached for her ball cap and pulled it from her head. "I remember Spence and I came home from Hilton Head one night and she had a flashlight in one hand and a paintbrush in the other. She was singing to *Tom Petty* on the radio and painting the shutters." He tossed the hat onto a box. "We just thought she didn't want to paint during the heat of the day. Later Mother told us she was bipolar and explained what that meant." He put a finger beneath Vivien's chin and lifted her gaze to his. "That must have sucked for you as a kid."

She shrugged one shoulder. "I didn't really mind when she talked about her dreams. She made them seem real and she'd entertain me for hours with things we would do when we ran off to Zanzibar or Bali. For a while she'd just be a normal mother.

We'd just be normal, and then I'd see her getting dressed up nice, and I knew she was going out to find some sorry excuse for a boyfriend. I hated her boyfriends, but I hated her sad moods even more." She shook her head and her brows furrowed above her beautiful eyes. "I figured out real quick the patterns of her moods. They were always the same: happy, normal, needy, and sad. I never knew how long she'd stay in one of her moods before moving into the next. Sometimes she wouldn't get out of bed for two weeks."

He brushed his thumb across her jaw. "What did you do when she was in bed?"

"Sometimes Mamaw Roz stayed with us or I stayed at her house. When I got older, I took care of her."

"She was lucky to have you."

She tilted her head to one side in thought. "I was lucky to have her. She taught me to dream big and that nothing was beyond my reach. She always told me that I could be anything I wanted to be. She never set limits on my imagination or had crushing expectations of me. Without her, I don't know that I would be where I am today." One corner of her pink lips curved upward. "I grew up in your backyard, but our lives were different."

"Drastically different. Growing up in boarding schools was lonely. Once we were sent away to school, mother's job was over. Spence and I had each other, but we were raised by headmasters and dorm advisers and Grandfather Shuler. I don't think Spence has ever forgiven her. If you add up the number of days we spent at home, they probably wouldn't even add up to a year."

"I think I'd rather have my momma than yours."

"You don't think, you *know* you'd rather have your momma." He chuckled. "I love my mother. God knows I do, but she is a hard nut to crack."

"Nonnie's a hard nut and my momma did nutty stuff sometimes. Maybe that's what they had in common after all."

"Macy Jane couldn't help her nutty side."

"I know." She brushed her cheek against his palm like she had the first time they'd made love. "She knew some of the kids at school made fun of me because of her. So one time, she stayed up for days and made pecan sandies for the entire school in hopes of winning them over."

"That's really nice. Did it work?"

"Not so much." She chuckled. "She didn't have baking powder so she used baking soda."

"I take it the two are not interchangeable."

"Not even close. Her cookies tasted like sodium bicarbonate. All five hundred. Not even the neighbor's dog would eat them."

She laughed now, but he imagined it hadn't been funny at the time. He could practically see the humiliation in her eyes. He probably *had* seen it. Vivien mortified to her core but pretending she didn't care. Pretending nothing hurt her. Hitting first before she got hit. He wrapped his arms around her and kissed the part in her hair. He hadn't understood her back then. He understood now, and he felt a *clunk clunk* like the chain drive snapping on his drum sander and wreaking havoc inside. If he wasn't careful, Vivien would wreak havoc in him.

That night as she lay curled up against him in her favorite spoon position, he thought of the day he would take her to the airport one final time. The day she would leave and not return. The thought made him turn cold and hollow inside.

They'd both agreed that the two of them didn't belong together long-term. They didn't fit outside of the bedroom. Except when they were at the carriage house packing her mother's things. At his house having dinner or driving the Mercedes with the top down. He always looked forward to picking her up at the airport, and he was going to miss her like hell.

Over the next three weeks, she made even more headway in the carriage house. He filled the bed of his truck with boxes for Goodwill and helped her stack "keep" boxes in one end of the living room. As much as he fought against it, the little clunk near his heart grew bigger and each time he took her to the airport he felt it snap a bit harder. Every time she left, it was a little bit harder to see her go, but even when she was gone, he could still see her. All he had to do was turn on the television and watch her segment on the Today Show, promoting her role in *Psychic Detectives*. Or he'd see her on the cover of some fashion magazine in the check-out line at Publix. She should look ridiculous wearing a pink feathery gown and a hat with a bird on it, but she didn't. He bought the magazine to read the article, only to discover it talked about her clothes and not her. It did have a nice photo spread of her, though. He especially liked the black-and-white taken of her in a corset and motorcycle boots. He liked all her pictures, but nothing was like the real thing. He got a kick out of watching her on television, but having her close enough to touch was much better. "I got the role!" she said the next time she jumped into his truck. A huge smile lit her face. "I got Dorothy Parker."

That night he took her to his favorite white-tablecloth restaurant to celebrate. He wore a blue suit and she dressed in the skirt and blouse she'd worn the day they'd had sex in the row house. They sat in a booth near the back of the restaurant, drinking champagne and eating steak and whipped potatoes. The meal was delicious and decadent, but not as delicious and decadent as his memory of her the last time he'd slipped that skirt from her hips.

"What are you thinking about?" she asked, a slight curve to her red lips.

"You. Me. Those red shoes and your momma's row house."

"I thought I recognized that look in your eyes."

"I didn't know I had a look."

"You have a look, Henry. It's kind of sleepy and ravenous at the same time."

Sleepy and ravenous? "Sounds scary."

"You don't scare me anymore, Henry."

"Were you ever really afraid of me, darlin'?"

"Terrified."

"You didn't seem terrified earlier when I washed your back in the shower."

She chuckled. "I'm a trained actress and my back needed scrubbing." Her laughter died and she tossed her napkin on the table. "I start filming in a few weeks. I won't be in Charleston as much."

"When you finish filming, we should find a secluded island. We'll lay on the beach and drink rum from coconuts all day." He took her hand. "Until then, I'll look forward to spending time with you when you return."

"I always look forward to spending time with you, Henry." She dipped her head and a smile beamed at him from across the table. "When I'm gone, I think about you. A lot. You're important to me. I trust you and—"

"Oh my God! Zahara West!" an excited girl squealed as she approached their table. "It *is* you!" Several more teenage girls and one boy with seriously complicated hair joined their friend. They spoke fast, as if they had to get it all out before their heads were chopped off, and Henry sat there wondering what Vivien had been about to say before they'd been interrupted by sci-fi fans who talked as if the *Raffle* films were real.

"I loooved the last Raffle movie," the boy said. "You were—"

"—*Zahara's Revenge* was—"

She'd said she thought about him and that he was important to her.

"—When you hotwired the calabrone intergalactic cruiser—"

He wished she wouldn't have said she trusted him.

"—And escaped the sotarian hoard!"

They all held up one hand and said, "—Defy, rebel, triumph."

Henry glanced from the worked-up teens in front of him to Vivien. She looked apprehensive, amused, and maybe a little terrified all at one time. If he were in Vivien's shoes, he'd be embarrassed as hell and looking for a back exit.

"We're members of Kings Street Cosplay—"

"—I'm Commander Trent—"

"—Vixen Star Chaser—"

"—can you say, 'Open and free for all humans!' just once? Or Maybe—"

"—Can we get a picture with you?"

The corners of her smile dipped a fraction. "I'd love to."

Henry signaled the waiter and reached for his

wallet. "We're in a hurry," he said as he handed over his card.

"Can you take our picture?" One of the Raffle fans shoved a cell phone at Henry before Vivien could even respond.

"Sure."

They crowded around Vivien and said, "Death over sotarian tyranny!" as Henry snapped the photo. As soon as he handed back the cellphone, he signed his credit card receipt and took Vivien's elbow in his hand. "Are you ready to go?"

"Yes." Her gratitude shone in her eyes, and as they walked to his car, she asked, "Are you sure you look forward to seeing me?"

"Always." She was becoming important to him, too. Maybe too important. So much so that the next time he took her to the airport, he felt like she was taking a piece of him and leaving a hollow place in his chest. "I have to tell you something before I go," she said as he once again unloaded the last of her suitcases from his trunk.

That didn't sound good. He stood at the curb of Charleston International, bus fumes clogging the muggy air and horns honking up and down the departure lanes. She wasn't just leaving a tidy hollowed-out hole in his chest. It felt more like she was ripping him apart. He looked down at the top of her straw hat and asked, "Am I going to like it?"

"I hope so." The airport concierge took her

bags and she tilted her face up to look at Henry. Her green eyes turned serious. "You know when I told you that you could see other people?"

"Yes."

"I'm rescinding that. I don't want you to see other women."

"Does this mean I'm more than just your meat?"

"Yes."

He laughed with relief. "So I should cancel the dates I have lined up while you're gone?"

"Don't tease." She frowned and the corner of her mouth trembled. "I'm falling in love with you, Henry." Then she turned on the heels of her red pumps and before she could walk away, he pulled her against his chest and dipped beneath the brim of her hat. His mouth found hers, and he kissed her, long and deep and filled with everything he felt inside. Everything that he couldn't say. Fear and longing and maybe he was falling in love with her too. "Have a safe trip."

She shoved sunglasses on her face and covered the deep furrow wrinkling her brow. Henry knew that look. He'd seen it before on the disappointed faces of women in his past. She'd wanted to hear him to say more. "Okay." Then Vivien Rochet the actress pushed her lips up into a beautiful smile. "Okay." When she turned to leave this time, he didn't stop her.

I'm falling in love with you. In Henry's experience, when women said that it was more than just falling. It meant they'd already landed but were testing his feeling. It meant love. Real love. Was Vivien really in love with him? Was it real love? Was he in love with her or was it just intense lust that drove him both mad and crazy? She'd come back into his life and turned it upside down, inside out, and knocked him for a loop. He didn't know what he felt other than deep affection, consuming passion, and a big dose of guilt. He didn't know what to think, other than it was impossible.

Vivien Rochet lived a gigantic life. He'd downsized his. He loved his new job and the calm he'd found. His life was in Charleston, hers in Hollywood. Even if they fit together in bed, their lives were at odds. They didn't fit together, and if he ever forgot that, he always had his mother to remind him.

"When is Vivien returning?" she asked, all stretched out like a cat on the chaise in the red parlor.

"I'm not sure," he lied. He knew the day and hour she would return. She was currently in Tokyo, making outrageous money for shooting a Honda commercial, and would be back in Charleston in two days. He crossed his foot over one knee and picked at the crease of his khaki pants. It had been three days since he'd dropped Vivien off at the airport. Three days since she'd said she was falling in love with him. Three days for him to figure out exactly what he felt for her. Not that he'd had much to figure out. He'd fallen in love with her, too. Plain and simple, only it wasn't so plain and simple. She'd trusted him when she shouldn't, and that made him feel guilty as hell. Now he just had to figure out what he was going to do about it.

"You are not fooling anyone." Nonnie reached for a cup and saucer on the table next to her. "I know you and Vivien are messing around. Did you really think you could keep it a secret?"

Since the night of her mother's funeral, she'd spent every night with him when she was in town. He'd hardly been trying to keep it a secret. "How's Spence?"

"Your brother is behaving badly." She lifted a cup of tea to her lips. "He got kicked out of his country club for bringing tawdry strumpets to a black tie event."

He hadn't seen his brother since the night he'd talked about running off to Key West and morphing into a cross between Hemingway and Jimmy Buffet. "Spence is a big boy. He'll figure it out."

"He's bringing shame and embarrassment to the family."

"I think we'll survive."

"I don't know if we'll ever live it down. Which is why you need to watch what you do with Vivien and be on your best behavior."

"We're all in this mess because of *your* behavior," he reminded her.

Her gaze narrowed as she set her teacup on the saucer on the table. "Mind your manners, Henry."

Earlier, he'd been at a meeting with the chamber of commerce and thought he'd check up on his mother before he drove home. Kind of kill two birds with one stone. Bad idea. "I came by to see how you're doing." He leaned back against the crimson couch and stretched his arm out across the top. "Not to get a lecture about Vivien. She's not your business."

"She certainly is my business. Since the day she and Macy Jane moved into the carriage house, she's been my business."

"I thought you and Vivien had buried the hatchet."

Nonnie frowned. "There was no hatchet, Henry. She was a child and it wasn't her fault that Macy Jane was unable to take care of either one of them. I don't have anything against Vivien. She's turned out to be a responsible woman. Admirable, given that she used to be such a terror. Her mother was very proud of her, as she should have been."

Henry tapped a finger on the heavily carved wooden armrest, but he didn't say anything. Why bother? He and Spence had learned at an early age that if they disagreed with their mother, trying to talk to her was futile. So impossible, they didn't bother. Short of tackling her and tying a gag around her mouth, she'd give her unsolicited opinion. She was his mother and he'd give her the respect of pretending to listen, then he'd do exactly as he pleased. And it pleased him to be with Vivien. It was going to please him even more when she returned to Charleston.

"Most of Macy Jane's affairs are settled. I'm going to speak to Vivien about selling the carriage house to me. Then there will be no reason for her to return to Charleston at all." She reached for her teacup once again. "Unless she returns to see you." She looked across at him. "If you get my meaning."

"I hear you."

"You have to leave Vivien alone. You've kept her distracted and away from your brother long enough. The sooner she's gone, the better."

Not for him, and he had no intention of leaving Vivien alone. "For who, Mother?"

"All of us. I said to keep her occupied. Not sleep with the girl."

He felt like he was sixteen again and his mother was berating him for dating "strumpets" he'd met at the Piggly Wiggly or Jean's Sunshine Café. Perfectly nice girls who hadn't been strumpets at all but whose last name didn't appear in Charleston history books. And just like when he'd been sixteen, he pushed back. "We don't get much sleep, Mother."

"I don't care to know the details." Her lips pursed and her nostrils pinched. "You're a good

238

son, Henry. You always do what's best for the family."

"Yeah," he said, the heavy burden of family responsibility weighing him down even more than usual. "You know me. No task is too distasteful."

"No need to string Vivien along further," she continued as if she hadn't noticed the bitterness in his voice. "Leave her alone now so she'll return to Hollywood where she belongs."

A flash of blue caught his attention and he glanced at the entry hall. Vivien stared at him, her eyes wide and her cheeks were red as if someone had slapped her. "You're not in Japan," came out of his mouth as his brain tried to absorb her sudden appearance.

Her gaze turned to his mother then back to him. One of her shoes fell from her hands, then she spun on her heels and disappeared, almost as if she'd never been there. Except now he could hear the heels of her bare feet echo into the silence. He wondered what she'd heard, and by the look on her face and quick retreat, he feared too much.

"Well, that's a shame." Nonnie confirmed his fear. "But I suppose it's for the best. Now she can return to her home and not feel as if she has anything keeping her here."

Henry stood and felt as if he'd been kicked in the chest. Vivien wasn't going anywhere. Not if he had anything to say about it. "I know you love nothing better than ordering people around and congratulating yourself when you think you succeed, but I haven't been spending time with Vivien because you commanded it." He moved toward the doorway and said over his shoulder, "I've been spending as much time as possible with her because I want to, and it doesn't have anything to do with you." He bent at the waist and picked up Vivien's stiletto. "She's not going anywhere." Not if he could help it. "I want her here with me."

"Henry." Nonnie swung her legs over the side of the chaise. "Vivien isn't a suitable woman for you. I like her fine, but her place in society is beneath yours."

"You don't get to tell me who's suitable or not." He pointed his finger at her then to his chest, filling with rage. "That's my choice to make that decision, and Vivien is my choice." He dropped his hand to his side. "You stay out of it."

"There is no way around the situation of her birth. You know it can't be sugarcoated."

God, she made it sound like it was 1850 and they were standing in the parlor of Whitley Hall. He looked over his shoulder at his mother. "Not like mine?"

"It's not the same, Henry. You have Whitley blood."

"Mixed with Olivier. Not even your blue blood could elevate a lowly cabinetmaker from Sangaree. Could it?"

— Chapter 16 —

The Diary of Vivien Leigh Rochet
Keep out! Do NOT read under Penalty of Death!!

Dear Diary,
  Momma didn't have any more babies after my daddy died, but I wish I had a brother. For a while I wanted a sister so she could do half my chores and we could share clothes. But I think I want a brother. If I had a brother, he could beat up Bubba for me. He could beat up Henry, and Spence, too. I'd give my brother my Kiss My Patootie list and he could take care of it for me.

Dear Diary,
  Momma's making me go to Texas again. I don't want to go. Kathy doesn't like Momma and me. She says Momma uses her sadness to make people feel sorry for her. That's not true and it's mean. Before we left Texas last summer, I broke Uncle Richie's fly rod

because brothers and sisters should stand up for each other. I told Momma that I don't ever want to go to Texas again. She said we need to be like Jesus and love and forgive each other. I told her I didn't want to be like Jesus. He got nailed to a cross. After that, I had to go to church for a whole summer. Even when Momma got the sadness and didn't go, the Mantis took me. No Fair. ☹ ☹ ☹

Dear Diary,
   Now that I got a bra, I'm going to get my period soon. I got a cramp in my stomach last week and I thought it started, but it was just from running in P.E. At school the teacher said to call it menstruation. My momma calls it her monthly visitor. Lottie says her sister calls it shark week. Ouch!! When I get my period, I don't know what I'll call it. The teacher said menstruating lasts for four to six days. Momma says that in our family the monthly visitor only visits for two days. She says I'll be happy about that.

Dear Diary,
   I've been thinking about boys lately. What if I can't find a boy to marry me?

Momma says I have a long time before I have to worry about that, but I think I should start making a list now of all the things to look for in a husband so I don't end up with someone like my momma's new boyfriend, Nile. I call him Vile because he wears too much cologne.

Things I Want in a Husband

1. Big house and pool
2. Can fix stuff so our door isn't broken for three months
3. Handsome like Jonathan Taylor Thomas
4. Trust him not to give other girls stuffed dogs and lifesavers
5. Doesn't stink

More to come.

— Chapter 17 —

Vivien sat at her momma's kitchen table. Boxes of her china and silver were packed up and waiting for her to rent a storage shed. She should have more done. The whole house should be done and ready for a cleaning crew but she'd spent her time with Henry instead of taking care of her mother's estate.

Her blue suede stiletto fell from her lap. She'd arrived two days early from Japan because she'd wanted to surprise Henry. A tear slipped down her cheek and she wiped it away with the back of her hand.

The last time she'd seen him, she'd told him she was falling for him. He hadn't said he was falling for her, too, but she'd been so sure he felt something. She'd been so sure of him that she'd flown in early and taken a cab to the carriage house. She'd been so sure he felt the same that she'd planned to surprise him. She'd wanted to change into the blue bra and panties she'd bought to matched her five-inch pumps. She knew how much Henry liked her pumps and she had it all planned out in her head. She'd call and tell him she was in town, and when he knocked on her door, she'd answer in her underwear and heels.

"Surprise." Only she'd been the one who'd been surprised. First by Henry's truck in the driveway and then by what she'd heard in the parlor.

A dull pinch pulled at her forehead and squeezed her brain. She was jet-lagged. She was tired. She probably hadn't heard Nonnie right. She probably hadn't heard Henry say that she was a distasteful task or Nonnie thanking him for stringing her along. She didn't want to believe it. Henry wasn't the kind of guy to play games. He wasn't that mean. He would never hurt her.

Or would he? Did she even know Henry? Vivien wished she could go back in time. Go back to half an hour ago and have the taxi take her to the house on Rainbow Row instead. Go back to when she was happy and excited to be in Charleston and impatient to see Henry. Go back to when her chest had been light and fuzzy with anticipation, before a bomb exploded near her heart.

"Vivien," Henry called out from the living room seconds before he appeared in the doorway of the kitchen with her toe-pinching killer pump that she'd taken off before she'd walked into the big house. He looked at her and opened his mouth as if to speak. He shut it again because there was nothing to say.

"Tell me it isn't true."

"It's not what it seems."

She wished he'd denied it. Vivien closed her eyes and covered her face with her hands. It was true. She'd heard both of them correctly, and she was an idiot to ever have thought either of them cared a bit about her. She felt him grasp her wrists and he pulled her hands away from her face.

"Vivien, you don't understand what all of that was about." He knelt on one knee in front of her.

"What part do you think I don't understand?" His handsome face was on the same level as hers, and his dark gaze bored into her head as if they were kids again and he wanted to read her brain. "The part where Nonnie was proud of you for keeping me away from Spence?"

"Vivien."

"Or the part where I'm a distasteful task?"

"It's not what you think."

"Then tell me I didn't hear Nonnie say you were stringing me along." Now it was her turn to search his gaze for anything that would make the pain go away.

"You have to understand—"

"Make me understand," she interrupted, her voice pleading with him to make it better. To make it go away so they could go back to the warm, cozy place where she'd felt safe and secure. Where his solid arms made her feel as if she stood on stable ground for the first time in her life. "Make me understand why you did this to me?"

He closed his eyes then opened them again. "It has nothing to do with you." He brushed his hair back with both hands and looked like he wanted to crush his skull. "It's about Spence."

"What does Spence have to do with me?"

"He's been reckless since his divorce."

"What? That doesn't make sense." But nothing that day made sense. "I don't get it. I haven't even seen Spence since Momma's funeral." She took a deep breath past the jagged shards of her heart. "What did I ever do to you to make you hurt me like this?"

"I didn't mean to hurt you, Vivien. You're the last person I'd hurt, but Spence would have kept coming on to you just to amuse himself."

She stood and walked across the room, putting distance between herself and Henry. Tears fell from her eyes and she didn't even try to stop them. "So you amused yourself instead."

"I wasn't amused. I found the whole idea offensive to both of us."

"Not so offensive that you didn't do it. Do you and Nonnie think I can't control myself around all men, or just the Whitley-Shuler boys?"

"Not at all." He rose and moved toward her.

"You wasted your time, Henry. I'm not the least bit attracted to your brother. He could have come on to me all he wanted but it wouldn't have mattered." She shook her head and laughed without humor. "Did Nonnie tell you to have sex with me? Was that part of her plan?"

"There wasn't a real plan, Vivien. I needed to

247

keep Spence away from you. That was it. I wanted to have sex with you because *I* wanted you. You wanted me too."

"I made your plan so easy for you. You didn't even have to *try* to get me in bed." The backs of her eye stung. "I just hopped in all on my own."

"Nothing about you is easy." He reached for her but she moved away from his grasp.

"I trusted you and you lied to me." He'd broken her trust *and* her heart.

"I didn't lie to you."

"Yes you did. Every time you made me think you wanted to be with me, and every time you made me think you cared about me, was a lie." She wiped a tear from her cheek. "Everything was a lie. God, even as I say it, it's hard to believe."

"I do care about you, Vivien."

"And I fell for it." Again he reached for her, and again she backed away. "All because you didn't want me to end up with Spence."

He simply looked at her. His silence more telling than words.

She shook her head. "There's something I don't get. Why were you asked to sacrifice yourself for your brother?"

"It was no sacrifice."

"It's so insulting, really." Again she swiped at a tear. She wished her eyes would stop leaking. She was an actress. She should have more control, but when it came to Henry, she'd never been able to control herself. "Why is Spence so special that you had to save him from me?" She put a palm to her chest.

"Spence isn't special. There are things about Spence that you don't know."

"Is he crazy?" Spence had seemed perfectly normal to her. "Is he a demented pervert or a serial killer?" She dropped her hand to her side.

"Of course not. He's reckless sometimes, but he's a good guy."

"That doesn't tell me why you threw yourself under the bus to save him." She wiped her hand across her nose. "I deserve the truth."

He took a deep breath and stared into her eyes. "You do, but I'm not sure I should be the one telling it. Macy Jane should have told you."

"What does my momma have to do with any of this? What does my momma have to do with Spence?"

He let out the breath he'd been holding and walked to the counter. He plucked a tissue from the box and handed it to her.

She grabbed it and almost said thank you. "What is so special about your brother that y'all had to protect him from me?"

He looked at her for several long moments then said, "You and Spence have the same father."

"What?" She thought he'd just said that her daddy was Spence's daddy too.

"You and Spence have the same biological father."

"Jeremiah Rochet?" He'd made her chest ache and now he was spinning her head around.

"No, Vivien. Fredrickk Shuler."

"My father is Jeremiah Rochet." She wiped beneath her eyes and placed a hand on her chest. "I told you that he was killed before I was born. On a three-masted schooner that went down in the Florida Straits."

"Saving Cubans. I remember."

"I have the old newspaper article." God, even as she said it, it sounded like a lie. "All the Rochets were killed that day."

"Your biological father is Fredrickk Shuler."

She moved to a chair and sat before her knees gave out. "No. Momma would have told me."

"Think about it, Vivien." He sat in a chair near her and reached for her hand. "Don't you think it's a little too convenient that all the Rochets were lost at sea so you never got to meet any of them?"

"It could happen." She'd seen the newspaper with her own eyes.

"You and Macy Jane lived in the carriage house."

"Because we were employees and your mother gave it to us."

"My mother didn't have anything to do with it. In fact, the day you two moved in she was livid." He paused and squeezed her hand. "Macy Jane was Fredrickk's mistress, and he gave her the carriage house. He probably would have given her more, but he died without providing for either of you financially."

"That's ridiculous." She pulled her hand from his and folded her arms. If all that was true, her momma had lied to her her entire life. If it was true, the woman who'd always worried that even the whitest of lies would make the poor baby Jesus cry, had lied about something as important as Vivien's father. It was crazy and she couldn't wrap her brain around it. "You want me to believe Fredrickk Shuler is my father and Spence is my brother."

"Yes. I know this all sounds crazy right now, but Jeremiah Rochet was just some guy who conveniently died around the time you were born."

She thought of Spence's face as he teased her about razzies and as he slid his hand up her knee. She gasped and felt her heart spasm. "Spence came on to me!"

"That's because he doesn't know." Henry shook his head. "He was never told, either."

Spence didn't know. She didn't know. Who did know besides her momma, Nonnie, and . . . *Henry?* "Sick!" She jumped to her feet as the blood rushed from her head. "Y'all are sick." She backed away from him. "If Spence is my brother, then you . . ." Her finger shook as she pointed to him. "Then you're my brother too, and we . . ." Her brain refused to grasp the fact that Henry was her brother and she'd had sex with him. She felt sick to her stomach and couldn't catch her breath. "It's no secret that some of you Whitleys married your first cousins. But brother and sister . . . each other . . ." She covered her burning cheeks with her hands. "Oh my God, you people are sick."

"Vivien." He stood and scowled at her. "I'm not your brother."

"If . . . if . . . Spence, then—"

"My biological father isn't Fredrickk Shuler."

Her hands fell to her side. "What?" What the hell was going on? Her father wasn't her father. Henry's father wasn't his father. Her mother was a liar. Spence was her brother. It was all too much and her brain went blessedly numb.

"My father is, was," he corrected himself, "a man who worked at Whitley Hall. Fredrickk married my mother when she was three months pregnant with me."

If that was true, she hadn't committed incest, praise baby Jesus. But if the rest was true, crazy Spence was her brother and Fredrickk Shuler was her daddy, Nonnie was a self-righteous hypocrite, and her momma was a big fat liar. Henry had pretended to care about her in order to keep it all a secret. She'd trusted him. She'd fallen in love with him and it was all a lie.

He put his hands on her arms and dipped his head to look into her eyes. "I'm sorry you had to find out this way."

Her brain might be numb from shock and information overload, but not so much that she forgot that while Henry had been playing her for a fool, she'd been falling in love.

"Now you understand why I had to keep you away from Spence."

"Oh, I understand. I understand that you used and manipulated me so that you and Nonnie could keep your secrets. I understand that I came rushing back today so I could be with you. You made me trust you and fall in love with you and it was all a lie." She swallowed hare. "I feel so stupid."

"You're not stupid, and what I feel for you isn't a lie." He looked into her eyes. "Vivien, I've fallen in love with you, too."

"Stop it, Henry." She balled her hands into fists and folded her arms to keep from slapping him. She didn't believe him for a second. "Stop lying."

"I'm not lying."

"Why are you trying to hurt me more than you have already? What did I ever do to you?" She racked her fuzzy brain for an answer. "Was it because I snooped through your stuff as a kid and I broke the lawn jockey?"

"I'm not trying to hurt you. I'm trying to tell you that I love you and you're not listening to me."

"I don't think I ever did anything bad enough to

deserve this." Her ears began to ring like they usually did just before she threw up. "Please go."

"Did you hear what I said?"

"This house might be on your momma's property, but it's mine now." She paused and stuck her chin in the air as if her life hadn't painfully shifted beneath her feet. As if her ears weren't ringing and her stomach didn't ache. "Apparently, my daddy wanted me to have it and I want youto leave." Even though she said the words, they didn't still feel real to her.

His eyes turned dark even as his cheeks paled. "I love you and you said you love me, Vivien."

God, he was a better actor than most of the men she knew in Hollywood, but not better than her. "I lied." With her heart and her life broken, she asked, "How does it feel, Henry?"

It felt like shit and got a whole lot shittier. Now that the family skeletons were out of the closet and littered all over the ground, there was one person left who needed to know the truth. Who needed to hear it from the horse's mouth. The horse being Nonnie.

"It's your secret." Henry looked at his mother across the room lounging on their great-grandmother's peach fainting couch. She wasn't fooling anyone. The woman had never fainted in her life. "You tell him."

Spence looked from one to the other. "What secret?"

It had taken Henry most of the day and half the night, but he'd finally found his brother at the Griffon Pub near Waterfront Park, drinking River Dog beer and eating nachos. Now that Vivien knew the truth, it was past time for Spencer to know, too.

After a search of the ground floor, they'd found their mother in the sitting room off the master suite, wearing her evening caftan and steadily drinking wine. They sat on one of her couches, a family heirloom from a gaudy era and as uncomfortable as hell. Instead of answering, Nonnie raised a glass filled with French Bordeaux to her lips.

"Don't tell me you're dying." Spence turned back to Henry and had real concern in his blue eyes. "She can't be dying! She's too tough to die."

Henry frowned. "She's not dying."

"If you want him to know so badly," Nonnie finally said, "you tell him." He'd never known his mother to cower from anything. Until tonight. Her eyes were pinched and she'd been drinking more than normal, yet the wine failed to give her liquid courage.

"I never wanted to keep your secrets in the first place."

"Tell me what?" Spence demanded.

"Secrets always get out." Henry kept his gaze

on his mother but pointed to his brother next to him on the couch. "And look what happens."

Nonnie lowered her glass. "None of this would be happening if not for Vivien."

"Vivien? What does Vivien have to do with your secrets?"

Neither bothered to answer Spence. "This isn't Vivien's fault." When he and Spence had pulled into the driveway, he couldn't help but notice that the carriage house was dark inside and the porch light off. "She's a victim as much as Spence. More, in fact."

"What the hell is going on?" Spence demanded.

Resigned, Henry turned and looked at his brother. "Have you ever wondered why Macy Jane and Vivien lived in the carriage house in our backyard?"

"No." He shook his head. "Someone had to live there."

Which confirmed what Henry had always suspected of his brother. Spence's thoughts ran as deep as a puddle.

"They lived there because . . ." He paused a moment and tried to think of a way to say, "Vivien is your sister."

Spence looked at him for several seconds. "You dragged me away from the bar just to pull my leg?"

"I'm not pulling your leg. The reason Macy Jane and Vivien lived in the carriage house is because Vivien is Fredrickk Shuler's daughter."

"The hell you say?" He looked at his mother. "Did you know this?"

"Yes."

"How long?"

"Since nineteen-eighty-five."

"God damn." Spence collapsed against the back of the couch. "When did you find out we have a sister?"

"She's not my sister. She's yours."

"If she's my sister, she's your—"

"Fredrickk Shuler wasn't my biological father."

Spence got that look in his eyes, the one Vivien had earlier, confusion bordering on mental collapse. It was understandable. "Who is your father?"

"A cabinetmaker mother hooked up with—"

"—Henry—"

"—He wasn't good enough to marry a St. Cecilia debutante, so she paid Fredrickk to marry her."

"I didn't pay Fred." His mother had the nerve to sound indignant. "Talking about money is vulgar."

"How long have you known?" Spence sound deflated. "About my father and your father and . . . everything."

"I figured it out when I was ten, when we charted our family blood types in school."

"And you never told me?"

Henry turned his gaze across the room to his mother sipping her wine. "No."

"When did you find out about Vivien?"

"The same time I found out about Fredrickk."

"What?" Spence jumped to his feet, suddenly agitated as if Henry had committed the bigger sin. "You knew about that, too, and didn't tell me?"

"No."

"No, what?"

"No, I didn't tell you."

"Does Vivien know?"

"She does now." And she wasn't home and not answering his texts.

"Jesus Christ! I almost had sex with my sister."

Now he was exaggerating. "You didn't almost have sex with Vivien."

"I tried!"

"Trying and getting it done are two different things."

"Wait." Spencer held up a hand like a traffic cop. "That's why you took her away the day of Macy Jane's funeral. I thought you cock blocked me because you were interested in her, but that wasn't it."

He'd been interested. "Mother was concerned that you'd slide your hand all the way up Vivien's thigh to the underwear."

Spence's jaw dropped a bit. "And you didn't think that maybe it would have been better to say, 'Hey Spence, don't slide your hand up your sister's thigh?' You thought lying and scheming was better than telling me the truth?"

"Not the time or place."

"What about before?"

"Before what?"

"I don't know, Henry. Maybe at some point before tonight you could have found the time to tell me the dirty family secret."

"It was not my secret to tell." Just his to keep. "That was for Mother and Macy Jane to decide."

"That's bullshit." Spence looked from Henry to Nonnie, then back again. Then he said something that blew Henry's puddle theory out of the water. Sort of. "I'm not surprised that she kept secrets from me. She is who she is. Leopards don't change their spots. They think they don't have to because they think they're better than all the other cats on the Serengeti." He pointed at Henry. "But you. You're my brother and we've always looked out for each other. I've always looked up to you, Henry. You always knew the answers and the right thing to do. You were always the good son. The strong one. The Eagle Scout. The guy who graduated summa cum laude from Princeton but never acted like he was better than anyone else." He shook his head. "I'm looking at you now, and you're not the person I thought I knew." He swallowed hard. "Who are you?"

Vivien had said the same thing. "I'm the guy who had to take on a load of shit at an early age

259

and carry it all my life." Henry rose to his feet. "I'm the guy who laughed with you and helped you with your homework and watched out for you so you weren't bullied at school. I'm the brother who hunted and fished with you and made sure you didn't drown in the ocean." He put a hand on his chest. "I'm the one who had to be responsible so you could be reckless. The guy who's had to take care of everyone and everything. Not you, Spence. Me."

Spence shook his head. "It doesn't matter how you justify it to yourself, you were dead wrong to keep the truth from me. I can understand why you couldn't tell me when we were kids. I understand why you had to do what she told you to do, but now . . ." He looked at Nonnie then back at Henry. "All these years, Henry. All these years you could have told me, but you didn't because you're so used to keeping secrets. You're so used to toeing the family line no matter who gets hurt. You just follow Mother's orders without question."

"Not without question, Spence." His jaw tightened at the truth of his brother's words. "I've questioned the right and wrong of a lot things in my life. Things you don't even know about because when it gets right down to it, you don't want to know."

Spence shook his head. "If you believe that, you're more messed up than I am."

— Chapter 18 —

Henry's life was a mess and getting messier by the day. He couldn't find Vivien and she wasn't returning his texts or phone calls. She hadn't been back to the carriage house since the day he'd told her that he loved her and she'd thrown it back in his face. He didn't have her e-mail address or any of her assistant's information. She'd mentioned once that she lived in the Hollywood Hills; her neighborhood secured by guarded gates. He was fairly certain he could get past the gates, notthat it mattered. Vivien was in New York filming her Dorothy Parker movie. Security would be extremely tight, and he was fairly certain he couldn't get past the muscle heads surrounding her.

Sawdust swirled around him as he fed a four-foot cedar plank through his ripsaw. The chain-driven blade chewed a line dead center. A pair of orange earplugs muffled shrill sounds around him, and the simple paper facemask kept the dust from his lungs. Several feet away, Hoyt fed a length of reclaimed oak across the joiner.

Lately, Henry had bid on quite a few jobs that involved wood reclaimed from dilapidated barns and uninhabitable buildings. A few months ago, he'd bought an old grange hall in Richland County. He'd taken up the pine dance floor and ripped out the old cabinets. Once the wood was refurbished, he'd put it in a restoration project in Smalls Alley.

Henry shut off the power to the ripsaw and reached for the cedar, now cut into equal widths. Vivien would have to come back to Charleston sometime. Macy Jane's belongings were scattered about the house or in boxes. It had been less than a week since she'd stood in her momma's kitchen and accused him of lying. Less than a week since he'd told her about Spence and she blamed him. Less than a week since he'd told her he loved her and she'd thrown it back in his face. Less than a week that felt a hell of a lot longer.

Vivien would be flying back and forth between California and New York while filming. He was sure she'd make a detour to Charleston. When she did he'd be waiting for her. He'd make her listen and make it up to her, but a week later, she had yet to materialize and he started to worry that she might not return at all. The thought of never seeing her, of losing her for good, weighed heavy in his heart and mind and gave him a knot between his shoulders.

After week three rolled around, Vivien had yet to turn up and Spence had gone missing as well. Henry had driven to his brother's condo on Bay Street several times and his mail hadn't been picked up for a month. Like Vivien, Spencer didn't answer texts or phone calls. He wasn't answering his e-mails, but if Henry had to make a wager on where his brother was hiding out, he'd put his money on Key West. He'd bet Spence was in some beach bungalow, still fuming while he wrote the next great American novel, downed pitchers of mojitos, and stepped on pop tops.

The only member of his family still talking to him was his mother, and he wasn't talking to her. He wasn't purposely punishing her, he just didn't have anything to say to the woman who had kept secrets that had torpedoed all their lives, then had sat back and refused to accept any blame.

He should have told his mother a long time ago to deal with her own baggage and leave him out of it. He should have freed himself from the pressure of making sure their names stayed free of the scandal Nonnie had covered up and feared most. He should have, but he hadn't. He'd been handed the responsibility of keeping the family secrets, and at the moment, he wondered why he'd ever thought it mattered. The family scandals and secrets hadn't been worth the pain and betrayal both Vivien and Spence felt.

He'd left his old job for the peace and calm of John's Island. He'd left the pressure and stress of his old life behind. In reality he'd just traded one source of strain for another. Compared to the pain he felt in his chest from loving Vivien, he'd take a heart attack any day. He could deal with that. He knew what to do to make that pain stop before it started. He knew the warning signs, but this, there'd been no warning and the constant ache never stopped.

For the first time in his life, Henry couldn't fix everything.

There was only one way to fix a broken heart. Martinis. Lots of martinis. Too bad Vivien couldn't stay oblivious for the rest of her life. At some point she had to sober up, and when she did, she still felt stupid for loving Henry *and* she was sick as a dog to boot.

She'd been a fool. She'd fallen for a lie, a façade, and she hardly knew what had been real or what to believe anymore. How could something that felt so real, not even exist? How could she still feel such a strong attachment to a man who felt nothing for her? How had that happened?

He'd told her he loved her. She didn't believe him at all. A lot of men in Vivien's past had claimed to love her. At some point, she always discovered they'd either lied or were in love with Vivien the actress. Not Vivien the woman. They were in love with what they saw on a thirty-foot screen at the local multiplex. Like her mother, she'd never been lucky in love, but unlike her mother, she'd never had any delusions about anyone with the last name Whitley-Shuler—at least not until a few months ago. Until a few months ago, she'd never believed they would ever welcome her into their lives. Not really, and now she felt so stupid for believing their lies.

After Macy Jane's death, Nonnie had been kind and helpful and she'd fallen for it. She'd fallen for Henry, too, and that was the worst pain of all. She'd known she'd fallen in love with him, but she hadn't known the depth of her feelings until he broke her heart. Until he took it all away, as if everything they'd said and done and been had meant nothing to him. As if she'd meant nothing to him.

In her head, she couldn't help reliving every moment between them, every conversation and text message. It had all felt so real and wonderful and fresh. She'd felt protected around him, and he'd made her happy. She'd never felt so good with a man, and now she'd never felt so bad.

Henry had reached out in several texts, and she'd been so tempted to contact him. Her heart urged her to talk to him. To listen to him and believe his lies, but her head knew better. Just one message. Just one call. Just to hear the sound of his voice one more time, but that would only make her feel worse in the end. Her heart and her head warred. Push pull. Push pull, until her head won and she completely deleted Henry from her life. Before she could change her mind, she deleted him from every electronic device she owned, and she changed her phone number. She wiped him out totally and completely so that in a moment of weakness, when her emotions swamped her better judgement, there was no way she could call or text. It was too bad she couldn't delete him so easily from her heart.

For the next week, she went through the motions of living. She read her script and went over lines with the scriptwriter. She got fitted for wardrobe, beginning with the first scene when she would become Dorothy Parker in a sable coat, cloche hat, and holding an ivory cigarette holder between her fingers.

During the day she was able to lose herself in her role, but at night . . . the nights sucked. Her mind was free from work and she'd forget. She'd smile and think, "I can't wait to tell Henry," or she'd chuckle at the memory of something he'd said or done. The worst were the moments when her heart would pound at the thought of walking into a room and seeing his smile. The smile she'd thought that he saved just for her. Then she'd remember that the smile had been as phony as the rest of him and unmanageable tears would slip from her eyes. Not in torrents, but like her pain, a relentless drip, drip, drip.

She tried to tell herself that she didn't want to be with a man who didn't want to be with her. She was better than that. She deserved better than to get played for a fool by Henry and his mother.

She'd been played before. For money or fame but never for the blood that flowed through her veins.

She hated Nonnie but, in hindsight, she really wasn't all that surprised. But Henry—Henry had taken their plan one step further. He'd made her fall in love with him, and she hated him for that. She hated him for making her miss the touch of his hands and the sparkly tingles he spread across her skin. She hated him for the warmth of his chest pressed against her as she slept. She hated that each morning she woke and her heart was still broken.

Most of all, she hated that she missed him.

She spent the next two months filming in New York and kept herself busy. She had to be on the set at six in the morning and it took two hours of make-up, hair, and wardrobe to be transformed into a theater critic for *Vanity Fair* in 1918. During the day, she didn't have time to be consumed by the elaborate lies of her own mother. She escaped into the role, immersing herself in a wit as sharp as a surgeon's knife. At night though, it didn't matter how tired she was when she got to her hotel room, the minute her head hit the pillow, her mind would race with questions that could never be answered by her mother. Why the lie? The truth was so much simpler. Did Mamaw Roz know? Did Uncle Richie? Who'd known that her mother had been Fredrickk Shuler's lover and not the widow of poor Jeremiah Rochet?

Henry for one, and he'd let her go on and on about the saintly Rochets, lost at sea while saving Cubans. He'd sat there while she'd gone on about how much she would have loved to know her father, and he'd said nothing.

Nonnie for another. Her mother had obviously legally changed her maiden name. Had it been as simple and serendipitous as an article in the *Post and Currier*? When had she concocted the story? Before or after Fredrickk's death?

And most of all, how could her mother have kept the secret for thirty years? Sometimes, she hadn't been able to keep days of the week straight, let alone the details of an elaborate lie.

Although when Vivien thought about it, she was fairly sure that Nonnie had fabricated the story and she'd gotten her mother to agree to it. Somehow, she'd managed to get the woman who hated even the whitest of lies, to go along with her scheme. Vivien didn't know how Nonnie had accomplished it or what sort of leverage she'd used. Someday she'd confront her nemesis and get her answers, but that someday wasn't today. It wasn't tomorrow or next week, either.

It wasn't two months later when she wrapped up filming in New York. Her wounded heart had yet to heal, and she might have made a side trip to Charleston to confront the Mantis, if not for the chance of seeing Henry again. In a way, it was worse than the death of her mother. She missed her mother, but she knew there would never be a chance meeting between them. She couldn't reach out to her. Couldn't stalk her on Google or Linkedin or search for her public records. Death was final, but this lingering love cut her to the pit of her soul.

It still lingered the two weeks she filmed in Paris and it continued to linger at parties where she smiled and chatted but felt empty inside. It especially lingered at night when she went to bed alone and remembered Henry's touch on her shoulder and down her arm, and when she remembered that he couldn't seem to keep his magic hands off her. She remembered falling asleep with her back against his chest and her behind cradled against his pelvis, feeling so safe and protected for the first time in her life.

In an effort to understand her confused feelings, she read books about breakups and articles on betrayal on the Internet. She took the advice she read to heart and practiced the art of loving herself more than loving a man who didn't exist. By the time she returned home in mid-August, her heart didn't ache quite so much and she didn't think about Henry all day long. Her tears had dried, and each day she could feel herself loving Henry a little less. Any day now, she expected to feel absolutely nothing.

The second half of the movie was to be shot at Paramount Studio, and Vivien planned to use the much-needed break in filming to sleep. She was exhausted and jet-lagged and she'd caught a flu bug that made her feel a little queasy at night.

"I got you some oranges and Airborne," Sarah said as she walked into Vivien's room and plopped the sack on the bed by her right hip.

"Oranges are for colds and you have to take Airborne *before* you get sick." She rolled onto her back and looked up into her assistant's frowning face. "But thank you."

"I made an appointment with your doctor. Get dressed."

"Now?" She was too tired to go anywhere. "I'm not that sick." She secretly wondered if she was more depressed than sick. That made her think of her mother and worry about her own mental health. Worrying gave her anxiety, which in turn made her stomach tumble.

"Chop chop. Pull yourself together."

Chop chop? Sarah had turned into a drill sergeant, and pulling herself together meant Vivien pulled on a pair of baggy sweatpants and a hoodie.

"You're going to die in the heat," Sarah warned as she pulled out the driveway in Vivien's Beemer.

Sarah was right but Vivien wasn't about to admit it. She hadn't told her assistant about Henry, not after Vivien had lectured her on man skanks and heartbreak. She was never going to admit to Sarah that she hadn't taken her own advice. She didn't know if Henry was a man skank, but he was a heartbreaking A-hole and she told herself she was well rid of him. *You're wonderful,* all her breakup books told her. *You deserve someone just as wonderful.*

When Vivien and Sarah arrived at the medical complex, they entered through a side door. A freight elevator took them up two floors where Vivien had her blood drawn and she peed in a cup.

"Have you ever noticed that doctor's offices smell like medicine and have hideous wall-paper?" Sarah asked.

"No." She glanced about the room and took in the vine wallpaper bordered with purple and green grapes. "It looks like Macaroni Grill in here."

"So two thousand and two." Sarah handed Vivien *US* magazine. "Someone got a shot of you on the set in New York."

Vivien didn't care and lay back on the paper-covered bed. She was either depressed or had some kind of cancer. The kind that made her sleep a lot. Sleeping cancer.

Her doctor came in and sat on one of the ubiquitous round stools that rolled around on wheels. He opened her chart and looked up. "You don't have the flu."

"That's good," she said as she rose to her elbows.

He stood and grabbed one of those special

doctor flashlights from the wall. He shoved a small black cone on the end and grabbed a tongue depressor. "When was your last period?"

"Period?" She thought back and sat up all the way. "July maybe."

"Say ahhh."

"Ahhh."

He removed the tongue depressor and tossed it in a flip-top trash can. "Could it have been the end of May?"

She held still as he looked up her nose. "No. I'm pretty sure it was in July because I was in Paris."

He checked each ear then tossed the little cone in the trash can. "You're pregnant."

The lid shut and Vivien thought she heard him say she was pregnant. "What?"

"Eleven weeks."

Sarah gasped. "Holy shit!"

"That's not possible. I . . ." She couldn't be pregnant. Eleven weeks? That was almost three months. She'd know if she was pregnant. Wouldn't she? She thought of her periods, and yeah she'd missed two and the one in July had been very light. She hadn't given it much thought because her cycle was always wacky, especially when she was under a lot of stress. She'd only had sex with one person and he'd worn a condom . . . except that one time when it broke, but what were the chances? It couldn't be true.

The doctor must have given her a bad test. One of those false positive scenarios. "I don't believe it." Yeah, because the thought that she might be pregnant with Henry's baby was impossible to wrap her brain around.

"You're pregnant." He showed her the test results, but her brain still refused to believe what her eyes saw was true.

"No. It's impossible," she scoffed, but just to make sure, she made Sarah run into Walgreens and grab a pregnancy test on the way home. Sarah, being the always prepared assistant, bought three. All different brands just to be certain.

"Doctors make mistakes," she said as they watched the three white and blue sticks. "I heard about a man who went in for prostate surgery and got his leg amputated instead."

"I think that's an urban myth, like Bloody Mary."

"Or the Slender Man."

Sarah laughed. "That one is so lame."

Vivien lifted her gaze from the sticks and chuckled. "When I was a kid, I believed that if you ate Pop Rocks and drank cola at the same time, you'd explode."

"Oh that one is true. I knew a guy whose cat exploded." Vivien might have pressed for more information on the possibility of a cat explosion, but Sarah's big gasp stopped her. "I see a pink line on this one. Oh my God, boss woman, here comes another pink line."

"Let me see that." The second line was so faint it didn't count.

"This one has a blue plus."

Vivien looked at the second test to make sure. She grabbed it from Sarah's hand as her face went numb. "It could be faulty," she said, but the third test was digital and the screen lit up with the words: pregnant, 5+ weeks.

"You're preggo," Sarah announced as she waved the white and blue stick around as if it needed to dry.

"This can't be happening to me." Vivien sat down in a kitchen chair. "I don't believe it."

"I'll make an appointment with your vagina doc. You're in denial."

Vivien liked denial. It made her life easier, and she decided to pitch a tent and stay firmly camped out in denial. She quite happily lived in the land of denial until the day her OB-GYN squirted clear goo on her stomach and the outline of a baby popped up on the ultrasound screen. She saw arms and legs and a beating heart.

"It's a boy," Sarah gasped. "And my God, look at that thing."

"You're looking at the umbilical cord," the doctor told her. "We won't be able to determine the sex for a few months."

"Oh."

Pregnant. She was pregnant with Henry's baby. What the heck was she going to do? She had no idea, but when she was all alone later, she remembered her conversation with Henry about the choice he and Tracy Lynn had made a long time ago. He'd said he felt more guilt than anything else. Then as now, there were only two choices and she had to make one.

She sat down with a legal pad and made a pros and cons list:

Henry's Lies and Betrayal

1. Heart still aches a little at the thought of seeing Henry again—con.
2. A lifetime reminder that the Whitley-Shulers have made a pathetic fool of me—con.
3. No family to help—con.
4. Nonnie would be in my life forever—con-con-con.
5. Career—con. Actresses with children are hired less often than actresses without.
6. Get fat—con.
7. Possibility of stretch marks—con.
8. The pain of pushing a baby out my vagina-ouch!—con.
9. Henry Whitley-Shuler is an a-hole—con.
10. Henry Whitley-Shuler is a gigantic a-hole—con.

When she was through, Vivien had a whole list on the con side and nothing on the pro. Not one thing. She thought of the tiny white outline on the ultrasound. She thought of how impossible it was to have a baby at this time in her life.

She reached for the phone.

Henry reached for the key on top of the door frame and unlocked the door of Vivien's pink row house. Everything had been restored to the satisfaction of Charleston's Historical Society. The house was ready to be put on the market. He walked through one last time and was flooded with memories. The garden reminded him of the afternoon he'd found her digging in the mud, of her drinking tea in the kitchen, and of her green eyes looking across the table at him. She'd complained about the stench of his lucky coat after he'd run outside in the rain to get it for her.

In the parlor, he recalled her narrowing gaze as she looked at the renovation work and her calling him a sneaky bastard for taking advantage of Macy Jane. He remembered the day she'd walked in the parlor wearing red shoes and blouse. He remembered having sex and breaking a condom. He remembered every word and touch, but three months after she'd disappeared from his life, the memory no longer felt like a knife slicing his heart. Now it was just a dull, manageable ache.

Henry backed out of the French doors and put the key in the pocket of his jeans. He needed to drop it off at the realtor's office on his way home, but first he made a quick stop at the Kangaroo Express for a fill-up and a six-pack. He grabbed a king-sized Twix and headed to the checkout. Third in line, he called Hoyt to talk about a dilapidated tobacco barn he'd found in Marion County. It was in rough shape, but still salvageable. "I got it for two grand," he said as the woman at the front of the line paid for a Rock Star and a pack of Camels. "But we have to do the demo and haul it away ourselves."

"No problem. I like demo."

Which was one of the reasons Hoyt made such a valuable employee. He was built like a tank and loved grunt work. "It'll take a few trips to haul it all back."

The kid next in line paid for a Slurpee with a handful of change. He dropped a quarter on the floor, and Henry's gaze followed him as he bent to pick it up. "I can sell it as . . ." his voice trailed off, his attention caught and held like glue by the *National Enquirer* in a rack at the checkout counter. The kid stood and blocked Henry's view.

"Excuse me," he said and reached in front of the boy. He pulled the tabloid from the rack and stared at the picture of Vivien, walking down a street somewhere and eating ice cream. The paparazzi had caught her eating, but it wasn't the ice cream that caught his attention. It was the enlarged red circle around her stomach and the red arrow pointing to it. "Baby Bump?" was written in bold black letters. Henry stared at the red circle and Vivien's belly and he felt the blood rush from his head. He thought he might pass out. Right there in the Kangaroo Express.

"Boss? Are you there?"

"Yeah. I'll call you back." He disconnected and stepped out of line. Balancing his six-pack, he thumbed to the center of the magazine. The same picture was blown up even bigger, and he could see a slight bulge, like she'd eaten a grapefruit. He studied the photo and it looked to him like she'd gone on an ice cream bender, like when she was a kid.

"Sources close to Vivien will neither confirm nor deny that the actress is pregnant," he read. Tabloids made stories up all the time. Like him fondling her bra in the sports bar on King Street.

He slid his gaze to her beautiful face and big dark sunglasses. There had been a bit of truth to the bra story. He *had* been holding it on his finger and . . . Henry's brows crammed together over his eyes and he brought the paper closer to his face. Right beside Vivien, as if he didn't have a care in the world, strolled Henry's missing brother.

While Henry had been going through hell in Charleston, Spence had been living it up in Hollywood.

— Chapter 19 —

The Diary of Vivien Leigh Rochet
Keep out! Do NOT read under Penalty of Death!!

Dear Diary,
 I'm supposed to write a paper on my family roots for history class. I know some of the kids have family that arrived on the <u>Mayflower</u> and others when South Carolina was still a colony. Their people have cities and streets named after them. I traced my momma's roots back as far as 1870 and found out my family is from Tennessee and they were share-croppers. Momma showed me a picture of them standing in a dirt patch. Some didn't have shoes but all the men wore suits and ties and even hats. None of them smiled.☹ I wouldn't have smiled either. Mamaw Roz said I should write about Great Uncle Cletus, who lived in a chicken coop. Uck!!! I didn't want to write about

my momma's family standing in dirt and sleeping in chicken poop.

Dear Diary,

Proof Spence Whitley-Shuler has a mental defect. Just today, Momma and I were in the big house with the Episcopal ladies. They were praying and talking about the Bible and I thought I might die from boredom. The only good thing about the Episcopal ladies is they bring cookies and tea. Yucky Spence and Butt Head Henry are home from spring break and Nonnie made them come down from their rooms and say hey to the ladies. They were all "pleased to meet you," and "how's your mama." All polished and polite until Louisa Deering asked if they wanted to try some of the ladies' special sugar cookies. Spence started to laugh so hard I thought he was going to give himself an internal injury. Henry's lips kind of twitched and he hauled his brother out of the room, probably to find a straitjacket some-where. What's so funny about sugar cookies? I love sugar cookies. I would eat sugar cookies every day if Momma let me. Yummy!! ☺

Dear Diary,

No Fair!!! I wrote my history paper about the Rochets, but I had to make some stuff up. Stuff like I traced my daddy's roots all the way back to the Boston Tea Party. It isn't a lie because it could be true. I would have totally gotten an A if I hadn't messed up today and forgot what I wrote. ☹ The teacher asked me if my great-great-granddaddy had been a member of the Sons of Liberty. I forgot all about the assignment, I said Daddy died rescuing Cubans and I'd never met anyone in his family. Now I have to write the paper again. ☹☹ My momma was mad and said big or small, lies are lies and Jesus hates lies.

Dear Diary,

I got a cramp in my stomach this morning and I wasn't running any-where. I think I'm going to have my period any day.

Dear Diary,

I've been thinking about boys again. If I want to get married, I have to think about who I might pick. Momma says I have my whole life ahead of me to think about it, but I think I should start now.

Husband List

1. Justin Timberlake
2. James Van Der Beek
3. Rider Strong
4. Zac Hanson
5. The boy who sells ice cream at Ben and Jerry's

More to come.

— Chapter 20 —

"This is the life." Spence lifted his empty hand as if he held a glass. "Here's to Hollywood, my dear."

Through her cat-eye sunglasses, Vivien looked at the script in front of her. She lay curled up on her side beneath the white canopy of her poolside cabana and read the stage directions: *Dorothy feels ambivalent about the move to Hollywood and about her marriage to Alan.* Just as she was about to say her lines, Spence's phone beeped and he broke character.

"Christ almighty! Henry's been texting me five times an hour." He tossed his script on the mattress. "He's definitely seen the cover of the *Enquirer* and he sounds pissed off."

Vivien lifted her gaze. "So? Let him be pissed. I didn't get *him* pregnant." She tossed her script aside and stretched out within the linen pillows. Beyond the shade of the cabana, the California sun bathed twelve Greek statues in bright light as they poured water from urns into an elaborately tiled pool. The house had been owned previously by a twenty-five-year-old computer-game developer who had more money than taste. Although at night, Vivien had to admit, the sound of water spilling from the urns was relaxing.

"When do you plan to talk to Henry?" Spence asked as he rose from the cabana and moved to a chaise a few feet away.

"I don't know." She'd avoided the subject. She wanted to get her current film wrapped up before she thought about him, but at some point she would have to tell him or Henry would make himself unavoidable. "I wrap up shooting Friday, and then I'm going to sleep for a week. I'll think about it after that."

"I don't know if he'll be put off that long." Spence whipped off his T-shirt and stretched out to sun himself. His chest was still pink from tanning the day before.

"Are you sure you don't want sunscreen?" When and if she decided to talk to Henry was not up to him. It was up to her.

"I spent every summer on Coligny Beach. I'll bronze up in no time."

He looked like a blister just waiting to happen. Vivien snuggled deeper into the pillows and put a hand over her slightly rounded stomach. She closed her eyes and listened to the water falling from the stone urns into the pool. She'd been so tired lately. All she did was work and sleep. All of the pregnancy books she'd read said exhaustion was normal. The lists of dos and don'ts for pregnant women was mind-boggling. The dos were commonsense stuff like make regular doctor visits and get lots of rest. The don'ts list was frightening. She'd read that she couldn't eat hot dogs or fish or soft cheeses. She should avoid microwaves, cat litter, and herpes. Although really, avoiding herpes was a given, pregnant or not. The others though . . . What if she forgot and ate a microwaved hot dog? Or there was some brie hidden in a tostada? Would she need her stomach pumped?

The warmth of the sun through the cabana curtains lulled her into the relaxing space just before sleep. All the baby books differed, though, on when she might feel movement from the baby. One of the books said sixteen weeks, the other twenty-two.

She wished she had someone to talk to other than Sarah and Spence. She wished she had her mother. For lots of reasons—not the least of which was to ask why she'd lied to Vivien her whole life—and because a girl needed her momma when she was expecting a baby. Spence was her closest living relative, and his only piece of advice had been to avoid hard liquor. To which she'd replied, *Duh*.

It was still weird to think she had a brother. Especially Spence, but the same day she'd written down her list of cons, she'd reached out to him. Without hesitation, he'd dropped everything and hopped on the first available flight to L.A. He'd arrived at her house wearing yellow pants, a white-and-yellow-checked shirt, and a gray jacket. The choice had been bold for a man living anywhere but South Carolina, where even the most hetero of men weren't afraid of pastels. Except maybe Henry. She just couldn't see him in yellow pants.

"I didn't know who else to call," she'd said as he walked in the front door.

"Of course you called me." He'd pushed his sunglasses to the top of his head and dropped his suitcase on the floor. "I'm your big brother."

That had sounded so odd. It still did. "I've always wanted a brother."

"Now you have me." He grinned.

"Yes. I have you and your brother's baby." She'd meant it as a joke, but her voice hiccupped and embarrassing tears filled her vision. She pretended she had something in her eyes and turned her face away, but he'd reached for her and she discovered that Spence gave the best hugs. He wrapped his arms around her and squeezed just hard enough to mean it but not so hard that she couldn't breathe. He smelled like cologne and starched cotton and not like his brother at all.

"It'll be okay," he'd said into the top of her head. "I'm here for as long as you need me."

That had been three weeks ago, and apparently he didn't have a job waiting for him in Charleston. As far as she could tell, he didn't do a whole lot. During the day, he putted a golf ball on the putting green the previous owners had installed. He swam in the pool and tanned himself. At night, he flirted with Sarah over a pitcher of mojitos and took a cab to the local hot spots. At the Rainbow Room, he swore he saw Tom Petty. At Whisky A Go-Go he claimed he bought a Playmate of the Year a snakebite. Even if Vivien hadn't been pregnant, she wouldn't have been interested in accompanying him. She'd been there, done that, and wasn't missing out.

He drank too much and slept too late, and every day he gave her the best hugs in the world. At night they talked for hours when she got home from filming. They talked about anything and everything, and the subject of Henry always came up.

"I knew there was something between y'all, but I didn't think you were . . ." Spence paused to look at her beneath his lowered brows. "As my grandfather Shuler used to call it, 'making honey.' " She wrinkled her nose and he laughed. "He was a good guy."

Vivien should have known that. She should have known a lot more about her grandfather instead of believing Hurricane Kate had sunk his schooner off the coast of Florida. Even now, when she thought of the lie she'd believed all of her life, she was embarrassed to admit that she'd never even thought to question her mother. For one, her mother had been staunchly opposed to lies. For two, she never would have thought that her mother had the mental endurance it took to keep such a fantastical lie. "Do you think your grandfather knew about me?" she asked.

"No. Family was important to him. Not the way family is important to Mother. Mother's biggest concerns are keeping bloodlines and appearances pure. The Whitleys care more about protecting the façade of a loving family. The Shulers truly love 'their people,' warts and all. Whenever you're ready, I'll introduce you to the cousins."

During those three weeks, Vivien was grateful to have Spence around. He helped her run her lines and brought her water or milk or juice when he thought she might need it. He was nice and funny and she discovered that he didn't have mental issues as she'd always suspected. He cracked jokes and laughed a lot and nothing much seemed to bother him, but there had been a time or two when she'd glimpsed something cold in his ice-blue eyes. Then he'd crack another joke and melt the sudden freeze with laughter.

Her mind drifted from Spence to a few promising scripts she'd read. The actual filming wouldn't start for at least a year. In some cases longer. The baby would be born by then and she'd hire a nanny to help out—Beneath Vivien's palm she felt a soft little flutter. Her eyes popped open and she got very still. She held her breath . . . waiting . . . then it happened again. A flutter like gossamer wings. It was probably just gas. All the books said women often mistook gas for move-ment. It happened again, and in that instant, the baby became real to her, more real than an outline on a monitor. She felt more attached and protective than before. Her life seemed to refocus, and suddenly nothing was as important to her as the tiny life making itself known.

"Viv?"

She looked over at Spence in the chaise and debated whether or not to tell him that she'd felt the baby. She decided against it because it just might be gas.

"Yeah?"

"You know I've always wanted a sister. Right?" Spence pushed his sunglasses to the top of his head and looked over at her.

"You've mentioned it." About a hundred times.

"A really good sister who invites hot friends over for a slumber party."

Vivien laughed. "I always thought a really good brother should beat people up for me. The problem is that you and Henry were tops on my list of people to beat up."

"I'll tell you what." He readjusted his sunglasses and pointed his face to the sun. "I'll beat Henry up for you if you have a slumber party and invite your hot friends." He paused a moment in thought. "Do you know any of the Kardashians?"

First Lottie, now him. "No. Sorry." She didn't feel more flutters and removed her hand from her belly.

"Katy Perry? She's hot. So is Elisha Cuthbert. The two girls could have a pillow fight."

She'd met Katy but seriously doubted the singer wanted to have a pillow fight at a slumber party. "Sorry."

He named off a few more celebrities, and Vivien didn't know if he was serious or joking with her. "How about that Kendra Wilkinson?" he continued. "I think her show is canceled now." He tried to keep a straight face but couldn't quite manage it. "After breaking it off with Hef and then Hank cheating on her, she might be desperate for a Southern gentleman who has a way with former playmates."

She laughed. "I don't know Kendra."

His cell phone beeped once more and he dug it out of his short's pocket. "Damn, he's persistent."

"Henry?"

"Yeah. He knows I'm going to forgive him." Spence sighed and set the phone on the pool deck. "But he needs to suffer more than . . ." He paused and cocked his head to one side. "What's that?"

"What's what?" In the distance a rapid *whop whop* came from the direction of Charlie Sheen's house. It grew louder and more distinct, like it was coming up Mulholland. "Oh. That's part of the helicopter tour that flies around Beverly Hills. It never comes this way."

"Are you sure?"

It sounded closer than usual. "Yes," she answered as whirling chopper blades rose from behind a row of trees at the far end of the property, whirling chopper blades that lifted a blue helicopter and whipped the treetops. Sitting in the open door, a man pointed the long lens of his camera right at her.

"Dammit!" This was her time. Her time to enjoy the first fluttering movement from her baby, or at least gas that she mistook for fluttering, and it was being ruined. She quickly dashed in the house, but Spence stayed right where he was, like he didn't mind the attention at all. He might have even waved.

The paparazzi were relentless since the baby-bump picture, making her life even more hellish than ever before. They posed as tourists to get near the movie set and they waited for her to drive away.

After the helicopter stunt, Vivien hired a car service to take her to the studio because she feared that they'd try to block her in traffic. The limo she'd chosen had blacked-out windows, and Spencer rode in the car with her to and from Paramount in case she needed "muscle."

"At least they're not killing themselves to take a picture of you eating," Sarah had pointed out.

True. Now they were fighting for pictures of her stomach and combing through her personal life more than usual.

On the last day of filming, Vivien only stuck around Stage Seventeen long enough to thank the production crew. She was tired and feeling harassed and all she wanted was to relax and concentrate on the tiny life that was sucking all her energy and making her queasy at night. She wanted to do the regular pregnant women things, like buy maternity clothes and look at baby shoes.

She slid into the dark limousine and leaned her head back against the soft leather. She could feel Spence's presence across the seat and she closed her eyes. She needed a vacation. Maybe she'd run off to a remote island and go all Marlon Brando for the next few months. Maybe she'd never come back.

"We should run off to Fiji." She rolled her head to the left and sat up so fast, it felt like her heart bumped into her ribs.

"Hello, Vivien. Is there something you need to tell me?"

Henry tilted his head to one side and waited for a response as the limo drove past building façades and continued beneath double-arched gates. Vivien looked just as he remembered. Her smooth, pale skin appeared translucent within the car's dark interior; she wore a white sundress and looked angelic. God, he wanted to shake the hell out of her.

"How did you get here? Where's Spence?"

"Spence is lying by your pool in deep contemplation about the many ways I'm going to kick his ass." He understood that his brother was angry with him. He understood why, but that didn't mean he was even going to try and understand why Spence would keep something so important from him.

She looked out the window, then turned her face back toward him. The color of her eyes was hidden in the shadowy interior, but he didn't need to see her clearly to know they were the color of magnolia leaves first thing in the morning. When everything was bathed in dew and morning light. He didn't need to press his mouth to hers to know the taste of her lips, and he didn't need to hear her laughter to know it sounded like sunshine and honey to his ears.

"He's bigger than you."

"I'm meaner." She was so close. A couple of feet, but it might as well be a couple of miles.

"That's true."

The last time he'd seen her, her beautiful eyes had been filled with tears and he'd felt like kicking his own ass. *Why are you trying to hurt me more than you have already?* she'd asked. If this was her idea of making him pay, she was doing a really good job turning the screws. She looked out the window again, as if she could ignore him. He'd loved her more than he'd ever loved a woman, and she'd angered him more than any other woman, too. "Are you pregnant, Vivien?"

"What did Spence tell you?"

"That I should ask you." Since neither would give a straight answer, he guessed he didn't need one. "When were you going to tell me?"

"Assuming it's yours?"

She wasn't done torturing him. "Yes, but if not, you need to tell me right now."

"It's my baby, Henry." She turned and looked at him. "I don't want to have anything to do with you or Nonnie."

"That isn't your choice to make."

The limousine made a right turn and an angle of sunlight slid across her lower face and throat. "You can go on with your life like before."

Too late. He hadn't been able to go on with his life. He was stuck in place. Somewhere between love and hate. Seeing her, he was caught between pleasure and pissed off. "Before what?"

"Like with Tracy Lynn. Just forget it happened."

Pissed off won, and he swallowed against the anger crawling up his throat. "What happened at that time in my life isn't even close to what is happening now." She wasn't going to be satisfied until she ripped him apart again. Things were different now. He was different. The thought of a child didn't send terror shooting through his eins, nor was he going to leave the decision solely up to Vivien like he had Tracy Lynn. "You should have told me before I saw it in the magazine rack at the Kangaroo Express." Although, he guessed, she'd already made a decision.

"I don't owe you anything." Her voice shook a little when she spoke. From hurt or anger he couldn't tell. Perhaps both. "You lied to me. You made me think you cared about me when you didn't. You took advantage of me at my time of grief."

"You're allowed to still be angry with me, but you're not allowed to rewrite history, Vivien. No one took advantage of you."

"You said I was important to you, and the whole time you were just playing me for a fool." She took a deep breath and raised her hands to the top of her head. "It doesn't matter. I'm over it."

It didn't sound like she was over it to him, but he wisely kept that observation to himself.

"I don't owe you anything." Her hands dropped to her sides. "I don't owe you my baby."

"Our baby." His gaze slid down the front of her dress, and he stared at her stomach as if he might be able see his child. Of course he couldn't, but it was there. Safe and warm, growing beneath the heart of the woman he loved. He'd fought like hell to get over his feelings for her, but the second she'd slid into the car, they all came rushing back. He was powerless to stop the chaos churning through him. "I'm the baby's father, and I'm going to be in that child's life."

"I was raised without a daddy, and I grew up just fine."

Henry didn't say anything. There was no need. He let the silence speak for him.

Vivien stared at the outline of Henry's shoulders in the dark corner of the car. Every emotion she'd ever felt for Henry Whitley-Shuler came at her like a hurricane. Conflicting emotions like love and hate tumbled with anger and the pure joy of seeing him again. The sound of his voice added a tempest of fear and longing and scattered her senses like a debris field. She tried hard to delete him from her heart when she'd deleted him from her life, but she hadn't. She thought she'd erased him from her soul, but she'd been fooling herself. Silence stretched between them and she heard herself say, "I didn't have a daddy and look at me now."

Again he said nothing. She was rich and successful. Men around the world wanted her. Women wanted to be her. Her life looked perfect. No, it *was* perfect. Perfect, except she was alone and pregnant, and even though she didn't want to admit it, scared to death.

"And I have Spence now."

That brought an unamused chuckle from his side of the car.

Okay, so maybe Spence would make a better uncle than a substitute daddy, and maybe growing up without a father hadn't been so fine. Oftentimes, it had been painful. She'd hated when other kids asked about her parents and why she didn't have a dad. She hated the tug on her heart when she'd see families in the park or at school, and envy had churned in her stomach whenever she'd seen daddies carrying little girls on their shoulders.

Not even a heroic, fake father cut from the newspaper was a substitute for the real thing.

There'd never been a father figure in her life. It had just been her mother, Mamaw Roz, and her. She wanted more for her baby. She wanted her child to know a daddy's love. Not a fake daddy like she'd had, but the real thing.

Vivien could give her baby the real thing. She might think Henry was a colossal, coldhearted jerk, but there was no doubt in her mind that he would be a good daddy. "Okay, maybe we can work something out." Like he could visit twice a year, and when the baby was older, go to Disneyland.

— Chapter 21 —

With a solid click, Vivien unlocked the deadbolt to the carriage house and walked inside. It looked the same as it had the day she'd left. Boxes and bins, some packed tight and labeled. Others left open, waiting for the rest of her mother's belongings to be organized and stored away.

"Are you going to be okay here by yourself?"

Vivien chuckled. "Yes, Spence."

He looked as jumpy as a cat in a skillet. He'd made it clear that he wasn't ready to be any-where near his mother. That included across the yard. "I'm going out to dinner with Henry tonight. If he buys me a good steak and a nice bottle of wine, I might forgive him."

"Really?" Vivien dropped her keys into her purse as Spence dropped her luggage on the floor. She looked across her shoulder at him. Today he wore a lavender polo shirt and some-how, the pastel didn't look so bad on him. She must be getting used to his choice of Easter colors. Either that, or being back in Charleston made him a less glaring fashion victim.

She was back. Back to the Charleston heat and carriage house and memories that resided here. It had been four days since Henry had turned up in her limo. Four days since the sound of his voice had touched a visceral place deep inside. She wasn't sure she was ready for any of it.

She was over Henry Whitley-Shuler. She didn't love him anymore. Despite those lingering feelings imprinted deep inside. What she felt for him most was anger, but she did want what was best for her child. That meant Henry. He'd flatly refused to be a "Disneyland dad," but it *didn't* mean he got to call all the shots or set the parameters. Toward that end, she and Spence had waited three days to fly to Charleston. Not the next morning as Henry had insisted. "I don't know how you can forgive him so easily." Henry had left L.A. alone, but only after Spencer had assured him that he and Vivien would return together.

"He's my brother." Spence shrugged as if that said it all. "What you need to understand about Henry is that he always tries to do the right thing. He was dead-ass wrong not to tell me about you a long time ago, but most of the blame should be placed on my mother and yours. Henry kept their secret, but they lied."

She understood that, but her mother hadn't sent in an understudy to seduce and distract her.

"Henry would take a bullet for me." Spence laughed as he headed out the door. "You never know when someone like that might come in handy in the future."

She was still getting used to Spence's ways of

saying and doing and living his life. Vivien shut the door behind her brother and leaned back against it. Without Spence's distraction, she felt the strong emotions from the last time she'd been in the carriage house. They were all still present. Like the boxes and bins, waiting for her to return and sort things out. Painful and confusing things from her past. Broken trust and heartbreak. Lies and unanswered questions.

Vivien kicked off her shoes and headed upstairs to her mother's bedroom. She couldn't fix broken trust, or heartache or lies from her past, but maybe she could find answers.

Three bins of photo albums and keepsakes sat on her mother's bed. The answer had to be in there somewhere. For the next three hours she looked at old photos and read old letters from Mamaw Roz and Uncle Richie. She found the old newspaper article with a photo of boat debris floating in the Florida Straits. She found her birth certificate, the father's name left blank.

Vivien sat on the bed and looked at the old document in her hands. Her mother had explained away the blank line by telling her that Jeremiah Rochet hadn't been alive to sign her birth certificate.

Little baby Jesus hates lies but loves the liar, had been one of her mother's mottoes, and perhaps that was how she'd been able to live with herself.

Vivien placed the certificate back in the album

and returned it to the bin. Her momma had been a rich man's mistress. The rich man was her father, but there was absolutely no record of him at all. Not even a photo of Fredrickk Shuler in the pile of albums that had recorded almost every moment of Vivien's life. The most important man in her life had been cleanly deleted, but not forever. Like trying to wipe Henry out of her life, the past was never completely erased.

The answers to Vivien's questions weren't in a box or bin. Not in a photo album or stack of old letters. Her answers were in the big house beyond the roses and wisteria, probably having her first cocktail of the night.

Vivien returned downstairs and shoved her feet into sandals. It was time to face Nonnie, *mano a mano* in the Mantis's lair.

Vivien had been right. She found Nonnie in the gold salon, reading a book and sipping a dirty martini. She appeared as always, like a queen minus a crown.

"I've been expecting you," she said as Vivien walked into the room. She set her book aside and took a sip of her cocktail.

"You know why I'm here then." Vivien moved to the chair closest to Nonnie and sat. She wasn't a kid. She wasn't afraid.

"Yes, Henry told me the happy news." She didn't sound or look happy.

"I'm not here to talk about that." If she had her way, Nonnie would have little contact with her child. "I want to talk about Momma."

The older woman raised a brow. "What do you want to know?"

"Why did you and Momma lie to me?"

"*Lie* is such a strong word. Macy Jane and I did what we thought was best."

"I can't imagine my momma coming up with such an elaborate lie when she had a hard time following through with everything else in her life. You had to have said or done something to her to make her go along with your lies."

Nonnie chuckled. "The day of Fred's funeral, your mother came to *me*. He hadn't even been put in the ground yet when she made me an offer I couldn't refuse." She wiped at the lipstick smudge on her glass as if she hadn't just quoted Don Corleone.

"Which was?"

"That I provide for the two of you financially, and she wouldn't tell anyone that my husband was your father."

Extortion didn't sound like the mother she'd known. "I don't believe you."

"It's true."

But lying like a cheap rug didn't sound like her either. "And you were happy to agree?"

"Not happy. Resigned. I couldn't have it known that Fred had an illegitimate child. Let alone that you were living under my nose." She set her glass on the table between them. "In my carriage house."

"My mother's carriage house." Vivien folded her arms across her breasts. "The carriage house was left to my mother."

Nonnie gave a sharp nod. "When my husband was alive, he took care of the two of you. When he died, the responsibility came to me."

"And you resented it."

"Of course. My husband had a child with his mistress, and he had the gall to move the two of you into my own backyard. He put the needs of his mistress above his wife and sons."

"That explains why you hated us." She wasn't so sure she wouldn't have felt the same.

Nonnie lifted her pointed chin. " 'He who hates his brother walks in darkness.' I don't hate anyone. I didn't care for your mother at first, but she didn't seem to notice. After years of Macy Jane blindly believing we were best friends, I came to care for her a great deal. She was a good-hearted woman." She reached for her drink and took a sip. "You, however, could try the patience of a saint. Your mother let you run wild."

Vivien had heard that all her life; she didn't care to debate it now. "Was your idea of providing for Momma and me putting us to work in your house?"

"Really, Vivien. You two did light cleaning for

extra money." Again she wiped at her glass. "Do you really think the money your mother made dusting some furniture was enough to support the two of you?"

She'd never known how much Nonnie had paid her mother, but who paid and how much wasn't her biggest issue. "The two of you seemed to have worked it all out."

"We both benefited."

"Who found the newspaper article about the Rochets?"

"I did. Your mother could handle the basics of the story. It was up to me to think of every angle and fine-tune it."

Vivien folded her arms across her chest. "Were either of you ever going to tell anyone the truth?"

"No. That was part of the deal. It was to be buried with us. It would have stayed buried if Spence hadn't started to behave inappropriately—"

"—And you naturally made Henry keep me busy—"

"—I can't make Henry do anything. I certainly didn't make him spend so much time with you. In fact, I didn't think anything good would come of it." Her gaze drifted downward. "I was right."

Vivien lowered a hand to her stomach, protecting the baby from Nonnie's evil eye. "I didn't imagine you'd be happy about the baby."

"It's not exactly an ideal situation."

"What? That Henry is having a child on the

wrong side of the blanket, or that he's having it with me?"

"Both. This is a disaster."

At least she was honest and consistent. Her feelings weren't all over the place. Not like Vivien's. One moment she thought she was doing the right thing by involving Henry in the baby's life, and in the next, she felt all panicky because that meant Henry would be involved in her life, too. He thought the idea of co-parenting meant she lived across town from him, which wasn't going to happen. She needed to set firm rules and boundaries with him the next time they talked. Vivien stood. "The good news for both of us is that you won't have anything to do with this disaster."

The bad news was that Henry arrived on her porch the next morning with bagels and fruit and she forgot all about boundaries and rules. "How are you feeling, darlin'?" he asked, his smooth accent pouring over her.

She used to love it when he called her that. "You should have called first." She stood in the open doorway wearing her pajama shorts and T-shirt from the night before, and her hair was a mess.

"I don't have your phone number."

Oh, yeah. She let him inside and followed him past the boxes and bins to the round table that still sat in the middle of the kitchen. "I'll give it to you, but you can't just drop in like a screw-worm anytime you feel like it."

He didn't acknowledge her personal boundary and she turned back toward him. "Did you hear me?" He didn't answer even though he was staring straight at her. "Henry!"

"What?"

"Did you hear what I said?"

"Something about your phone number." He moved to the counter and pulled a bagel out of a bag.

"I said you can't drop in like a screwworm anytime you feel like it."

"Okay." The corners of his mouth twitched. "I don't want to be a screwworm. What days work best for you?"

Oh. She hadn't given it any thought and gave an arbitrary answer. "Mondays and Fridays."

"Okay," he said, but he didn't stick to it. He came the next morning with fruit and yogurt.

"It's Wednesday," Vivien pointed out.

"You don't say."

He pulled out a chair for her and put yogurt and fruit on the table. So much for their talk about dropping by like a screwworm.

"I met Spence for dinner the other night."

"I know. He said he was ready to forgive you, but I don't think he'll forgive Nonnie anytime soon," she replied.

"That's between the two of them." He got two plates and sat across the table from her. "I'm out of the business of taking care of my mother and Spence."

"Have you talked to your mother lately?" She and Henry were behaving so civil, this co-parenting might work out after all—if he respected boundaries.

"Not since I've been back in town." He sat across from her. "Have you?"

"Yes. I talked to her Monday night." Vivien placed strawberries and cantaloupe on her plate. Maybe she and Henry could even become friends someday.

"How'd that go?"

"She answered some questions about my momma." She took a bite of cantaloupe and licked the juice from the corner of her mouth. "She's not happy about the baby."

He paused in the act of raising a fork, suspending a strawberry in front of his mouth. "Did she say that?" he asked before he popped the fruit in his mouth.

"She said it's not an 'ideal situation.' She called the baby a 'disaster.' "

"She said the word disaster?" He didn't look happy.

"Yep. I guess this means she won't be throwing me a baby shower anytime soon."

He looked across the table at her, his gaze went from anger to speculative, but didn't say anything.

When Henry didn't appear the next morning, she told herself that he was respecting her boundaries. It was a good thing and she was glad. She wasn't disappointed. Not at all, but Friday morning when she opened the door and he stood on the porch with a paper bag in one arm, she felt like her whole body smiled. Which was not a good thing.

"Good morning, darlin'."

Again with the *darlin'*.

He brought Greek yogurt and granola this time. "When are you going to finish packing up your momma's belongings?" he asked as Vivien took two bowls from the cupboard.

She was dragging her feet. She knew she was, but packing up the last boxes felt so final. "I have to finish going through all the closets upstairs." The pink row house had sold the day before, and it felt as if she'd sold off a piece of her past. She hadn't expected to feel sad and sentimental about the Candy-Button house her mother had dreamed about but never lived in. "I'll be finished before the baby comes."

"The baby has started growing toenails today," Henry said as he took his usual seat across the table and dug in to his breakfast.

She looked at him, his dark eyes and hair and handsome mouth crunching away. "How do you know that?"

"I downloaded an app from *Today's Parent*." The corners of his mouth turned up in a big smile. "It sends me weekly alerts."

The yogurt in Vivien's mouth suddenly tasted

sour and she felt like she'd been punched in the heart. He was looking at her like he used to. Giving her that smile that had melted her and lit up her insides. The smile that used to make her think he saved it just for her. She swallowed hard. "I can't do this." She stood so fast her chair fell back. "I thought we could be civil to each other for the baby's sake." She shook her head. "I thought maybe we could be friends, but we can't."

Henry looked up at her and set down his spoon. "I don't want to be your friend, Vivien." He kept his gaze locked with hers as he slowly rose. "I can never be your friend. Too much has happened between me and you."

He was right. In the past few days she'd forgotten that he'd only pretended to care for her. He'd broken her heart once before. Almost smashed it to pieces, and she wasn't such a fool that she would let him finish the job. She turned away and he grabbed her hand.

"You're having my baby, for God's sake."

She looked back at him over her shoulder and the warmth of his touch spread to her wrist. "This is about the baby."

"What?"

"This." She pointed at the table. "Bringing me breakfast all the time. You just want to make sure I eat right." Why had she thought it meant more?

"That's part of it."

She should be grateful, but she'd let her stupid heart convince her head that he might care for her a little. She pulled her hand from his before the warmth in her wrist spread up her arm to her chest.

"The other part is that I love you, and it's an excuse to see you every day."

In her heart, she wanted to believe him. She wanted it so much that she felt like she was being inflated with happy gas. Her head knew better. "I don't trust you, Henry." She folded her arms over her chest as if they could shield her heart.

"I know."

"You lied in the past to get what you wanted."

"I never wanted to lie to you. I never wanted to deceive you, either." He reached a hand toward her but dropped it by his side. "I never wanted to hurt you. I never wanted to fall in love with you, but I did. I fell so hard that all these months later, I still can't catch my breath." He grabbed his car keys off the table. "You don't trust me and I don't blame you. You don't believe me and I don't know what I can to do to change that."

She wanted to believe him. Even after all he'd put her through. She wanted to believe him so much that she had to fight the urge to throw herself on his chest. He turned and walked away and she had to fight the urge to run after him, too. Her gaze slid from his dark hair and broad shoulders, down the back of his T-shirt to his jeans. She wanted to believe him so much that even after all the self-help books she'd read to get over him, she fought the urge to grab on to his bumper as he drove away.

She shut the door before she gave into her urges. To take her mind off her troubles with Henry, she packed up more boxes then got on her computer and ordered maternity clothes. Lots of maternity clothes. When that didn't work she met Spence for dinner. He ate crab and lobster and she ordered steak, medium-well, because she'd read that pregnant women shouldn't eat shellfish or rare meat. They talked about growing up across the yard from each other and she felt herself relax more than she had in weeks.

Later that night, as Spence pulled his car to a stop in front of the carriage house, he turned to her and said, "I was thinking about something the other day."

She was almost afraid to ask. "What?"

"My brother and sister are having a baby. That makes me both a maternal and paternal uncle. I bet there aren't too many people who can say that." He thought a moment. "Well, not in this generation of Whitleys, anyway."

He made her laugh and she would have invited him inside, but she knew he didn't want to be near his mother. Not even in the same zip code, which was fine with Vivien. Spence had exhausted her brain and all she wanted was her bed. The minute her head hit the pillow, she fell into a deep peaceful sleep until the doorbell woke her the next morning. She grabbed her robe and walked down the stair. Her hair was a mess and she needed a shower. She was going to have to insist—again—that Henry call or text before he came over, but it wasn't Henry standing on her porch, sunlight glistening within the deep luster of the family pearls.

"I wanted to hand deliver this personally." Nonnie shoved a white envelope at her.

"What is it?"

"You'll have to open it to find out." She turned on the heels of her sensible pumps and moved toward the garage, the tail of her peach scarf flapping in her wake. Vivien watched her jump in her Cadillac before she stepped inside the house and closed the door. She looked at the envelope in her hand, almost afraid to open it, afraid Nonnie had found some way to evict her.

It wasn't an eviction notice, though. It was a card with a stork holding an umbrella on the front, and *It's a Baby Shower* printed across the top. Inside the card, Nonnie had written the time and date and location for the baby shower of *Vivien Rochet and baby Whitley-Shuler*.

She wouldn't have been more surprised if the card had turned into dynamite and exploded in her face, Wile E. Coyote style.

A baby shower? For her? This had to be a joke.

It wasn't a joke. Just a really bad nightmare. Vivien sat on a white wicker chair, surrounded by cupcakes with candy rattles, stacks of gifts wrapped in baby-shower paper, and the Episcopalian ladies from her mother's church. They all wore sun hats and sipped tea in Nonnie's rose garden like this was all somehow normal.

"Your mother would be so happy," one of them said. "It's not like in my day, when girls got sent off if they got pregnant."

That comment brought a round of commentary ranging from the morals of society today to who'd been sent away "in their day."

"Oh" and "uh-huh" were Vivien's contributions to the conversation. She kept her smile in place. She was an actress. She could do this.

"I remember my first child. I was so sick I had to get better to die," someone else said, which turned the conversation into a competition over who'd been the sickest.

"Oh." Vivien drank tea and ate a cupcake and wondered what the hell was going on. She glanced at Nonnie several chairs away, but her smile was stuck in place, too, like she wasn't anymore a happy hostess than Vivien was the guest of honor.

They were both faking it, tacitly keeping up the charade as Vivien opened gifts of handmade quilts and knitted booties and a kit to mold her baby's hands that looked so creepy she hid it beneath a blanket.

"When I gave birth, I didn't take drugs to block the pain. I had my children the way God intended. Just me, the doctor, and several nurses." She paused her childbirth horror story long enough to take a sip of tea. "And the woman screaming down the hallway like someone cut her arm off."

"I tore something fierce."

"Uh-huh." Vivien tried to block those comments from entering her brain as she blessedly opened the last gift. A handheld breast pump.

"You're going to nurse that baby, aren't you?"

She feared an incorrect answer. "I believe so."

"Good. Best to get your nipples all toughened up now as later."

She raised her hands to her breasts. She didn't want tough nipples. Now or later. What was wrong with these women? Was Nonnie's purpose in having this party to torture Vivien with harrowing stories from old church ladies? If it had been her goal, it was working.

She folded the wrapping paper because they seemed to expect her to keep it. She'd been at the party for two hours now and figured it was time to make her escape. She gave a tired sigh and even faked a big yawn to set up her getaway.

"Thank you ladies so much," she said sincerely.

"You have one more gift," Nonnie pointed out.

Vivien glanced around, expecting to see another

gift wrapped in paper, but the only thing sitting on the table was a wooden box. "This?"

"Yes."

The box barely filled both palms and had different wood inlays. It was beautiful, but when she tried to open it, she couldn't. She turned it upside down and looked at it from every angle. She shook it and heard something rattle inside.

"What is it?" someone asked.

Vivien smiled. "It's a puzzle box." Henry. It suddenly became clear who was really behind the baby shower. "If y'all will excuse me, I need to rest." She thanked everyone again and carried as many gifts as she was able across the yard. The wooden box sat on top of the breast pump, and once inside the carriage house, she tossed everything but Henry's gift on a clean spot on the sofa, then moved to the kitchen table. She sat in the same chair she'd sat in as a girl, and skimmed her fingertips across the wood, which had been carefully sanded until it was as smooth as satin. She'd been fairly good at opening Henry's boxes as a kid, but after an hour, she figured she must have lost her touch. She slid one piece of tiger wood one way and walnut another. One strip up, another down. Back, forth—up, down, and just when she felt like getting a hammer and smashing the beautiful box, she heard a soft click. A victorious smile curved her lips and anticipation pumped through her veins.

A weathered cork sat inside the box lined with

green velvet. It had turned a darker brown and was a little shriveled, but the name *Moet & Chandon* was still clearly visible.

Vivien reached inside and pulled out her mother's cork. The one she'd searched for in the bed of red impatiens. To anyone else, it was nothing. Just a weathered piece of nothing. To Vivien, it was everything.

Henry turned off the shop lights and locked the door behind him. Vivien's baby shower should have been over hours ago. He had no idea what usually took place at a baby shower, but he hoped like hell his mother had behaved herself.

As if thinking of his mother had conjured her up, Nonnie's Cadillac turned into his driveway. After his little chat he'd had with his mother, he hoped she'd been nice to Vivien. Or had, at least, faked it. If not, he was going to stick to his promise of cutting her out his life.

The car pulled to a stop and the door swung open. Instead of his mother's tall, bony frame, Vivien stepped out.

"You wouldn't happen to know why your mother threw me a baby shower, would you?"

"Wouldn't know a thing about that." For a second he thought something must have gone wrong, but she smiled and the knot between his shoulders relaxed. "If I had to guess, I'd say it's because she's such a warm-hearted woman."

"Thank you," she said through her smile. "But next time, don't leave the guest list to Nonnie."

Next time.

She held out her hand and the old cork he'd found for her rested in her palm. "Thank you for this, too. This is the best gift anyone has ever given me."

"It's not exactly gold."

"It's better." She stared at him, solemn as a judge. "I love you, Henry."

He placed his hand on her arm and slid it up soft skin to her shoulder. "Are you just saying that because I'm charming and rescued your cork before the new owners moved into the row house?"

"No. I love you because you're a good man and no matter how hard I tried, I couldn't stop loving you."

He pulled her against his chest where she belonged and looked down into her upturned face. "I've missed you like crazy. You're sunshine and honey. Whiskey in a teacup, and everything I want in my life." He pushed her hair behind her ear. "I love you, Vivien Leigh. I loved you before the baby. I love you even more now. I would do anything for you. Give you anything. I want you. I want us. I want—"

"Shhh. . . . Henry." She rose onto the balls of her feet. "Just kiss me."

Henry, being a Southern gentleman, gave the lady what she wanted.

— Chapter 22 —

The Diary of Vivien Leigh Rochet
Keep out! Do NOT read under Penalty of Death!!

Dear Diary,
 I'd forgotten that I'd written you so long ago until I found the three spiral notebooks in the back of my closet. I started with the first and read every word. I'd forgotten the thirteen-year-old girl who wrote about drama and heartache. I remember her now and it's a little embarrassing to be reminded of my apparent obsession over getting breasts, boyfriends, and my future husbands. I didn't marry Justin Timberlake. I married someone better.
 SHOCKER ALERT #1 Spence Whitley-Shuler is my brother!!!! He won't do my chores, ☹ but he gives the best hugs. ☺ He's not as stupid as I used to think, just restless.
 SHOCKER ALERT #2 Henry Whitley-Shuler is my husband!!!! He can fix

stuff ☺ and he smells good. ☺ ☺ He's not as scary as he used to be, just more hand-some.

SHOCKER ALERT #3 The Mantis is my mother-in-law. ☹ ☺ To date, she has not bitten anyone's head off—that I know of!!! She's not as mean as she used to be, just resigned to faking it.

SHOCKER ALERT #4 Henry and I are having a baby girl. We're naming her Macy, after Momma. I had to learn to accept momma's faults and love her for who she was to me. She was a kind and loving woman whose big dreams set my feet on the path to my life today.

Dreams that Came True List

1. I am an actress—duh
2. Pool
3. Wear bra like other girls
4. I know my daddy's people
5. The man who loves me and doesn't give stuffed dogs and lifesavers to other girls

Center Point Large Print
600 Brooks Road / PO Box 1
Thorndike, ME 04986-0001 USA

(207) 568-3717

US & Canada:
1 800 929-9108
www.centerpointlargeprint.com